HEARTWARMING

The Rancher's Family

——

Barbara White Daille

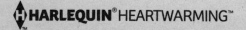

Recycling programs
for this product may
not exist in your area.

ISBN-13: 978-1-335-51082-2

The Rancher's Family

Printed in U.S.A.

www.Harlequin.com

He ruffled Neil's hair, dark and thick like his own.

"Son, what made you think this lady was going to be your mama?"

"She came home," Neil said instantly.

For a long moment, Wes froze. Then he forced himself to move, dropping his hand lightly onto Neil's shoulder. "'She came home.' You mean, like Mama always did?" And as no other woman on her own had done since. Until today.

Neil nodded.

Cara wrapped her arms around her middle, almost as if to stop herself from reaching out to his son.

"Car accident," he muttered. "Last year. Jed and Andi probably filled you in." He stared at the back door. Now would be a good time to leave the kitchen and head out to the barn—if he didn't need to step up and be the daddy he wanted to be. He gave Neil's shoulder a little squeeze. "Son, Miss Cara is not here to be your mama. She's not here to stay. She's just come for a visit. You understand?"

Dear Reader,

I'm thrilled to share my first Harlequin Heartwarming with you! The focus of my writing has always been "heartwarming characters... hometown charm." Sounds like I've now made the perfect match, doesn't it?

Speaking of matches, in *The Rancher's Family*, a matchmaking grandpa is in for a surprise when he attempts to bring together two family friends. To put it bluntly, they just want him to butt out of their business.

Widower Wes Daniels is focused on protecting his two young children from any more hurt. Cara Leonetti, a woman suffering from a devastating double loss, no longer believes in happy-ever-after. They definitely don't need a matchmaker interfering in their lives.

While this book is my first Heartwarming, it's part of my ongoing series The Hitching Post Hotel. Though family and friends from previous books often drop in to visit, you can enjoy reading the stories in any order.

If you'd like to get in touch, stop by barbarawhitedaille.com or write to PO Box 504, Gilbert, AZ 85299. I would love to hear from you!

All my best to you.

Until we meet again,

Barbara White Daille

Barbara White Daille and her husband still inhabit their own special corner of the wild, wild Southwest, where the summers are long and hot and the lizards and scorpions roam.

Barbara loves looking back at the short stories and two books she wrote in grade school and realizing that—except for the scorpions—she's doing exactly what she planned. She has now hit double digits with published novels and still has a file drawer full of stories to be written.

As always, Barbara hopes you will enjoy reading her books! She would love to have you drop by for a visit at her website, barbarawhitedaille.com.

Books by Barbara White Daille

Harlequin Western Romance

The Hitching Post Hotel

The Cowboy's Little Surprise
A Rancher of Her Own
The Lawman's Christmas Proposal
Cowboy in Charge
The Cowboy's Triple Surprise
The Rancher's Baby Proposal

Visit the Author Profile page
at Harlequin.com for more titles.

To Kathleen Scheibling and Johanna Raisanen with my endless gratitude for their above-and-beyond support this year.

And the same to Rich.

CHAPTER ONE

THOUGH THE SCORCHING southwestern summer had turned to fall, Cara Leonetti spent part of her long drive from Arizona to New Mexico thinking about ice cream. Focusing on all the different flavors kept her mind away from thoughts she desperately needed to avoid.

The highway off-ramp led to the winding two-lane local road that would take her to Cowboy Creek. With the flat, dusty land all around her and the mountain range off in the distance, she might never have left Phoenix.

Frowning, she reconsidered. *Left* didn't come close to describing what she had done today. She had fled. Escaped. Abandoned her life in her hometown. Or at least, what she had left of that life. Thanks to her own mistakes, that now amounted to lots of good friends and happy memories but nothing more.

Fighting tears, she stared at the road ahead of her. Better to look forward than back.

When she hit the town's main street a half

hour later, her car slowed to a crawl almost on its own—and not just due to the reduced speed limit. She had spotted the ice-cream parlor that, naturally, had become one of her favorite places since her first visit to Cowboy Creek.

The warm afternoon sun made her even more eager for the cold, creamy distraction of ice cream.

The teenage girl behind the counter at the back of the Big Dipper welcomed her with a big smile. "Hi! Give me just a minute."

"No rush. It's going to take me a while to decide." This detour wouldn't throw her schedule off at all. She had started out sooner than planned for her trip to the Hitching Post—the ranch hotel owned by Jed Garland, her best friend's grandfather. No one expected her to arrive this early. And as excited as she was about seeing Andi, her two kids and the rest of her family again, at the same time, she dreaded their first conversation alone.

She had told Andi about almost everything that had gone on these past few months—her move, her breakup, her new homeless and jobless statuses. All that was bad enough. But Andi didn't know the worst news.

The teenager finished packing a gallon-sized tub with ice cream and set the container into a freezer. "Okay, now what can I get you?"

"I haven't made up my mind yet." Wrong. She hadn't even checked out the options. "Do me a favor. Don't let me go too crazy or I'll spoil my appetite. I'm on my way to check in and have dinner at the Hitching Post."

"You must be Cara!"

Surprised, she looked up from the display case. "How did you know?"

The girl rolled her eyes. "In case you haven't noticed, this is a *very* small town."

A quiet one, too. Cara was the only customer, surprising for a sunny Sunday afternoon. Then again, the business section of town might be small, but it was surrounded by a big ranching community, and as she'd learned on previous visits here, ranchers worked seven days a week. It was probably too early for most people to have quit for the day.

"I'm Lizzie," the girl continued. "And no, I'm not psychic. Andi was just in here yesterday, all excited about her best friend moving here."

Temporarily. Andi wanted her to stay indefinitely, if not forever. That couldn't happen. Eventually, Cara would heal from her loss and put her life back together. She could only accomplish that by going home, by proving to herself she could stand on her own again. But for now, she was beyond grateful to Andi and her family for offering their support and a place for her to stay.

With effort, Cara brought her mind back to Lizzie's chatter.

"Andi also said you've got beautiful strawberry blond hair. And she was right. Wish mine was red or black or anything but this boring brown." She turned her head to point to her own curls, held back by a wide band.

"I wouldn't call light brown with golden highlights boring at all."

The teenager giggled, suddenly looking like a mischievous twelve-year-old, though Cara would put her age closer to sixteen. "Thanks. That's what my boyfriend keeps telling me, but I tell *him* he's only saying that because—" she placed both palms over her heart "—he *lo-oves* me."

"I think you can believe him." Cara ignored the twinge of pain knifing through her stomach. She'd believed in love, and look where that had gotten her—craving extra calories. "I'd better make a decision now, or I'll miss my chance for dessert before dinner. How about a scoop of chocolate chip in a sugar cone?"

"With a shot of whipped cream and some sprinkles?"

"Sounds great to me." A few more calories would never solve her problems, but they couldn't hurt. Much. Digging into her shoulder bag for her wallet, she moved to the cash register.

Lizzie soon followed and handed the cone across the counter.

"Wow. You've really made this a work of art." With one bite, Cara devoured most of the extra toppings. The second mouthful finished them, leaving a drop of whipped cream on her chin. She grabbed a napkin from the dispenser on the counter.

Lizzie laughed. "I hope you know you've just destroyed a masterpiece. But it's ice cream, right? Even plain, it's still special."

True for people, too. What was inside mattered more than what the world saw on the outside. Hopefully, Lizzie would come to understand that on her own soon.

"Come in again when you get a chance," Lizzie said. "But just so you know, I usually only work Saturdays and Sundays, unless somebody calls in sick." She handed Cara her change. "You're lucky to be going out to Garland Ranch," she added with obvious envy.

"There's a lot to do out there—horseback riding and trail rides and cookouts and hanging out with all the guests at the Hitching Post."

"There's definitely enough going on to keep everyone busy," Cara agreed. She knew from past visits that the ranch offered all those activities and more. Eventually, she might feel an interest in them again. For now, all she wanted was calm and quiet and lots of opportunities to catch up with Andi.

Since her best friend's relocation to Cowboy Creek the year before, Cara had come for Andi's wedding and visited for a weekend every few months. But those trips didn't give them nearly enough time together, especially compared to seeing each other daily when Andi had lived in Phoenix.

"I'll try to stop in again soon," she promised Lizzie.

"I sure hope so. We only see new faces around here every decade or so."

Laughing at the exaggeration, Cara turned away from the counter. The afternoon sunshine blasted through the picture windows, making her squint.

On the sidewalk in front of the store, a couple stood close to one another. The man's cowboy hat shaded his face as he looked down at the woman, who rested her hand on his arm as she smiled at him. A dark-haired boy about three or so tugged on the man's free arm, clearly wanting the adults to hurry up and get his ice cream.

The sight of the child sent another pain lancing through her stomach, another reminder of what she had lost. Only months ago her body had held so much promise, so much joy, from the moment she saw the positive result on the home pregnancy test. Yet only weeks later that joy changed just as quickly to sorrow. Ever since, the sight of any child made her ache.

One look at this little boy triggered her biggest worry over this trip. Between Andi's and her cousins' kids, not to mention the younger guests at the Hitching Post, how would she survive?

She took a deep breath, forcing her anxiety to ease. She had promised herself she would stay strong. And she would keep that promise, no matter what.

Outside the store, the woman walked away. The little boy ran to the heavy glass door and strained with both hands to pull it open. As he eased the door away from the frame, he laughed, clueless about the help he was getting from the man standing behind him.

Kudos to the cowboy for lending a hand.

The boy flattened his palms against the glass panel. "See," he shouted, "I'm a big boy, Daddy!"

The man looked down. "That you are."

Cara frowned. He'd answered in a light tone but without the trace of a smile. Couldn't he at least have made an effort for his own son?

She took another deep breath. She needed to quit overreacting, to stop being this sensitive about kids. To let go of the guilt her doctor assured her she shouldn't feel. Losing the baby wasn't anyone's fault, including hers.

The boy ran in her direction, waving to Lizzie at the back counter. Before Cara could move aside, he darted between her and a small round table for two. As he rushed past her, his head bumped her elbow. The scoop of ice cream fell from the cone and plopped onto her shoe. Unaware, the boy kept going.

"Mark," the man called, no lightness in his tone now.

"It's okay," she said quickly. She grabbed a couple of napkins from the metal dispenser on the table.

"Come over here, son," the man said.

Immediately, the little boy reversed his steps. Smiling, he focused on his father. He probably hadn't even seen the ice cream, now sliding from her shoe to the store's tile floor. As the man approached, his boots slapped ominously against those tiles.

She tensed. This cowboy seemed ready to make a big deal over such a simple mistake.

Father and son met halfway, coming to a halt beside her. "No worries," she told the man. "It was only an accident."

Focused on the boy, he nodded. "One we need to make right."

She stooped to pluck the ice cream from the floor just as the cowboy crouched in front of his son. Almost eye level with them both, she could now see the rest of the man's face—a very nice face, tanned and topped by a pair of dark eyes and darker eyebrows. As he looked at Mark, one side of his mouth curved in a wry half smile. Finally.

That sign of caring filled her with relief. Yes, another overreaction, but so worth the reminder some men cared about their children.

He said quietly to his son, "You knocked this lady's ice cream on the floor when you ran past her."

"I *did*?" Mark's mouth dropped open in surprise. He stared at Cara, his eyes the same dark brown shade as his father's and now rounded in dismay. "Sorry, ma'am."

He seemed so sincere and sounded so polite, just like the cowboys out at the Hitching Post. She could almost see Mark tugging on a hat brim.

"That's okay," she told him. "You didn't mean it to happen—I know. It was an accident."

"What do you think we ought to do about it?" the cowboy asked his son.

"Buy new ice cream," the child said instantly.

Again, the cowboy gave that half smile. "Sounds like a plan, pardner."

He and Cara rose at the same time. "I appreciate the offer, but actually, it's not necessary. I'm having dinner at a friend's soon. I probably—" *definitely* "—didn't need the cone, anyhow. You don't have to worry about getting me another one."

"Sorry, ma'am." He sounded exactly like a grown-up version of Mark. "My son thinks otherwise. And so do I."

Mark stood beside them, hopping from foot to foot, obviously eager to have his dessert but just as interested in this conversation.

Shrugging, she gave in. She tossed her

ruined cone into the nearby trash bin and grabbed some napkins to wipe her shoe and hands. "Okay, then."

Mark's daddy wasn't going to change his mind, especially not after he'd made a point of getting the boy to accept responsibility. And how could she fault the man for that? In fact, she admired him for making sure his son did what he thought the situation demanded.

Besides, replacing the cone had been Mark's idea. And while she might be able to say no to the daddy, she couldn't turn down his child.

After smiling at the boy, who grinned back, she nodded at the cowboy now standing expectantly by the counter. "If you insist on a replacement, who am I to argue? Not when it comes to sweets, at least." Not when an ice-cream treat didn't matter, compared to a little boy's feelings. "Let's make it a scoop of chocolate this time. And thanks."

As she walked toward the back of the room, Mark skipped along beside her. "You like ice cream?" he asked.

For a moment, she tensed. She hadn't expected him to start a conversation. Why hadn't she just refused the cone and gone on her way? "I do like ice cream. How about you?"

"Yeah!"

"What kind do you like best?"

"The cold kind."

She couldn't help but smile. He seemed so smart. So sweet. "Me, too. But really, anything with chocolate in it is my favorite."

Lizzie already held out a fresh cone, again complete with whipped cream and sprinkles. At this rate, she'd have no appetite left for any dinner at all.

"No charge for this one," Lizzie said. "That'll teach me to make my cones more accident-proof."

"I'll take care of it," the cowboy insisted, frowning.

"That's okay," the teen said. "But you might add a bigger tip in the jar before you go."

"Bigger than usual, you mean?"

Cara glanced at him in surprise, but Lizzie laughed, taking the comment as a joke, as he had probably intended it to be. He might not smile much but at least he had a sense of humor—with the right person. And he did seem to have a good relationship with his son.

The reminder made her stomach twinge again. Forcing a smile, she held up her cone. "I guess you'd call this freebie one of the perks of living in a small town. I'd never expect the same courtesy back home."

If he'd planned to respond, she would never know. Mark tugged on her shirt, stealing her attention. "Where is home?"

"Phoenix," she said. "That's in Arizona. Do you know where Arizona is?"

"Next door," he said promptly, eyeing her cone. "Good ice cream?"

"It's great." Judging by the way he stared with his eyebrows nearly meeting in concern, he didn't buy her answer. She took a lick of sweet chocolate and didn't have to fake her response. "Mmm…it's yummy. Thank you very much."

"Welcome." Now Mark grinned.

His father simply turned back to the counter to place the boy's order.

No sense trying to be sociable with this cowboy. Either he was the strong, silent type or he just didn't feel the need to show the same manners he expected from his own son.

Add yet another who-cares checkmark to the list. With luck, she would never see Mark's daddy again.

While she was in Cowboy Creek, she and Andi might make a few trips to the local sandwich shop and here to the Big Dipper. Other than that, she would spend her time out at the ranch—where, unlike this cowboy, everyone made her feel welcome.

CHAPTER TWO

THE MINUTE CARA pulled into the long drive-way leading up to the Hitching Post, the front door of the hotel opened and a woman stepped outside.

At this distance, Cara couldn't make out features, but the woman's long wavy blond hair gave a good clue as to who might be waiting for her on the porch.

As she drove past the hotel to the parking area on the side of the building, she practiced a few slow steadying breaths. Between Andi's concern and her grandfather's bright-eyed scrutiny, Cara would need lots of calming techniques during her visit.

As much as she appreciated and wanted their support and sympathy, she also needed to hold herself together. At least, until she and her best friend had a good, long talk.

When Cara climbed from the front seat, Andi wrapped her in a hug. "It's about time you got here! I've been pacing the floor all day."

She laughed. "Now, that's an exaggeration. It couldn't have been *all* day. You knew I wouldn't get here until at least the middle of the afternoon."

"Whatever. I'm just glad to see you. Come on, let's start taking your stuff up to your room."

An older pickup truck came around the corner of the building. The driver pulled to a stop a few spaces away. Andi's grandfather emerged from the truck, settled his Stetson on his head and loped toward them.

Jed Garland was slim and long-legged. In his seventies, he had white hair and bright blue eyes that could be unsettling at times. Those eyes always seemed able to see more than anyone else's did.

"Well, look who's finally turned up like a lucky penny. Welcome." He wrapped Cara in a bear hug, then stood back, looking searchingly at her. "How's our girl?"

From the minute they'd met, Jed had treated her like another granddaughter, and he'd become a substitute for the grandfathers she'd lost when she was a little girl.

She gave him an extra-big smile. No way could he find anything suspicious about that. "I'm just fine and thrilled to be here again."

"Good. We've all been looking forward to your visit. Andi most of all."

"I didn't know you'd gone out, Grandpa," Andi said. "What have you been up to?"

Unlike the cowboy from the Big Dipper, Jed smiled easily and often. Surprisingly, his face suddenly wrinkled in a frown. "Went to Sugar's for a cup of coffee." SugarPie's was a combination bakery and sandwich shop in town. "I stopped by Wes Daniels's place, thought maybe I'd talk him into going with me. But I couldn't get him out the door." He looked at Cara to explain, "Wes is an old friend of the family, a widower now, lost his wife just over a year ago."

"I'm very sorry to hear that." Instantly, she sympathized with this Mr. Daniels. Now more than ever, it hurt even to think of anyone losing someone they loved.

"Something's got to be done about that man," he said. "He's had a hard time of things, but if he keeps on the way he's headed, he'll wind up a hermit."

"Not if you can help it," Andi said. "I'm sure you'll come up with a way to get him over here for a visit soon."

He tilted his head slightly, considering Cara again. Now would be just the time for him to ask exactly the wrong question. Instead, he only said, "We'll do some catching up once you get settled in." And even that sounded ominous.

Mentally, she shook her head. Jed knew everything that went on in Cowboy Creek, but even he couldn't know she'd been holding out on Andi.

"We were just going upstairs," Andi told him.

"Good enough. I'll tell Paz to get supper going." He touched his fingertips to the brim of his Stetson in farewell.

Cara opened the trunk, revealing four canvas carryalls.

Andi gasped. "This is all you brought?"

"I packed light and left everything else in storage for now. And I brought a lot of quarters for the laundry."

"Very funny." Andi took two of the bags. "Let's go in through the front door and grab your room key. The dining room's closed on Sundays, remember, so we'll be eating in the kitchen. Grandpa and Paz waited to have supper with us, too."

And while her hosts held up their own dinner, she'd eaten ice cream at the Big Dipper. "They didn't have to do that."

"They wanted to."

Inside the hotel, Andi went behind the registration desk spanning the long right-side wall of the lobby. Opposite the desk was the entrance to the sitting room, large enough for the extended Garland family and all their guests to move around comfortably.

And comfort was the keyword at the Hitching Post, from the sitting room's oversize couches and chairs to the guest room's down-filled pillows.

The southwestern decor reminded Cara of home. Supple leather, heavy wood and wrought iron accented the furnishings. Bright glazed pottery sat on tabletops and on shelves hanging from the walls. Everything together turned the Hitching Post into a warm and welcoming haven.

Knowing this haven waited for her had made her even more eager to return to Cowboy Creek.

"Are you okay?" Andi dangled a key in front of her. "Have you been hypnotized?"

"No, I'm just looking around," Cara said. "It seems like nothing's changed since my last visit."

"Nothing has," Andi said. "When I spent every summer vacation here, that's one thing I always loved about the Hitching Post. Every

time I came back, it felt like I'd never left."
She waved the key ring again. "Second floor.
Your own favorite room. Elevator or stairs?"

"Elevator? What's the matter—are you out
of shape since you quit the gym?" They had
met at their local gym, when they'd indepen-
dently walked out of a killer aerobics class and
wound up sharing a booth in the coffee shop
next door. Cara plucked the key from her fingers. "Give you one guess."

THEY HAD TAKEN the stairs.
Cara set her bags on the floor and plopped
onto the bed. The bedspread's rich turquoise-
and-cream colors echoed in the curtains and
two upholstered chairs near the window, with
a small round table between them.

Not that she ever got much reading time in
on her visits.

Andi took one of the roomy chairs and
curled her legs beneath her. Cara recognized
the signs she was settling in for one of their
heart-to-heart talks.

Those talks were what Cara missed most
since Andi had left Arizona.

When they'd met, Cara had already gone
up the ladder of a local department store, and
when Andi unexpectedly needed a job, Cara

had recommended her for an opening. Since they'd worked different shifts, she had volunteered to babysit for Andi's two kids, watching them at her apartment.

Cara loved and missed Trey and Missy, yet she dreaded seeing them again. Being with them would remind her of her own child, the unborn baby she loved and missed with all her heart.

"I know you've been busy," Andi said, "but your emails and texts have been almost nonexistent for a while now. So fill me in on all the latest."

All described it perfectly. Cara unthinkingly brushed her palms across her stomach, then froze. She'd kept quiet about her pregnancy, wanting instead to share her joy in person. Now she almost wished she hadn't waited. Telling Andi the bad news face-to-face was going to be so much harder than she'd expected.

She'd hesitated for too long, and Andi spoke again. "I really had hopes for you and Brad after you finally decided to move in together."

You finally decided... Key words there. More than a sign—a roadside billboard. How could Cara not have seen it?

"Your hopes couldn't have been any higher than mine," she admitted.

Instead of Brad coming down to Phoenix, they had agreed to live in his condo in Flagstaff, and at the start of spring, she had relocated. Almost immediately, she had gotten pregnant.

And Brad, the man who'd said he wanted to be with her…who'd claimed to want the family she'd longed for, too…suddenly changed his mind.

"Moving in together turned into a trial period by default." Swallowing hard, she shrugged. "A good thing, after all, since we figured out being together permanently wouldn't work. *We* wouldn't work."

Being left without a home or a job didn't matter. She'd clung to what was most important. She still had her baby to love and all the joys of motherhood to look forward to.

By the early summer, she had lost those, too.

"I'm sorry about what happened with you and Brad," Andi said. "But I'm glad you're here to stay with us."

"For a while, anyhow. And even though Jed's nice enough to give me a free ride as far as my room—"

"There's no nice about it. Besides, I live here

now, too." After Andi remarried, she and her family moved into the Garlands' private wing of the Hitching Post. "And I'm sure not going to charge a friend to stay at my house."

"Yes, but this is a hotel." She tried for a laugh and almost made it sound natural. "How is Jed going to make a profit if he's covering my room and all my meals indefinitely? Don't get me wrong—I appreciate his generosity, but I'm not destitute, you know. I've got savings. Though that's another thing that won't last forever."

"Cara. You would do the same for me, and you know it. We've got your room and board covered. Now, what happened when you told Edie?"

She had called the manager at the store where she'd worked, and where Andi had still had a part-time job until moving to Cowboy Creek. "She said she would have taken me back in a minute—and I believe her. But they had already replaced me and didn't have any other openings available."

It was Andi who had convinced her not to look for a permanent job yet and to come to Cowboy Creek for an indefinite stay. To be honest, it hadn't taken much convincing.

Andi sighed. "I wish I could tell you just to

get a job here, but as much as I love Cowboy Creek, it's a small town."

Exactly what Lizzie had emphasized at the Big Dipper earlier. "And with a very small business district."

"True. It's not like there are dozens of openings just waiting to be filled. At least you can commute. I've been looking around lately, but with the kids and my work here at the hotel, I want something local. But there's nothing here."

"Don't you have enough to keep you busy already, between taking care of the kids and handling wedding preparations?" Along with reservations for staying guests, the Hitching Post catered weddings and other special events. Andi and her two cousins handled most of this side of the business for Jed.

"It's not as much work as you'd think. The catering business is picking up, we're all happy to say, especially Grandpa. We have a wedding reception booked a few weeks from now, but with three of us dividing everything up, there's never too much for any one of us to handle. And..." Andi ran her hand along the edge of the table.

"And what?"

"Tina and Jane have other jobs, too. You

know Tina's assistant manager and bookkeeper for the hotel. And Jane's photography business is doing great. That's why I've been thinking about finding another job, too. And…" Her friend cleared her throat too late to hide the break in her voice.

"What else?" Cara asked gently.

Andi shook her head.

"What's the matter, Andi?"

She looked up, her eyes hazy with tears. "Mitch and I are trying to get pregnant. But it's been a while, and nothing's happening yet." She added in a rush, "I was thinking about a job long before we started trying, though. One thing's got nothing to do with the other." She sighed again. "Well, I really didn't plan to tell you all that right now. We don't need it hanging over us, and you have enough on your mind."

Andi stood abruptly. "You probably want to freshen up, and I should go see if Paz needs help. By the way, except for Paz and Grandpa, it's just us for dinner tonight. All the adults took the kids in to town for some bowling. Tina and Jane thought you might appreciate a quiet grown-ups-only dinner your first night here."

They couldn't have been more right, though for the wrong reasons. "I'll have to remember to thank them." Or send them flowers for buying her some time.

"I'll see you in the kitchen." Andi left, closing the door behind her.

Cara slumped on the bed.

At least she hadn't made the situation worse. Who could've known months ago that not sharing about her pregnancy would be the right decision? A decision she had to hold on to for a while. With Andi so upset right now, she didn't need to hear that her best friend had lost a baby.

JED GARLAND MADE his way into the hotel kitchen, where Paz, the Hitching Post's cook, was preparing their Sunday dinner. Paz was also his longtime friend and the grandmother of his youngest granddaughter, Tina.

"Cara's here," he announced. "She and Andi were headed to Cara's room. Something's up with that young lady. I need to find out from Andi what's going on." He snatched a wedge of green pepper from Paz's cutting board, then laughed and ducked as she swatted at him. The two of them went through the steal-and-swat ritual nearly every day.

"I suppose there's no need to question your feelings." The silver strands in Paz's hair danced as she shook her head. "You always just seem to know."

"It's a gift," he agreed.

Brows raised, she simply stared at him.

"Well…" There was no hiding anything from Paz. "It also appeared obvious when I talked to her outside. I asked how she was, and she gave me the most reassuring response. It wouldn't have convinced a greenhorn to saddle up Daffodil, and she's the sweetest mare I've ever owned." The oldest, too, and long retired to live out her days on Garland Ranch.

As he took his favorite spot at the table, Andi walked into the room. When he saw the frown on her pretty face, he frowned, too, and beckoned her to the table. "Have a seat, girl. We haven't got much time, and we need to do some talking."

"About what?"

"Your innocent act needs some work. You know what I'm about to say as well as I do. It's plain to see Cara's worried about something. And I'm thinking you're worried about Cara."

"I am. Guess I'm not very good at hiding my feelings, am I?"

"And I wouldn't have you any other way." He squeezed her hand. "Now, we already know the girl's got no job and no home. That's not a problem. She can stay here as long as she likes. You told her so, I hope."

"Of course. But that's just it. She doesn't want to take advantage of your hospitality."

"Well, let's hope you set her straight on that point, too. We *all* extend hospitality here. To our paying guests. Cara's not a guest—she's part of the family."

"She knows how we feel. And that I want her to stay. But she's already hinting around about leaving."

"Well, we'll just see about that."

Andi's blue eyes gleamed and at last she smiled. "You're scheming again, Grandpa."

"Darned right, I am. Would you expect anything less?"

"No. And I wouldn't have *you* any other way." This time, she was the one to squeeze his hand as she echoed his words. "Though I'm not sure Cara's ready for your matchmaking services."

"Who said anything about matchmaking?"

Naturally, he planned to spend plenty of time on that, too, but his granddaughter didn't need to know all the details up front. "I'm thinking of getting her to help us around here somehow. She can hardly insist on leaving if she's doing us a favor, can she?"

"I wouldn't think so. But we can't use the wedding business as a reason. I've already told her Jane and Tina and I have that covered."

"No worries," he said firmly. He beckoned to Paz, then waited until she had joined them at the table. "I've got an idea. Now, you two listen up…"

CHAPTER THREE

AFTER A HUG from Paz, Cara had joined her along with Jed and Andi at the table. Large enough to seat a dozen or more people, the table was still dwarfed by the Hitching Post's huge kitchen. Paz had set out bowls and platters filled with her spicy southwestern specialties.

While they ate, they caught up on the latest news in Cowboy Creek. As always, Jed seemed to know everything that went on in town.

As they finished dessert, Cara said, "This was all delicious, as usual, but I'm very sorry about holding up your meal. I could just have stopped to eat something along the way." Besides that ice-cream cone.

"No worries," Jed told her. "This is our usual suppertime any other day of the week. Sundays are different only because the dining room is closed."

As Andi topped off their glasses with iced tea, Jed slumped back in his chair.

"What's the matter, Grandpa?"

He shrugged. "Just thinking about Wes Daniels again."

Paz shook her head. "It's not good for him to brood, day after day. We need to do something to help him."

"Grandpa's tried."

He nodded. "At one time or another most of the folks in Cowboy Creek have made an attempt. I think we need to shake the man up. He needs something to take him away from his troubles. And you know what they say—a trouble shared is a trouble halved."

His gaze met Cara's, reminding her she needed to be extra careful around him. He had ways of making you reveal your most personal thoughts before you realized you'd opened your mouth.

She didn't trust the smile he suddenly gave her, either. "Cara, I think we could use your assistance."

"Mine? But I don't have any idea how to help your friend."

"I've got the idea. And I believe you're the one who could help us put it into action." He set his glass aside and leaned forward. "We've all encouraged Wes to take a first step, to start clearing his wife's things out of the house. I know it's not an easy thing for him to do, especially on his own. It was hard when I went through it, and I had my family to help. But I also know the time comes when it has to be done. It's been over a year now for Wes and he hasn't even made a start."

She could imagine Jed's old friend deliberately putting off the job, dreading having to face painful memories. To make final decisions. To deal with a lifetime—and most likely a houseful—of possessions.

Hadn't she faced the same dilemma just a couple of months ago, on a smaller scale? One drawer in a dresser. One drawer she'd used to hold all her hopes and dreams, all the clothes and blankets and toys she'd collected for her baby-to-be.

Fighting to keep her voice from breaking, she said, "I feel for your friend, Jed, but what can I do? I've never even met him."

"Exactly my point. It might make things easier for him to have a stranger's help. We won't know unless we try. But I think it's worth a good shot. I'll give Wes a call, see what we can fix up."

Before she could respond, the hallway outside the kitchen suddenly filled with the sounds of shrieks and running footsteps, all coming from the direction of the Hitching Post's back door.

What had sounded like a half-dozen kids— but in reality were only two—burst into the room. "Aunt Cara! Aunt Cara!"

She barely had time to take a deep breath before Tina's son Robbie launched himself at her for a hug.

Then a blond-haired toddler climbed into her lap and wrapped her arms around her neck. "Hello, Aunt Cara!"

"Hello, Missy." Just the sight of Missy's chubby little face made her heart hurt. She had helped raise Andi's daughter almost from birth until the day she and her family had moved from Phoenix.

A tall, dark-haired man ambled into the kitchen.

"Hey, Mitch," Andi said. "Everyone back already?"

He shook his head. "No, just us. Trey wasn't feeling well. He overdid it on the hot dogs and popcorn, I suspect. He went off to his room saying he wanted his mommy."

"Then I'd better go check in. Come here, Missy—you're strangling Aunt Cara. And I have a feeling you need your face and hands washed."

Missy laughed and reached up, ready to go into her mother's arms, and Cara saw a vision of another little girl with her own strawberry blond hair.

She blinked, trying to chase away the vision. She had to stop dreaming about a baby she would never have and a future that would never be.

Coming to Cowboy Creek was supposed to give her the chance to leave all those thoughts and dreams behind. Instead, everywhere she looked, she had seen—would see—nothing but reminders. Andi and her happy family… Tina's baby and young son… Jane's two children… Even the cowboy with his little boy at the Big Dipper.

Watching him with his child made her see what she wanted so badly. What she had so recently lost. The chance to start a family of her own.

Why hadn't she just stayed home? Back in Phoenix, she couldn't avoid kids completely, but she wouldn't have to be around them nearly every minute, the way she would here.

Jed shifted in his chair, drawing her attention and making her think about his old friend again. She hoped he could convince the man to let her help him. Suddenly, sorting through someone else's memories—memories that couldn't touch her, that wouldn't break her heart into even smaller bits—sounded like a great idea.

An hour later, Cara found herself following Jed's brief driving directions to his friend's nearby ranch and the small two-storied house on the property.

She braked to a stop next to a pickup truck needing a good wash.

This late in the day, with the sun melting on the horizon, a few lights shone through the curtained windows of the house. She pushed the doorbell and listened to the chimes ring, then fade, as she glanced around her.

A thick layer of dust covered the porch swing. In one corner of the front window, the fine strands of a cobweb turned golden from the light shining through the panes.

Her heart went out to the widower who lived here. Obviously, the man had no housekeeper and now no wife to help him with all the little chores that made this house their home. Or else he couldn't summon the energy to worry about those things once he lost the person who meant everything to him.

Cara looked at her car only a few yards

away. Maybe she should get in it again and leave. Maybe Wes Daniels had decided he didn't want help.

And after all, who was she to come here and disturb a stranger still so wrapped up in grief that he might *wind up a hermit*, as Jed had put it?

The door swung open. Her jaw almost dropped.

A man stood in the opening, silhouetted by the light from a lamp in the room behind him. Not Jed's *old friend*. A much younger man, twentysomething, with broad shoulders and sturdy arms and dark brown eyes beneath dark brows. A man she already…sort of…knew.

The unfriendly cowboy she had met that afternoon at the Big Dipper.

He looked just as surprised to see her. "Did you make a wrong turn on your way to somewhere else?"

"That might be impossible in Cowboy Creek."

"Yeah. We're not like the big city."

A point in his favor—he'd remembered her telling him where she was from. He seemed more relaxed than he had earlier. Maybe he'd just been in a bad mood. Or—be honest—

maybe her own stress had led her to misread the situation, and the awkwardness was all on her.

Then and now. "Well, I'm…" Nerves suddenly stole her power of speech, but that had nothing to do with the man in front of her. She wasn't worrying over hurting a stranger. Instead, she was anticipating what was coming next—being reminded of her own loss and reliving her own grief.

This is not about you.

She tried again. "I'm here to see Wes Daniels."

"That would be me."

"Then I'm looking for Wes, senior."

"There is no senior. I'm the only Wes Daniels I know."

She blinked. "My mistake. Jed said you were a widower. And I saw you with a woman outside the Big Dipper—"

"She was a friend of my wife's."

"Oh." She'd definitely looked like she wanted to be friends with Wes…or something more. His tone said he didn't feel the same. Maybe *that* explained his attitude. "Okay, then you're just the person I want to see. We never had the chance to introduce ourselves this afternoon. I'm Cara Leonetti. Jed and Andi sent me."

He stepped back and swung the door open wider. "Come on in."

The entryway led directly into a small living room. Magazines and children's books lay every which way across the coffee table. A flowered afghan trailed from the brown leather couch to the floor.

Wes picked up the afghan and tossed it onto the back of the couch. "Have a seat."

"Thanks. In case Jed didn't tell you, I'm staying with them at the Hitching Post. His granddaughter Andi is my best friend..." Unsure how to continue, she stopped. He didn't seem overly enthusiastic about her being here. "Jed told me your wife passed away not too long ago. I'm sorry for your loss."

His face went blank, as if she were a magician who had put him into a trance. "Car accident," he said, his voice just as expressionless. "Last year. Jed probably filled you in on that, too."

Suddenly, she found she did care, after all—about this virtual stranger, so close to her own age and already a widower, and about his adorable young son, now left without a mother. Jed Garland's *old friend* made her heart crack in a few more places.

She looked down at the books and magazines on the coffee table, giving them both a chance to pull themselves together.

Even from friends, condolences were hard to accept. She'd learned that firsthand once people heard about her breakup with Brad. How much worse would it have been if they'd tried to express their sympathy for her losing her baby? Except no one had known about that loss, more proof she'd made the right decision in waiting to tell Andi.

Wes didn't have that option.

And here she was, a stranger to him, trying to comfort him over the loss of a wife he loved, a woman she'd never met. Awkward or not, now she had been put into this situation, what else could she do but tell the truth?

"Jed and Andi thought it might be easier for you to have someone you didn't know sorting through your wife's things. But I don't mean to barge in where I'm not wanted. If you're not comfortable with the idea, please tell me and I'll go."

Still, he didn't respond. Instead, he stared across the room as if silently confirming he wanted nothing to do with the idea. Or with her.

Then she heard what might have distracted him. The sound of shoes slapping against floorboards. Very small shoes, judging by the noises now growing louder and closer.

A moment later, Mark burst into the room waving a sheet of construction paper. "Daddy, I finished my picture!"

The boy caught sight of her and came to a screeching halt. Eyes wide, he sucked in a deep breath. The paper slipped from his hand and fell, *shushing* to a stop on the hardwood floor. "Hello! Are you my new mommy?"

CHAPTER FOUR

WES STARED AT the woman sitting across from him. Cara's wide open eyes showed she was as dismayed by his son's question as he was.

He stared down the hall to the kitchen. Now would be a good time to head out the back door and over to the barn—if he didn't need to step up and be the daddy he wanted to be.

"I like my new mommy," Mark said with a grin.

Looking at Cara, Wes shrugged in apology. "Once he gets an idea in his head, he doesn't let go."

"Like most kids, I guess." Her smile looked strained and her gaze didn't quite meet his.

He swallowed a sigh. Now wasn't the time to have a discussion with his son, especially with this woman still here. But what choice did he have? Mark, who had started asking questions around the time he'd learned to say *dada*, would never let this one go unanswered. And waiting would only let him set the misunderstanding more firmly in his mind.

"Hey, buddy, come over here a minute."

Mark scooped up the sheet of paper and trotted over to him. Wes ruffled his hair. "What made you think Miss Cara was going to be your mommy?"

"She came home," Mark said instantly.

For a long moment, Wes froze. From the corner of his eye, he saw Cara wrap her arms around her middle. Forcing himself to move, he rested his hand on Mark's shoulder. "*She came home.* You mean, like Mommy always did?"

Mark nodded.

Yeah, Mark and Tracey's mommy always came home—at least by the end of the night, because she spent as little time on the ranch as she could. She didn't invite her friends to visit because she saw them in town. The woman now on his couch was the first adult female he could remember stepping into the house in a year.

"Son, Miss Cara is not here to be your mommy. She's not here to stay. She's just come for a visit. You understand?"

Mark's face fell. Biting his lip, he nodded.

"Good. Now, how about we go in the kitchen, and I'll dish you up some ice cream."

"Miss Cara, too?"

"Of course, Miss Cara, too, if she wants some."

Mark rounded the coffee table. He grabbed Cara's hand and grinned at her. "You *love* ice cream!"

Her blue eyes softening, she smiled. Good for her. Her rigid shoulders told Wes she still felt uncomfortable, but she hadn't looked to him for a way out.

"Yes, I do love ice cream," she agreed. "You remembered I said that to you at the Big Dipper this afternoon?"

"Yes!"

"Along with never giving up, my son's got a great memory." Too great once in a while and usually at the worst possible moment. Like now. But heck, his boy deserved some credit of his own. "And he's smart. So smart, I sometimes think he's three going on forty."

Cara's laugh put dimples in her cheeks. Her shoulders relaxed a fraction.

"C'mon." Mark tugged on her hand.

Only then did she shoot a glance in Wes's direction. Giving in, he gestured toward the hallway. Mark led the way, towing Cara along like a cart behind a pony, leaving him in their trail dust.

As he passed the stairs, Wes slowed his steps, listening. All seemed quiet on the second floor. Tracey must still be sleeping—and with luck, that would last a while longer. His cranky little girl definitely needed extra rest.

He followed his son and Cara down the hall to the kitchen.

Crayons and construction paper covered the table where he had settled Mark after supper. He liked having his kids close in the evenings. "Don't mind the mess. This is about the only chance we have to spend some quiet family time together. Well...considering all Mark's chatter, maybe not so quiet."

Mornings were rushed, between getting them fed and dressed and to the sitter's in town, then hurrying back home alone to tackle the day's chores. Young as they were, he didn't like the kids being so far away from him all day. But with the ranch to take care of, again, what choice did he have? Even before the accident, Patty took any chance she could get to go on the run—

"I don't want to interrupt your time together," Cara protested.

"Not a problem." Neither was the fact she'd

interrupted his thought, too. No sense going down that familiar rocky road. "Mark's making a picture to bring to his sitter's in the morning."

"You come to Miss Rhea's," Mark said to her. "We have milk and cookies."

She shot Wes a glance. "Maybe it would be better if I just come back tomorrow."

He shrugged. "You're here now."

Mark nearly dove onto his bench at the table. He liked to kneel there when he drew or colored pictures.

"Take it easy, champ," Wes said. "You'll fall off if you're not careful."

"I won't fall."

Over his son's head, Cara's eyes met his. He tried for a smile. "As you said, like most kids. Can't tell them anything, can you?"

She glanced down at Mark then scanned the room as if she still felt uncomfortable around him. She'd seemed okay talking to Mark at the Big Dipper this afternoon. No surprise she felt uneasy here, considering that the moment Mark had seen her in the living room he'd tried to claim her for his mother.

Mark held one of his drawings up for her to see.

"Very nice," she said, examining the lopsided barn and stick figure horse as if she'd just discovered a masterpiece in the making.

She pointed to the paper, then said something Wes didn't hear. But he couldn't miss his son's laugh, a sound that lately he hadn't heard nearly as often as he liked.

"You sit here," Mark told Cara. He patted the chair beside the bench. The same chair his mother had always sat in.

Cara obligingly took her seat.

Mark stared at her, a crayon clamped in his motionless fist. He seemed afraid to move or even to blink, as if in that second of time she might disappear. The way his mother had.

Wes's throat suddenly threatened to shut down.

He rummaged in the utensil drawer for the ice-cream scoop.

"Here." Mark handed Cara a crayon and slid a sheet of paper toward her. "You color."

They sat close together, with her head tilted down toward his son's just the way Patty had when she'd drawn pictures with Mark. Only then, their two dark-haired heads had matched, underscoring the fact they were family.

Cara's reddish-blond hair threw the scene off-kilter, as if warning him he shouldn't let her into his kids' lives. Look what happened the minute she'd set foot in his house.

All right, he couldn't blame her for Mark's misunderstanding. And being a friend of Andi's would normally provide a solid recommendation for her. Emphasis on *normally*. Throw that scheming Jed Garland into the mix and all bets were off.

"Clear off the table, buddy," he told Mark. "You don't want to get ice cream on your pictures."

"Okay, Daddy."

As he and Cara put the crayons into the box, Wes set their bowls near them and took his own chair at the head of the table. He eyed Cara. "You said you're here staying with Andi."

"Yes." She started in on her ice cream. "I'm between jobs, so right now my time is my own. Eventually, I'm going back home. Probably sooner than later. But don't mention that if you talk to Jed or Andi. She's trying to convince me to stay permanently."

"Will she succeed?"

For a moment, her spoon hovered over her bowl. "No. I have to go back home." Her voice matched her expression. Determined. Or just this side of grim.

She said nothing else. Normally, Wes could

rely on Mark to carry any conversation, but now not even a mumble came from his son. Somebody had to break the dead silence. "You and Andi been friends a long time?"

Immediately, her expression lightened.

"Best friends. We met at the gym a few years ago, then found out we're the same age and like a lot of the same things. Not everything, though." She smiled. "I knew Andi was close to Jed and loved to visit the Hitching Post, but I'd never thought she would be happy living on a ranch."

"Not everybody's cut out for it," he said evenly, forcing himself from going down another rocky road.

"Well, meeting up with Mitch again changed everything for Andi. And as the saying goes, the rest is history. When they got married, I came to be maid of honor. I…guess you weren't there for the wedding."

"No." Or much of anywhere else this past year or more.

She glanced at Mark, who had his entire attention focused on his dessert, then said carefully, "As I told you earlier, Jed and Andi thought I might be able to help out, but that's completely up to you."

The look in her eyes made his stomach

clench. After all these months, he still couldn't handle the sympathy, the kindnesses he didn't deserve. Kindnesses he—

Pull yourself together, man.

She was talking about Jed's call. The reason behind it hadn't come as a surprise. He'd had repeated offers of a helping hand from Jed and his granddaughters, some of the older ladies in town and Patty's friend Marianne. Everyone wanted to help him.

And he didn't want everyone he knew getting into his business.

Maybe that was why he'd agreed to Jed's plan to send this woman over here tonight. Better to have assistance from someone he didn't know. Keep things formal and businesslike. Keep him away from well-meaning friends with questions he didn't want to answer and concerns he didn't want to face.

But he didn't need to share any of that with this stranger.

"I guess it's about time I took care of clearing out some of the stuff upstairs. There's an office full of crafts, too. My wife talked about starting a business selling things over the internet but never got very far with that plan."

"When you say *an office full*, what do you mean?"

"Just that. There's a spare room with boxes and bins piled halfway to the ceiling, filled with all kinds of stuff she sewed and knitted and crocheted. She'd developed kind of an obsession about her crafts."

An expensive obsession, almost as costly as the one she'd once indulged in with her friends, the trips to Santa Fe and Albuquerque and Las Vegas.

I've got to do something with all my spare time, she'd said resentfully after Mark had come along and she'd had to cut back on her travels.

Wes wouldn't have minded her overdoing it with the crafts, if she'd just spent less money on them and more on the kids.

"She was planning to sell all that inventory online?" Cara asked.

"Yeah. Why?"

"I was just thinking Andi might want to try some kind of online business. She's been looking for a job, but opportunities are slim here in town."

"Yeah, Patty used to complain about that, too. She said there wasn't enough of anything here."

Why can't Cowboy Creek have a few name-brand stores? Some trendy restaurants? A nightclub or two? And while they're at it, can't the town council bring in a casino? That's what his wife had always wanted. *The bright lights and excitement of the big city, not all the stale, dusty air in this hick town.*

No, she'd never been happy in Cowboy Creek.

Too bad she hadn't said so until long after their wedding.

He dragged his thoughts back to the present to find Cara looking thoughtfully at him. Those clear blue eyes unnerved him. Why, he didn't know, but he rose from his chair as if he'd been lassoed and jerked to his feet.

"You done with your ice cream, buddy?" When Mark nodded, Wes took his and Cara's empty bowls to the sink.

A whimper erupted from the monitor on the counter.

The sound of a startled gasp came from behind him. He looked over his shoulder. Cara's face had turned candle-wax white, and she'd rested one hand against her belly.

What now? He set the bowls on the counter. "You feeling okay?"

"I—I'm fine. The monitor just startled me. You have a baby?"

As if on cue, Tracey let out a louder cry.

Sounded like they were in for another bad time. "My daughter. She's fifteen months and lately not too happy about sleeping through the night. Or at all, sometimes. I'd better get up there before she starts yelling."

Showing off her perfect timing once more, Tracey gave another yelp.

He shook his head. "See what I mean? And Mark, it's bath time. You need to get out some clean pajamas."

"Okay, Daddy." Mark climbed down from his bench.

Wes watched him leave the room, then turned back to Cara. "Listen, I appreciate your offer of help. But you're right, it'll be better to hold off on that till tomorrow."

No matter what she'd told him about feeling fine, the relief now flooding her face said otherwise.

Her expression now…her blue eyes and the contrast of her hair with Mark's earlier… Why was he taking note of anything about her? A typical male reaction? A reflex?

Those had better be his reasons, because he wasn't interested. His kids had already lost their mother, and he wasn't letting them get attached to anyone else, especially not to a woman planning to leave town soon.

CHAPTER FIVE

NIGHT HAD FALLEN by the time Cara returned to Garland Ranch.

She found Andi on the front porch, perched on the wooden swing. Joining her, Cara pushed against the floor with one foot, setting the swing into motion.

From inside the hotel came a shout followed by an outburst of laughter.

"Don't tell me. The Garlands and their guests have settled down in the sitting room for their usual evening's entertainment."

"Good guess. And you know if you'd come back earlier, you'd be in there with us."

"You're right." As ordinary as the card and board games would have seemed back home, here they fit right in. Just the way her best friend had settled in to her new home with her new husband. Though Cara missed Andi more than she could ever say, on her first visit to Cowboy Creek she had been thrilled to see that perfect match.

"I have news to report," Cara said. "Wes Daniels agreed to let me help with his wife's things."

"What a relief. He told Grandpa he was okay with the idea, but we weren't sure he'd actually let you go ahead with it."

"And here's something interesting. His wife planned to open an online store, selling crafts she made herself. Wes says he has a roomful of them at the house. If you're interested, I'll ask to take a look. If the quality's good enough, maybe you could pick up her plans where she left off."

"That's a *great* idea." Andi pulled her feet up beneath her on the swing and turned to face Cara. "We've got a website for the ranch. Jane does all the updates, and Tina handles the online registrations and email. Between the two of them, I'd have all the help I'd need with that end of the business. And if I sell Patty's crafts, I could split the profits with Wes."

With a laugh, Andi went on, "I don't expect quality to be a problem. Patty once told me that in grade school, her mom dragged her to the local women's club meetings. She hated having everyone trying to teach her to knit. But I'll bet she learned something there." She shrugged.

"Anyhow, you'll see for yourself when you go back to Wes's."

"I will. I'm meeting him tomorrow morning after he takes his kids to their sitter's. Which reminds me. Andi, why didn't you tell me he has such young kids?"

Andi sat facing the light over the door, which left Cara able to read her puzzled expression. It seemed genuine, but...

"What does that have to do with anything?" Andi's confusion sounded like the real thing, too. "You said you're meeting him *after* he takes Mark and Tracey to their sitter's. They won't get in your way while you're working."

"It's not that." She gave the swing a bigger push. "It's all that buildup you and Jed did, feeding me info about your *old friend*, the *widower*. You had me thinking Wes was an older man. Instead, he's our age, and he has two small kids."

"Actually he's almost two years older than we are."

Cara rolled her eyes. "That's not the point."

Andi laughed. "It sure sounds like it. And you sound like you're interested in him."

"After what happened with Brad? I won't be interested in a man again for a long, long time.

If ever. No, I'm just wondering what you and Jed are up to."

"Nothing. You're thinking of Grandpa and his chief hobby, aren't you?" Suddenly serious, she said, "Cara, I would never do anything to hurt you. You know that."

"Of course, I do."

"Then you know I understand you're not ready for Grandpa's matchmaking services. Our reason for sending you to Wes was to help *him*. And trust me, you've already made great progress."

"I suppose." Andi did sound sincerely happy about Wes.

Maybe she had jumped too quickly to her suspicions about Andi and matchmaker Jed. Maybe tonight had just been too much for her at once—hearing Mark call her *mommy*. Feeling so much sympathy for Wes. Learning he had a little girl… All that must have rattled her more than she'd realized.

She had been so relieved when he'd agreed to postpone getting together until tomorrow.

"It will be good to have something to take your mind off Brad," Andi said. "And being around Wes could let you see how someone— with help—can get through a major loss. You're dealing with grief, too."

More grief than Andi knew. "He told me about his wife. Only that she'd been in a car accident sometime last year." Cara shook her head, trying to drive away the image of Wes's blank expression. "It must have been so hard on him and the kids."

Especially Mark. He seemed so smart, so aware of what was going on around him, especially for a *three-going-on-forty*-year-old. At the memory of Wes's teasing description, she wanted to smile but couldn't push away her concern. Did Mark know the details of his mother's accident? Had he managed to make the connection, understanding she was never coming home again? Is that why he had looked so imploringly at her when he had asked if she was his new mommy?

"It *has* been really hard on them all," Andi said. "That's why agreeing to let you help him is such a big step—the biggest step Wes has made since Patty passed away. Seriously, Cara. Grandpa managed to get him out here to the ranch with the kids a while ago, but we all could see his heart wasn't in it."

Cara couldn't tell Andi how well she understood that. After she lost the baby, she'd spent her days at her friend Shelley's house pretending nothing was wrong, her nights curled up in her borrowed bed until she finally fell asleep, her mornings… Mornings were the worst of all, when she woke up with her mind blank for a few seconds, until the memories came crashing down.

Then she would force herself out of bed and go through it all again.

Obviously, Wes Daniels's answer was to shut himself off, to become nearly a hermit, as Jed called it.

If Cara was going to help the man, if she had questions while she was sorting his wife's personal possessions, she had to know what painful topics to avoid. "What happened to Patty?"

Andi shivered, wrapping her arms around herself as if she'd gotten a sudden chill. "Let's take a walk."

They went slowly down the steps and along the front of the hotel. Moonlight added just enough glow to reveal shadowy shapes across the ranch.

"It was awful," Andi said, her voice hushed. "Patty had gone up to Santa Fe for a friend's birthday party. She was driving back home after midnight and crossed over into oncoming traffic. Somehow, she avoided hitting anyone head-on—or they avoided her. But her car spun out, slammed into a guardrail and flipped over. And she didn't have her seat belt on."

"Then…she didn't survive the accident?"

"At first she did, if you can call it that. They had to cut open the car to get her out. She lasted a few days in the hospital, in a coma." Andi shook her head. "Wes and the kids never had the chance to talk to her again."

Cara's breath caught in her throat.

Driving back here, she had wondered about the accident. Reality was so much worse than her imagination. No wonder the man had isolated himself and his family. She would have, too…if she'd had a family.

She blinked rapidly, staring into the shadows.

She didn't want to go to Wes's house tomorrow, to talk about his adorable son or think about his baby daughter or, worst of all, to see the sorrow in his eyes.

Wes still grieved. Her wounds hadn't healed.

We have nothing at all in common and yet we're so alike.

Knowing Andi and the rest of the Garlands were waiting for her to visit had given her a lifeline she'd desperately needed. Wes Daniels had their support, too, if only he would reach out and take it.

He had always refused. Until tonight. She had gone to his house and offered her help, and he had accepted.

She couldn't walk away now.

WHEN WES OPENED his front door the next morning, Cara gave him the most natural smile she could manage. He swung the door wide, and she stepped inside. "Good morning. Am I too early?"

"Right on schedule. I'll take you up."

His abrupt response surprised her. He hadn't seemed uncomfortable talking to her last night. Maybe he wasn't a morning person. Or more likely, he had a long day of work ahead of him and didn't have time to chat.

On the second floor, he gestured toward a doorway halfway along the hall and waited for her to enter his bedroom ahead of him.

Trying not to seem overly curious, she quickly surveyed the room. A large bed almost lost in a sea of dressers and chests. Table lamps on two of the dressers. Another lamp and an alarm clock on one side of the bed. Mini blinds covering the two windows. That was it. No curtains or bedspread, no designer pillows, no knickknacks or framed pictures or family photos.

She'd stayed in hotel rooms with more personality.

Chances were Wes had made changes here after his wife passed away. Because he preferred a pared-down bedroom? Or because he couldn't bear the reminders in this private space Patty had once decorated for them both?

"You can skip the nightstands. But I'd appreciate it if you'd go through my wife's share of the bedroom and the closet. These are hers." He pointed out various pieces of furniture and indicated Patty's sections of the walk-in closet.

Patty's *share* included most of the dressers and chests, as well as nine-tenths of the closet. With all the sweaters and shirts and skirts and jeans, his wife could have opened a clothing store of her own.

Cara stepped in to take a closer look. "Most of her clothes in the closet don't look very worn. A lot of them still have the price tags attached." Why did Patty have so many clothes she didn't wear? But that wasn't her question to ask. "From what I can see already, it looks like most of the decisions are going to be easy to make. Once I go through the tagged clothing and accessories, I'd recommend you try selling them at a clothing consignment shop or flea market. I'll divide the rest into donate and toss piles."

"Sounds good. I'll be out on the ranch until late this afternoon. You'll have the place to yourself."

He had almost reached the doorway before she could blink. "A minute?"

He turned back, his brows raised.

"You remember last night, when I said starting an online business might be a good idea for Andi?" He nodded. "I mentioned your wife's crafts to her and she's definitely interested. I was wondering if I could take a look. Andi might be able to use some of it to get herself started. She said to tell you she would be happy to sell it for you, on consignment if you're interested or just outright if you'd prefer."

"Forget it. I don't want charity."

She resisted the urge to snap back at him. "Andi's not offering you any. She'd just like to have stock on hand. She's willing to sell the crafts for you and split the profits." She added in a softer tone, "I think Jed would call this *being neighborly.* I have the impression the Garlands all consider you a good friend."

Unfriendly seemed a better description, both now and when she'd met him at the Big Dipper. What he'd gone through this past year didn't excuse his attitude but could very well explain it.

WES SCUFFED ONE FOOT on the floor, wanting to kick himself for blurting out that remark about charity. Why give the woman ideas?

"The Garlands are good friends. And I imagine Andi's plans are on the level," he admitted, "but I wouldn't put it past Jed to... Never mind." He would see Jed himself. From the time Wes was a child Mark's age, he'd looked up to the man. That wouldn't keep him from calling him out on his interference. Jed had a reputation for knowing everything that went on in Cowboy Creek. Not one-hundred-percent true. There were things his old friend didn't— and would never—know about him.

"I'll show you Patty's craft stuff before I head out," he told Cara. "We've got a spare bedroom. Patty converted it into her office and stored everything there. It's at the far end of this hall."

He hesitated at the office doorway. It had been more than a year since he'd set foot in here. If he had his choice, he wouldn't enter it again. *Coward.*

As though someone had shoved him between the shoulder blades, he shot through the door and didn't stop till he reached the center of the room.

When Cara followed, he gestured toward the multiple storage chests and dressers, the stacks of boxes, the closed but—as he well remembered— overflowing closet. "Everything's packed full. But I don't know much about what Patty stock-piled in here."

Her eyes widened. "This is all inventory she'd planned to sell?"

He nodded. "As I said, she spent a lot of time on her crafts."

"I can see that. Mind if I browse?"

"That's why we're here." He leaned against the door frame, watching her check out the contents of half a dozen boxes and bins.

"Amazing. If all the rest is like this, Andi should be thrilled to have it for her start-up stock, if you're interested."

"That'll work."

"Great. Then once I finish up in your bed-room, I'll start making an inventory in here. It's going to take time, though less of it if I can work from an existing list. I'd guess your wife made one." She glanced around the room. "Do you have a computer?"

"Not me. Patty did. A laptop. I'll get it out when you're ready for it."

"Since you said you'll be gone most of the day, if you don't mind, I'd like to take a look at it before you go. The sooner the better, don't you think?"

"You read my mind," he said truthfully. Just as he'd read the look in her steady gaze. Her eyes held the same sympathy they had the night before. He'd seen too much of that from too many people this year.

Somehow, last night, he'd imagined he could accept her help. That with her being a stranger, her sympathy wouldn't bother him. Now he wished he'd never opened the door this morning. Wished he'd never seen her on the porch with the rising sun turning her hair a fiery golden red.

She had shown up promptly, and he had returned the favor, wasting no time in ushering her toward the stairs. No small talk. No offer of coffee. Definitely no mention of ice cream. Forget manners. The quicker she took care of clearing Patty's things from his bedroom, the sooner she'd go on her way again.

Or so he'd thought.

"I'll get the laptop." Forcing himself not to hurry, he loped across to the doorway and down the hall. The exit did nothing to ease his racing thoughts. Like a crazed horse with a fallen rider caught in his own stirrup, he fought against the weight of memories dragging him down no matter which way he turned.

A memory from last night punched him in the heart.

He'd watched Mark's face fall and his teeth bite down to worry his bottom lip. All his boy had cared about was making sure he could still have his ice cream, as if dessert had become the most important thing left in his world.

This past year, how had he lost sight of his son's needs, of what was best for both his kids? For their sake, he needed to do anything that would make him a better father. Clearing out that office down the hall was a start.

In his bedroom, he took the laptop from the closet shelf.

There were older memories he didn't want to think about. Memories of the mistakes he'd made with Patty.

How had he missed so many clues? That admission she'd made a while after their wedding about hating Cowboy Creek. Her boredom at spending all day alone on the ranch. The solution she'd come up with—her constant running with her friends.

He hadn't missed the rest. Patty had made sure of that when she'd flat-out told him she had never loved him. Had married him only to get out of her parents' house. She'd never wanted to be a rancher's wife.

CHAPTER SIX

CARA PROWLED THE bedroom-turned-office, checking out the storage boxes and dressers. Patty Daniels's interests had covered many kinds of crafts, with the results arranged in no particular order. In fact, they were a regular mess, with Christmas stockings piled on top of cotton place mats, woven leather belts tangled up with woolen scarves. And the list went on.

Cara hadn't exaggerated when she told Wes this inventory would take a while. How had he felt about that?

She didn't need to wonder how he felt about this room. The way he'd left, with his face strained and his eyes unfocused, answered that. Obviously, the office upset him. How long had it been since he'd come in here alone? What memories did this space hold for him?

Did she really want to know?

She crossed the room to open the door of what turned out to be a walk-in closet. After one step inside, she froze. Unlike the mixed-up piles in the office, the closet was so perfectly organized from top to bottom, it could have been lifted whole and set down in any department store.

Her heart thudded once, then picked up speed as she took everything in: infants' dresses on hangers suspended from clothing rods. Shelves of pint-size neatly folded shirts and pants. Rows of plastic bins, some filled with knitted caps, others with tiny pairs of booties, still others with one-piece cotton pajamas. As her gaze raced from one item to the next, her pulse skyrocketed. She stumbled to reverse her step out of the closet.

Her lower back slammed against an unyielding object. The collision knocked a startled yelp from her.

"Hey." Wes's deep voice sounded just inches from her ear.

She jumped and swallowed a second yelp. She hadn't even heard him come into the room again.

"Easy there. You okay?"

Her face burning, she turned and saw what she'd hit, the laptop he had gone to get for her. "I'm fine," she managed. But she wasn't. Seeing all those baby clothes had thrown her, almost literally.

"Good to hear. By the way, you nearly cost me a computer." His expression looked solemn, but she caught a trace of amusement in his voice.

Grateful for the distraction, she tried to match his light tone. "I can top that. That computer almost cost me a kidney."

"You didn't hit it that hard."

"Well…probably not. To tell you the truth, I think my pride hurts the most. I'm not usually startled that easily."

"Jumpy."

"That's another word for it. But I guess I'm off the hook. Since you say I didn't hit the laptop that hard, you won't be planning to charge me for any damages, will you?"

"Why not? We all have to pay for our mistakes." No amusement now. He sounded grim, as if the statement brought back a memory he'd rather forget.

She understood, not because of something she wanted to forget but because of something she simply wanted…but couldn't have.

Wes set the laptop on the edge of a dresser.

Still shaky, she crossed her arms. *Get a hold of yourself, woman.*

When he turned toward the door, she said quickly, "Do you want me to print out your wife's inventory list so I don't have to keep the laptop?"

He shrugged. "I don't use it much. I've got no idea what she has on there as far as files. You'll most likely need access to other info, so you might as well hang on to it."

"Then I'd feel more comfortable if you stay here while I go through the files. Just in case there's anything you need to see and I don't."

They both moved to the dresser, where he stood close enough for her to pick up the fresh-laundry scent of his blue T-shirt. He shoved his hands, large and strong-looking, into his pockets and hooked both thumbs on his belt.

As she focused on easing the laptop backward on the dresser to open it, she had to push away thoughts of the man beside her and that closet yawning like a bottomless pit just inches from her back.

Maybe agreeing to do this job wasn't a good idea at all.

They both stood silently as the computer powered up. On the surface of the black screen, she caught a glimpse of their reflections, both grim. Their shared expression reminded her of the thought she hadn't been able to get out of her mind last night.

We have nothing at all in common and yet we're so alike.

No matter how strongly she denied it to Andi, she could feel Wes's pain. She could see how much his son longed for a mother. And even a child his daughter's age must realize her mommy was gone.

How had she gotten so wrapped up so quickly in worrying over a man and a little boy she barely knew and a little girl she hadn't even met?

The computer screen came to life. She opened the documents folder, then frowned. There were only a half-dozen files, none of them with a name that sounded like craft inventory. "It doesn't look like she kept anything about her business—"

"Potential business."

"—potential business on the laptop. Are you sure you don't want to do this yourself?"

"Go on."

She shrugged. One by one she opened the files, letting Wes see the contents, mostly receipts for online purchases. "Guess I'll be starting from scratch as far as making a list."

"Yeah." He sounded irritated. Or upset.

"Having second thoughts?" she asked.

"Nope." He stepped back a pace and gestured at the laptop. "There's nothing on there I need to worry about. Feel free to do whatever you need with it and to stick around here as long as necessary."

"Thanks."

Time for her to start work, too. First in Wes's bedroom, then back here. It seemed suddenly important to wrap up both jobs as quickly as she could.

Yes, a break from being around the kids at the Hitching Post had sounded like a great idea at first. And of course she wanted to help Wes and now Andi. But almost every word Wes said and every expression that crossed his face reminded her of his grief, making it impossible to forget hers.

And then that closet. Eventually, she would have to deal with all those baby clothes, a seemingly innocent task that would revive so many other memories she wanted to forget.

Turning her back to the closet, she hurried to follow Wes from the room.

HE'D HAD GOOD REASON for returning to the house sooner than he'd intended. As he kicked off his boots on the back porch, Wes repeated that reason to himself. Common courtesy, nothing more. Maybe it would make up for forgetting his host duties that morning.

Of course, he could have used his cell phone to get in touch with Cara, but what were the chances she'd pick up the phone in a stranger's home?

Out in the living room, he looked up the stairway. If she hadn't heard the noises he'd made down here, he had better warn her he was around. Another courtesy. He called her name.

"Be right with you," she called back.

A moment later, he heard her footsteps in the hall.

As she leaned over the second-floor railing, her hair spilling over her shoulder. "Hi." She crossed her arms and rested them on the rail. "I didn't expect you this soon. I thought you told me you'd be back later in the day."

"Finished checking out the northeast pasture." No lie. He just hadn't gone on to the next pasture as planned. "I know it's long past time, but I forgot to tell you about lunch. There's plenty of fixings in the refrigerator. You can help yourself."

"Thanks, but I brought some snacks along with me and I've already eaten. Have you got a minute? I want to show you something up here."

"About the crafts? Not necessary. Between you and Andi, I'll trust you both to figure out what to do with everything."

"No, it's not about the crafts. Or it is, in a way. There's a drawer stuck in one of the dressers. I didn't want to force it or go looking around your house for your tools. If you'll just give me something to use to pry it open, I can handle it myself."

"I'll take care of it. I know which drawer you mean. The wood's warped." As he climbed the stairs, he added, "My wife picked up the piece secondhand on one of her flea-marketing trips."

"I love going to flea markets back home, especially around the holidays. You can get great deals on handmade crafts and antiques and find brand-new merchandise, too. I haven't been to the market here in Cowboy Creek yet."

"Patty shopped out of town."

Cara's silence said he'd spoken too abruptly. They got halfway down the hall before she spoke again, gesturing toward his bedroom door. "Since we're here, I want to show you what I've done."

She stepped into the room before he could answer.

Hanging back in the doorway, he stared at the bed. Hard even to see the bedcovers beneath the piles of clothes. So many shirts and sweaters and dresses Patty had bought and never worn. She had never had enough chances to wear them. One more thing she'd made sure he wouldn't forget.

Cara shifted. Realizing she'd been waiting to get his attention, he dragged his gaze away from the bed.

"I've already bagged up what you should probably toss. It wasn't much." She pointed to a large plastic bag in one corner of the room, then to the bed. "These piles are things you might like to donate. And this one is some tagged accessories I'll see if Andi might want to try selling online."

Still staring at the bed, he nodded, impressed and glad now he'd taken her help. Organized and businesslike help—just what he'd known he wouldn't get from the women at the Hitching Post or the older ladies in town. They meant well; they always had. But he needed someone who would focus on the job. Who didn't ask personal questions. Who wasn't sticking around.

When it came to this job, he needed Cara.

Startled by the thought, he looked up. She stared back.

Organized and businesslike she might be, but the one thing she had in common with all those other women was the one thing he didn't want to see in her blue eyes. The one thing he saw again now. Sympathy.

He crossed the room to the nightstand. Jerking open one of the drawers, he said, "How about jewelry? There's a box of it here."

"Well, I…" She sounded uncertain. Or tense. "I don't know that Andi would want to sell anything too expensive."

"It's not." He set the box on top of a pile of clothes. "The only things of value we ever had were our wedding rings. Patty's tastes didn't run to jewelry, just clothes." Good thing, too. Between clothes and crafts, she'd strained their budget enough. Not that she could see it that way. "I'm talking fake…plastic…whatever you call it."

"Costume jewelry."

"That's it."

"Okay. Some of that might fit in at the online store. Everything else with tags still on I've left in the closet for you to take a look at. Like I said, I'd recommend you try a clothing consignment shop or flea market for those."

"Whatever you think is fine with me."

"In that case, I'll bag those up, too."

She'd gone back to her businesslike tone again, much better than the tension he'd heard. Or thought he'd heard.

Maybe that had been all on him. Maybe he just hadn't wanted to be the only uncomfortable person in the room. "You were wanting to show me that drawer?"

"Yes."

They went to the office at the end of the hall. Earlier he'd hated having to enter this space. Now grateful for the diversion, he strode into the room.

"I spent most of my time in the bedroom," she said. "I only came in here once the questions came up about the clothes. I'm moving slowly, trying to organize as I go. There's so much here and no order to how it's been stored."

"Yeah. My wife was good at doing what she liked, not so good at following through on things she didn't choose to." To give her credit, she had taken great care of the kids. When she was around.

At least he'd had sense enough not to say that to Cara. He hadn't intended to volunteer the rest of the information, either. He hoped he'd kept any bitterness from his tone, not just for her benefit but his own. What right did he have to feel bitter?

"It's over that way." She pointed to a small oak dresser in the corner of the room, with one bottom drawer open only a few inches.

"Yeah. Patty had trouble with that drawer all along." He crouched in front of the dresser. "You've gotta know the secret. Push the whole thing back an inch, shove this side in another notch, then give it a yank and out it comes."

As he spoke, he demonstrated. The drawer flew loose, still in his hands, the momentum throwing him onto his butt. The drawer landed in his lap. Balls of knitting yarn bounced all around him and across the floor.

From behind him, he heard Cara's laugh, light and cheerful and directed at him. He'd earned it. But it proved his point about his own tension.

She leaned down to pick up some of the yarn, coming to his eye level. It made him think of the day they'd met at the Big Dipper.

"If that's the secret, I wish you'd kept it to yourself." Her smile took the sting out of her words and revealed those dimples he'd seen last night.

"You're not alone."

"Or were you just showing off, cowboy?"

"No, ma'am." He shook his head for emphasis. "What man wants to make a jackass of himself in front of a lady?"

"I wouldn't say you did that. But I wish I'd had my phone here to catch a video of you in action."

"I'm just as glad you didn't. I don't need anybody to believe I'm more of a fool than they already think."

"A fool?" Frowning, she dropped the balls of yarn into the drawer. "Why would anyone think that?"

"Forget it." He scrambled to his feet. This woman somehow made him run off at the mouth. And now he was just plain fixing to run.

He picked up the remaining balls of yarn and tossed them into the drawer. Once he'd put the drawer back, half-open, he rose. "The dresser is far enough out of your way, you should be okay leaving it like this for now. And speaking of leaving, I've got to clean up before I go for the kids."

It was too early to get them from Rhea's, but he needed more air. More space. Some time away from... From this room.

"I'd like to work here for a while yet," she said. "If that's okay with you."

"No problem."

She did have a problem, though, considering she hadn't stopped frowning since he'd said too much. Why he had felt he could let down his guard with her, he couldn't understand. He never should have said anything about Patty. And he never should have opened his mouth about what folks might think of him.

Maybe he *was* even more of a fool than they thought he was.

JED FOUND ANDI in the office behind the registration desk. "Is Cara still over at Wes's?"

"Yes. I just talked to her a little while ago," Andi said.

Why that conversation would have made her look so grim, he didn't know. But he didn't like seeing any of his girls upset about anything. He took the chair beside the desk and studied her. "Why don't you seem happy?"

"Because Cara didn't sound happy. She had a chance to look at Patty's crafts, and everything's great with that. There's literally a roomful of handmade things of all kinds, and she says the quality is exactly what she'd hoped." Her brief smile settled into a frown again. "But there's something wrong. I don't mean about the crafts. Something else worrying her, more than what she already told me about breaking up with Brad."

Jed didn't like seeing any of his granddaughters' friends unhappy, either. "If she's not volunteering the information, maybe you need to ask her straight out."

"You're probably right. I feel terrible. Ever since she got here, I've been so focused on getting her to help Wes and now the idea of selling the crafts and… Well, that's almost all I've talked about. I can't believe I didn't notice before now there's something else bothering her."

He patted her hand. "That's not all on you. Cara's a quiet one, always has been. You told me that, and I've seen it for myself. If you didn't catch on, it's because she didn't want you to."

"That makes it even worse. I'm her best friend."

"Which means she'll have her reasons for not telling you, I'm sure."

"She won't after I get her alone for a while tonight."

He laughed. "That's my girl."

"And I have to do something to convince her to stay. The good thing is, at least the inventory she's going to make of all Patty's crafts will take a while."

"If you're busy here getting ready for the next wedding, you won't be able to help her out, will you? That'll make her job take even longer."

"Oh, I like that!"

"I thought you might." He grinned. "Then when she's close to finishing, we'll move on to the next step—getting her more involved in your ideas for the business. That'll provide some reasons you need her here. And if she starts up about her room, you make sure to tell her I won't hear about her paying for it."

"I will."

"You know, this is one of those times I think it's wise to call in reinforcements. I'll get in touch with Mo." His old friend Mo O'Neill belonged to every women's group at the community center.

"Another great idea. I'm going to want to talk to *all* the ladies in the crafts circles."

"And you may want to give Rhea a call."

"Rhea? Why? She's too busy with the day care to have time for making crafts." Her eyes narrowed. "You mean because she watches Wes's kids. Grandpa, you *are* trying to get Cara and Wes together, aren't you?"

"If I admit the possibility, you're not going to make a fuss, are you? You agreed they'd make a good match?"

"Definitely. But I don't want Cara to get hurt again if something goes wrong."

"Wrong?" He laughed. "You need to have more faith in your old grandpa. My matchmaking skills have never let us down."

"WE'RE HO-OME!" MARK sang out from the back seat of the pickup truck, as he always did when they made the turn into the front yard.

"Ho-ome!" Tracey echoed.

"Yes, we're home." Wes gave the expected response while half-distracted by the car still parked outside the house.

He looked at his dashboard clock. Nearly two hours since he'd showered and left to go into town to the sitter's. Normally, he'd have arrived much later, after most parents had already picked up their kids. Today he'd walked into a full house. Rhea's other charges had greeted him like a long-lost friend. Mark had insisted on showing him the finger-painted pictures he'd done that day, then had him look at all his other friends' creations.

Wes checked the clock again. Yep. Nearly

two hours, and Cara hadn't left yet. Good thing he didn't need to pay her overtime.

He helped his son from his car seat. Mark, usually more aware of his surroundings, raced from the truck to the kitchen door at the rear of the house without seeing the car. Also a good thing.

"Ho-ome, Daddy," Tracey said, as if she felt he needed the reminder.

"Right. Let's go, little girl."

"Go, go, go," she chanted all the way to the back porch. *Go* was one of her favorite words.

In the kitchen, as expected, Wes found Mark already at the table with his coloring supplies. "Be right back. I'm going to take Tracey upstairs. It'll be a little while before we start supper." Yeah, he'd picked up the kids *that* early. Maybe he should have stopped at the hardware store first to kill time.

This afternoon, he'd been driven to leave the house. Now he was just as drawn toward the rear bedroom down the hall. To see how far Cara had gotten. To judge how soon she would be ready to finish the job.

She knelt in front of a pile of opened boxes. If he'd taken the same position when he'd yanked open that drawer earlier, he wouldn't have landed the way he had or made any stupid statements. Maybe. She looked over her shoulder, then scrambled to her feet, eyeing him and the baby.

"This is my daughter, Tracey," he said.

"Hi, hi, hi," Tracey chirped. Another of her favorite words.

"Hello, Tracey." Cara's smile seemed forced. "She's very cute. I didn't expect—"

She stopped, her cheeks turning as rosy as Tracey's did when she was cranky from being overtired. The thought left him swallowing a laugh.

"I mean, you're back already." She glanced at her watch. "Forget that. It's later than I thought."

"How far along did you get?"

"Not that far. I finished up in your room first. And I just got off the phone after talking for quite a while with Andi. In between, I made a start on the dressers. They're mostly filled with yarn and thread and crafting supplies. I don't think those will be something she would sell."

"Me, neither."

"She's planning to come out to look everything over with me, though, so I'll show it to her."

"Sounds good. Tell her I'd be happy if she'd

donate the supplies to the women's clubs. They do a lot of knitting and sewing and everything else."

"That's very nice of you."

Yeah. Nice of him to find a way to get rid of more memories.

He crossed the room to look down at the boxes she'd returned to kneeling beside.

Squealing, Tracey leaned forward, almost toppling from his grasp. "Whoa, girl." He wrapped his free arm around her to hold her close but hadn't counted on those long arms of hers.

She grabbed a strand of Cara's wavy hair and tugged. "P'etty!"

"Yes, it's pretty." Hadn't he warned himself again and again not to notice? And now before he could stop himself, he'd gone and put it into words. Hopefully, Cara thought he was just echoing the word for the baby. "But we don't pull hair, Tracey." He reached for her fingers at the same time Cara did. Their hands collided.

"It's okay," she said. "I've got it." Carefully, she pried open Tracey's fingers. Tracey promptly clamped them around her thumb. Cara's laugh sounded shaky as she worked her way out of the new hold. "She's a strong little girl, isn't she?"

"Yes, she is. Aren't you, baby?" he asked, tickling her under her chin till she giggled. "Strong, just like your big brother."

Cara knelt beside the box again, moving out of hair-pulling range. "Before I go, I just want to finish sorting this box I've been working on."

"Sounds good." He should go, too, to put Tracey down for her nap. Somehow, his feet didn't want to move in the direction of the door. Instead, he wandered over to the closet. "Looks like you didn't get going in here yet."

It took her a moment to answer. "I'll probably wait and tackle that last."

"You make it sound like a challenge. Considering it's so neat inside, I'd think it would be the easiest part of the room to handle."

"That's why I'm leaving it till the end."

Her voice didn't ring true. "Any reason you don't want to go in there?"

Her gaze snapped to his. "No."

Tracey yipped and rubbed her eyes. Crankiness factor on the rise. "She needs a nap. See you downstairs later."

Wanting to kick himself, he left the room. Cara's comment about letting the easiest part of the job go till last made sense. So what if his curiosity nudged him, making him wonder why her tone and words didn't match?

He wasn't interested in her. Couldn't be interested in her. And he needed to start reining in his thoughts. Now.

CHAPTER SEVEN

IN THE KITCHEN AGAIN, Wes got busy assembling what he needed for supper, determined to distract himself from thoughts of the woman upstairs. What did it matter to him how she wanted to handle her work? Or how her hair looked?

And here he was, thinking of her again.

Mark still knelt at the table with his crayons and drawing paper. He looked up now, as if just realizing Wes had come back to the room. "Where's Tracey? Nap?"

"Yes. She's going to sleep now."

Footsteps sounded overhead, followed by the creak of a floorboard.

Mark's eyes opened wide. "Who's there?"

"That's Miss Cara. She's upstairs."

"Oh." He smiled. "Miss Cara going to sleep now, too?"

Imagining Cara cranky had made Wes laugh. The image now springing to mind did anything but that. He shook his head, both to chase away the vision and in response to Mark. "No, Miss Cara's not going to sleep now."

He appreciated knowing his boy had an extensive vocabulary and a great imagination, yet he didn't always like the answers he had to supply to Mark's questions. Considering what his son had said last night, this answer would be one he disliked giving most of all. He took a seat at the table. "Remember, I told you, Miss Cara is only here for a visit."

The sight of his son's crestfallen expression lodged a lump in Wes's throat. While Mark had cried for his mother during the months after her death, he'd never asked where Patty was or when she was coming home. Wes hated to admit it, but put to the test, he didn't know how he would have answered.

"Miss Cara is upstairs working," he amended. "She's…going to be helping Daddy with some…some baby things he needs to send away."

Mark's mouth fell open. *"Tracey?"*

"No, not Tracey. I would never send the baby or you away." This was too close to the questions he had feared he'd get from Mark about his mother. But until Mark asked outright or became old enough to understand, Wes wouldn't bring up the issue. He ruffled his son's hair. "Miss Cara is just taking care of some things your mommy made with her crafts."

"Miss Cara help?" Mark asked. When Wes nodded, the boy dropped the crayon on the table and slid from the bench. "I help, too."

"I don't think she needs any assistance right now."

"I'm not 'sistance. I'm Mark." He nearly ran from the room.

Shaking his head, Wes watched him go. How had his son grown so big in such a short time? Become so determined, so sure of himself? However it happened, Wes was glad to see Mark's independent streak reassert itself. Over the past year, he'd gotten too needy, too clingy.

Wes had himself to blame for that.

Mark rushed back into the room, followed by Cara at a slower pace. "Daddy, Miss Cara's here!"

Wes forced a smile. "Are you both all done working?"

Mark nodded and took his seat at the table again.

Silently, Wes looked at Cara.

"He wanted to help," she said. "I told him I'm sorry but I'm finished for the day."

"Sounds good." He rose. "I'll walk you out. Be right back, Mark." He kept the door open and stood on the porch beside Cara. Just the way it had this morning, her hair shone golden red in the sunshine.

"Will the same time tomorrow morning be okay with you?" she asked.

"That works." After a glance into the kitchen, he kept his voice low and asked, "Did you tell Mark you'd be coming back?"

"No. I thought that might not be a good idea."

"You thought right. If he knew you were on your way here, I'd probably never get him out of the house to go to the sitter's."

"I'll plan to be gone earlier tomorrow afternoon. He won't see me at all." She paused. "But he does seem…eager for company."

The hesitation—the signal she had worded her statement carefully, the way he had with Mark—made Wes's spine stiffen. "He's a friendly kid. And he gets plenty of playtime with his friends at Rhea's nearly every day."

"I'm sure he does. Still, he's got a lot of energy, and kids can't turn that off. I bet they wouldn't mind if you brought him over to the Hitching Post to play with the kids there once in a while, too. On the weekends, maybe."

Wes knew the signs. Jed Garland, at it again.

Gesturing, he led her down the porch steps. "Did Jed put you up to this?"

She frowned. "To what?"

"Trying to get me to visit the Garlands. To hang out. To socialize. Bad enough Jed sends his invitations through my brother—he's a hand on the ranch over there. Is the man using you as a messenger, too?"

"*Using* me? Put me *up to this*? Why would you think that? You just told me yourself Mark's friendly, which I've already seen for myself. And *friendly* kids like to play with their *friends*."

"Yeah." Wes sighed and ran a hand through his hair. "Guess I sounded half-paranoid. Not my intent. I meant, Jed's been trying every way he can to get me over to the Hitching Post."

"What's wrong with that?"

"He thinks—" He snapped his jaw shut.

After a moment, she asked, "Does this have something to do with what you said this afternoon?"

Like his son, this woman didn't miss much. "About folks thinking I'm a fool? Maybe."

"But why?"

What? Why? Darned if she didn't sound like Mark, too, with all the questions. And darned if he didn't want to do his best to answer, only because that's what he did with Mark. But unlike with his son, he didn't owe this woman a complete answer. "They think I need to get out more," he said. "As if I have the spare time."

"I don't know much about running a ranch, except what I've seen at the Hitching Post. That's enough to tell me it's a huge job, even with all those cowboys on the payroll. I can't imagine what it's like for you to do the work all alone."

"It's no problem," he said flatly. "My brother gives me a hand if Jed can spare him, or if not, the local ranchers are good at helping one another. And when it's a busy time for us all around here, I hire transients and day laborers, good men who come back to me every season. So don't waste any sympathy on me. Jed and everyone else shouldn't, either."

"Maybe they're concerned about your kids, too," she said in a softer tone.

"I love my kids."

"I know you do. That's plain enough for anyone to see."

"And I can take care of them."

"Of course, you can. But—"

"No buts. We're doing just fine. And if Jed Garland asks, that's exactly what you can tell him."

BY THE TIME Cara arrived back at the hotel, the Garlands and their guests had gathered in the dining room. Everyone was still swarming around the room, which was now full of the party atmosphere that usually kicked off the evening meal at the Hitching Post.

Andi saw her and came to her side immediately. "We thought we were going to be minus a guest at the family table tonight," she teased.

"No, I just left Wes's house later than I'd planned."

What had gotten to him tonight? Something beyond grief seemed to make him fly off the handle. Paranoia, as he'd jokingly claimed? A chip on his shoulder? Guilt connected to his kids? He'd sounded defensive when he insisted he could take care of them. Or was she just imagining things?

Cara refocused on Andi. "I thought about calling to let you know I was on the way, but in the time it would've taken me to reach you I'd almost be on your doorstep. It's not that far from Wes's place to here."

"True. So, how did the rest of your day go?"

"Fine."

We're doing just fine. Why had Wes sounded as though he needed to remind himself of that even as he tried to convince her?

Maybe she'd imagined that, too.

Jed stopped in front of them and handed Andi a tall glass. "Your iced tea. And I brought one along for you, Cara." He held out a second glass.

"Thanks." She accepted it gratefully. It had been awhile since she'd finished her last bottle of water, and though Arizona would win in any argument over which state had the driest air, New Mexico was arid, too.

"How did things go over at Wes's house?" Jed asked, almost echoing Andi's question.

Cara eyed them both. Maybe her imagination wasn't working overtime, and maybe Wes wasn't as paranoid as he thought. "Patty Daniels had a room filled with crafts."

"So Andi says." Laughter from conversations around them almost drowned out his deep voice. He gestured to the wide doorway. "Why don't we step out in the hall to continue this conversation?" As soon as he'd ushered them from the room, he said, "Did my girl get the chance to tell you her news?"

Cara looked at Andi, who grinned. "I'm going to be opening a store."

"A store? Where?"

"Right here in town. I hope, anyhow. There are some vacant storefronts on Canyon Road."

"You sound like a woman with a plan." Obviously, this idea excited Andi too much to let her drop it. At least *one* of them had their future lined up. "You've got this all thought out, haven't you?"

"Not too much beyond what I've just said," Andi admitted. Although she sent an almost uneasy glance toward her grandfather, her cheeks turned pink at the compliment. "I'm just getting started," she told Cara.

"Andi…" She held back a frown. "You know I'm the last person who would want to talk you out of a career. But starting a business is a completely different proposition than selling products online. You'll need to think about overhead costs, especially in a small town. What are the options on the square footage?"

"I don't know. I haven't looked yet."

"And what about future inventory?" This business had nothing to do with her, but as much as she wanted to avoid getting caught up in the planning, she had to ask questions. What kind of friend would she be if she didn't help Andi see all the angles and avoid potential problems? "What are you going to do when you make sales and your stock runs out?"

Jed laughed. "I knew Andi had a smart idea, roping you in on this."

"The inventory is the best part," Andi said, her eyes shining. "If I can get this business off the ground, I can also help some of the women in Cowboy Creek. They don't have much opportunity to earn money here, either, but so many of them are good at crafts."

"There are active groups at the community center," Jed put in. "A knitting club…a sewing club…"

"Grandpa's right. Not everyone's going to be interested, of course, but I imagine plenty of the women will love the chance to earn some money."

"That's probably true." And it might mean Andi could manage without her help. "In that case, maybe you won't need Wes Daniels's inventory, after all."

"Exactly the opposite," Jed said. "Andi needs it more than ever if we're going to give that boy a hand. We've seen some progress with him, thanks to you. And we want to help him get to the point where he can move on."

His simple statement opened a floodgate of questions. How long would it take for Wes to feel ready? For her to feel the same? How long did grief last? It had already been more than a year for him. Did everyone need the same amount of time?

She didn't have answers to any of the questions, couldn't argue Jed's statement and didn't want to. No matter what Wes thought, he and his family did need help. And she would help... for as long as she was around.

"Wes mentioned the crafts clubs."

"Did he?" Jed studied her, his white eyebrows raised.

Andi stared at her just as intently.

Quickly, she explained about the supplies she had found. "Wes understood you wouldn't sell crafting material, so he asked me if you'd donate it to the clubs."

"No problem," Andi said. "It was nice of him to offer that."

"That's what I told him."

"And he's a nice guy, don't you think?"

"Sure. But his being nice—or not—has nothing to do with bringing you customers. And how will you sell anything if everyone in town can make their own crafts?"

"That's more good news. Grandpa heard from a town council member there's going to be an exit opening up off the highway, just outside Cowboy Creek. Isn't that perfect?"

"For Andi's store and the Hitching Post, too," Jed said with a smile. "Of course, construction will take a while, but that'll give

Andi time to get set up. Then think of all the tourists we'll be able to attract. Speaking of which…"

He stopped to greet a small group of guests coming down the hallway.

Once he'd escorted them into the dining room, Andi tilted her head in that direction. "Come on. I've got to get in there and mingle, too. Never a dull moment around this place. Or a quiet one. But I've taken care of that. Mitch is going to keep an eye on the kids after dinner while you and I have some best-friend time."

Her suddenly serious tone gave Cara the first signal something was up. The second hint came from Andi's smile. A warm, sunny smile that didn't match the concern in her eyes.

CARA SETTLED IN a chair in the Garlands' private wing with a mug of tea cradled in her hands.

She and Andi had left the dining room before most of the Garlands and their guests had gotten up from their tables.

"Hope you don't mind if I take care of laundry while we chat." Andi laughed. "It seems like there's always a basket at the washing or drying or folding stage around here."

"I don't mind." But Cara did. Watching Andi

smooth a small pink T-shirt on the couch cushion reminded her of the closet at Wes's house. And the closet at Wes's reminded her of—

"The new exit is great news, isn't it?"

Grateful for the distraction, Cara nodded. "On the upside, it could be fantastic if it actually brings people into town. If you decide to take Patty Daniels's inventory—and she's definitely got enough to get you started in business—and supplement that with stock from your local crafters, you could have a very good thing going."

"That's what I was thinking."

"Then add in a line of southwestern-themed gifts, and you might be looking at a potential gold mine."

Andi paused midfold and stared, her eyes wide. "I love that idea!"

"Remember, that's the best-case scenario," Cara cautioned. "And that's based on having enough tourists or travelers come to town. On the other hand, I hate to point out the downside of your plan, but you need to consider it, too."

"And what's that?"

"A lease on the property alone could put you in a financial hole. With a family to worry about, I'm not sure you'd want to go that route. Couldn't you start off small and here at the hotel?" She gestured in the general direction of the Hitching Post's entrance. "I'm sure Jed would find space out in the lobby or somewhere close to it for you to set up some shelving and displays."

"We already talked about it today. The only space available is the room behind the reception desk. That's the management office, Tina's domain. And I want to do more than set up a few displays. With all the women I expect to be interested in making crafts to sell, I'm going to need at least a small store."

"Start-up costs are expensive."

"I know. And Grandpa offered to take care of those. But Mitch and I discussed it, and for now, anyhow, I want to try handling everything on my own." She smiled. "Don't worry. This is going to work out. I can feel it. Here." She held up her tea mug and leaned sideways toward Cara's chair. "For good luck."

Their mugs clinked together.

"I'm sure I'll be able to keep to budget," Andi went on. "Of course, I won't know details about what's available for lease in town till I start looking. I'm going to the realty office tomorrow."

"Tomorrow? What happened to looking over inventory with me?"

"That can wait for a few days. You said you've barely sorted through anything yet. While you're taking care of that, I'll make looking for the store my priority. I don't want to miss out on a good deal."

Andi dropped her hands to her lap, apparently unaware she was crumpling a freshly washed T-shirt.

"Since we won't have much time to talk in the morning, we'd better make the most of tonight. So, tell me what's wrong."

Grateful she didn't have to help fold those little clothes, Cara wrapped her hands around the hot tea mug. "Nothing."

"Oh, no. I don't buy that, just like you didn't buy it when I said the same thing yesterday. Something else is wrong. I mean, besides Brad. I know you're upset about breaking up with him—"

"No, I'm over him." She'd answered honestly but now, too late, realized her mistake would cost her.

"Really?" Andi tilted her head, eyeing her thoughtfully. "I'll admit, you seem to be okay. But there's *something* still bothering you. Since you've gotten here, you haven't acted like yourself around Trey or Missy or any of the kids. And you haven't once held Emilia."

No, she hadn't held Tina's baby. But she had hugged Robbie and Trey…shared hugs and kisses with Missy…caught Tracey's hand to untangle her hair from those little fingers… All those moments had been more than enough for her.

Cradling an infant might push her over the edge. Even now, just the thought brought tears to her eyes.

Tears Andi didn't miss. "Tell me."

"I…" She sighed, then blinked to clear her vision. "I would have told you sooner, but we've been so focused on Wes and his kids, and then talking about the store, and then—"

"Cara, please."

"I know. This is just so hard to say." She took a deep breath meant to pull herself together. It didn't help. "I told you what happened with Brad. I wasn't up in Flagstaff with him very long, just a few weeks in early spring, before I found out I was pregnant. We'd talked about having a family and we both wanted kids. But when I told him the news he…he said he'd changed his mind."

Andi gasped.

"That's when I broke up with him." Cara rushed on, knowing she had to get this out while she still could. "And then at the beginning of the summer, I—" Her voice broke. "I lost the baby."

"Oh, Cara." Andi reached out to give her a hug. "I'm so sorry." She grabbed a tissue from a box on the end table, then handed Cara the box. "You shouldn't have gone through that all alone."

"I know." She dried her eyes. "I planned to tell you. When I found out I was pregnant, I didn't share the news with anybody, not even the friend I stayed with when I went back to Phoenix. I wanted to wait till I got here. To surprise you. And then when…when I lost the baby, you were the first person I wanted to tell, too. But I couldn't share all that over the phone. Not the good news and the bad news in one call."

Andi nodded, her eyes tearing again.

"I know I could have asked to come sooner," she admitted. "Except by then I was having a hard time just making it through the days. And after I got here and you told me what you did, about you and Mitch trying to get pregnant—"

"Oh, no. You shouldn't have kept it to yourself just because of that."

She gave a shaky laugh. "You didn't plan to tell me either, remember?"

"Well, all right, that's true. But I still wish

you had called me instead of going through everything on your own. That's what best friends are for, you know."

"Yes, I do know."

"Are you okay? I mean, physically?"

Cara nodded. "I had a follow-up appointment just before I left home, and everything checks out. The doctor doesn't have any answers about what happened. She said they don't always know." She would never know why she had lost her baby.

She pressed her hand, warm from holding the tea mug, against her stomach. Her skin heated beneath her shirt, but the warmth couldn't reach the cold emptiness inside.

CHAPTER EIGHT

AFTER A RESTLESS NIGHT and a quick breakfast, Cara again drove to Wes's ranch at the promised time. She rang the doorbell, waited awhile, then tried again. By now, he should have gotten home after dropping off the kids at their day care center. Maybe he was working in the barn she'd seen yesterday.

She wandered around to the rear of the house. At the back porch steps, she spotted a small sheet of paper protruding from the edge of the screened door. Most likely a note for her.

Off to work. Door is open, Wes had written. He hadn't signed the note, just scribbled a phone number.

People in small towns certainly trusted their fellow man—or woman. Back home, she wouldn't have left her door unlocked to go to the mailboxes at the end of her block.

She slid the note into her jeans pocket on her way into the kitchen. Since she had missed lunch at the Hitching Post yesterday, Paz in-

sisted on sending a sandwich, fruit and cookies along with her today. When she tried to
protest the care package wasn't necessary, Jed
had jokingly—or maybe not so jokingly—said
refusing food would upset Paz, and nobody but
nobody was allowed to upset his cook.

Cara had given in and accepted the offering
with much gratitude. To tell the truth, those
snacks yesterday afternoon had barely kept
her hunger satisfied until dinnertime.

Wes had left the kitchen clean and tidy. She
noted the dishpan and Tracey's toys air-drying in
a drainer, Mark's artwork covering the front of
the refrigerator, his crayon boxes and construction paper stored neatly on a handy counter—
all proof of how much Wes cared for his kids.
But she had seen the signs of that before today.

When he had told her he loved his children,
she'd already had no doubt. Every time she was
with him, she saw the evidence in the way he
ruffled his son's hair and squeezed his shoulder, how he tickled his daughter beneath her
chin, making her giggle. She heard the caring in his voice when he talked to both kids.
Whether he knew it or not, Wes's every word
and gesture revealed how much he loved them.

If only—

No. If-onlys came from the past, from what

might have been, from what had never happened. Hadn't she promised herself she would look only toward the future?

Needing a distraction, she stored her lunch bag in the refrigerator, then stepped back to examine the outside of the door. It served as a gallery for Mark's crayoned drawings, finger-painted creations and a few ragged-edged coloring book pictures.

Beside one of the drawings, a couple of magnets held photos of the kids to the door. One photo showed Mark on the living room couch with his arm draped across Tracey's shoulders. Stuffed animals filled every available space on the couch around them.

The other photo was of Tracey. Newborn Tracey, wrapped in a baby blanket and cuddled against her daddy's chest. The photo blurred as though it had fallen into a dishpan full of water.

Before she could block it, an if-only slipped past her defenses.

If only everything had gone as it should, which would she have held in *her* arms one day, a tiny son or daughter of her own?

She grabbed her purse and laptop from the table, then nearly fled from the kitchen. She'd made it halfway to the stairs off the living room when she heard the back door open.

Blinking, she turned. "Wes? Did you forget something?"

One step into the kitchen again, she froze. The man framed in the doorway wasn't Wes.

He smiled broadly. "Hey. Hope I'm not interrupting anything."

That smile turned him into one good-looking cowboy. Yet he didn't interest her a bit...except for making her see how Wes could look if he'd just let himself relax.

"I'm meeting Wes," he said. "I'm early and thought I'd catch up with him here, instead of where we'd planned. I'm Garrett, the older, better-looking brother."

"I can see the family resemblance." Garrett was tall and broad-shouldered, with Wes's thick, dark hair and—as she saw when she walked closer—Wes's dark brown eyes. "He mentioned having a brother."

"Did he?" Another smile. "No offense, but he's never told me about you."

"We just met this weekend."

"Is that so?" His brows rose, relaying his thought as clearly as if he'd said it aloud. *Well, somebody sure moved fast.*

She would need to clear up that misconception just as quickly. Whether it was Wes's reputation or her own she wanted to save, she didn't know. "I'm Cara Leonetti. I'm a guest at the Hitching Post."

"You're Andi's friend. *Jed* did tell me about you." She couldn't miss the emphasis. "Speaking of my boss, he let me have the morning off to give Wes a hand. And as Jed would say, time's a-wasting. Wes around?"

He glanced toward the doorway into the hall as if his brother would materialize behind her. Then he looked up at the ceiling. Listening for footsteps? For the sound of the shower running? "He isn't here," she said. "He's already gone off to work for the day."

"And left you all alone at home."

Before she could protest, he went on, "I'd better head out, too. I know where to find him." He stopped in midturn toward the door. "Any message you want me to pass along when I see him?"

Who knew what Garrett would make of anything she could say. Maybe best to let Wes explain what she was doing in his house. "You can just tell him I'll be here when he gets…back."

So much for her good intention. Judging by the man's grin, he'd noticed her careful sidestep around the word *home* and now thought the worst anyway.

FROM THE DRIVER'S SEAT of his truck, Wes watched a roadrunner scratch at a patch of bare earth near the sagging fence line he'd come to repair. Some local tribes claimed this bird warded off evil and brought good luck. He could use both.

In the distance, he saw a familiar truck headed in his direction. Garrett.

Wes frowned. His brother had gotten here ahead of schedule. How long had he been sitting, thinking, when he should've been working as hard as Cara probably was? The dashboard clock reassured him Garrett wasn't early after all.

Why Wes had left the house so soon, he didn't want to admit. Still, he couldn't avoid the answer. He didn't want to see Cara again.

Not a problem he'd face much longer. She'd finish her job, then his life would go back to normal. As normal as it could ever get.

He watched his brother climb out of his truck, both hands full, and shove the door closed with his elbow.

The roadrunner cocked its head as if evaluating the situation. Even with a wingspan nearly equal to their length, roadrunners preferred to stay grounded. Those wings, held close to their bodies, combined with their long, sleek tail feathers, gave the birds an advantage on land. Their speed easily exceeded the limits on the county roads.

His speed when he'd left home would have beaten any roadrunner's. Of course, he hadn't actually run from the house this morning, but he couldn't get out of there soon enough to suit himself. No need to stay. Cara would find the note he'd left her and get to work more quickly without him hanging around. Exactly what he wanted—along with getting her out of his mind.

He focused on Garrett, carrying a monster-sized insulated mug in each hand. Wes leaned over and opened the passenger door.

"Nice to see you didn't start without me, bro. Here." Garrett held out a mug. "Courtesy of Paz, since she knows how much you like her hot chocolate."

"Yeah, like you don't. You knew she'd send some along for me. That's probably why you volunteered to help me out today." To tell the truth, he'd looked forward to the drink. It had been a long time since he'd had some of Paz's chocolate.

And whose fault is that?

Ignoring the voice in his head, Wes swallowed some chocolate. "Yeah, that chili powder really gives it a kick, doesn't it?"

"Makes it good and hot," Garrett agreed. "Like that lady you left behind."

Wes froze with the mug halfway to his mouth. "You stopped by the house."

"I was early. Thought I'd catch you there. I didn't expect to catch you up to something, too. She's *definitely* a hot one."

"I wouldn't know, and I'm not up to something."

"Wouldn't know?" Garrett conveniently skipped over the second half of the response. "How could you miss it? All that red hair."

Golden red. He blinked, trying to drive away the automatic thought. To chase away the memory of Cara standing in the sunshine. Where had this fixation on color come from lately? Spending too much time sorting out Mark's crayons?

"And those big blue eyes," Garrett went on enthusiastically. "For sure, she's worth a second look. Good thing you're staking a claim before all those lonesome cowhands at Jed's meet her at the next cookout."

"Knock it off, Gar. You always did talk too much."

"I wouldn't have had to if you'd talked enough."

History, old and new. Now he made the convenient conversational jump. "I said I'm not interested. I haven't staked a claim. And it's not her first visit to the Garlands. Those boys must've seen her before." Because Garrett was right. No red-blooded male would have let Cara's arrival go unnoticed.

"Where was I when she was around?"

Wes swallowed another mouthful of chocolate. "Probably dancing till closing time at the Cantina." Everybody in Cowboy Creek knew how his brother liked to spend his nights off. Wes eyed Garrett, who was just as likely as Mark not to give up till he got answers. At this rate, they'd never get any work done.

Briefly, Wes explained about Andi's new business and Cara's part in helping her. "She's only coming by the house for a day or two, sorting through some of Patty's crafts for Andi."

He expected a smart remark somewhere along the lines of *strike while the iron's hot*, but to his surprise, Garrett nodded, straight-faced. "Good idea. It's time you started thinking about clearing up all that stuff. Started looking at moving on."

"The only place I plan to move on to is over by that fence."

"What's with the sudden rush to get to work?"

"Not sudden." Wes forced a laugh and gave an obvious lie. "I've been waiting half the morning for you." He climbed from the pickup truck and made his way to the rear.

A moment later, Garrett's door slammed.

The roadrunner cocked his head, evaluating again. Now obviously suspecting danger, the bird took off in its typical hop-run. Wes wouldn't have minded going along. Leaving the truck hadn't left the conversation behind. Yeah, Mark definitely got his stick-to-the-subject trait from his uncle, Garrett.

Swallowing a sigh, Wes let down the tailgate and set the mug of chocolate to one side. Sure enough, before he could hoist himself onto the bed of the truck, Garrett clapped a hand on his shoulder.

Wes looked toward the horizon and considered, as the roadrunner had. Maybe the bird had gotten it right about the danger. He turned, shaking off his brother's hand. "Now what?"

"I'm serious, bro." Garrett shrugged. "All right, maybe you're not interested in the woman back at the house. When you're ready for that, you'll be ready. But you need to be careful."

Wes choked on a laugh. He'd never forget being a teen and having his brother—the only family member he had left—sit him down for "*the* talk." Girls and birds and bees and all the rest of it. Looking back, he had to give Garrett credit for trying, especially when he hadn't expected the overnight promotion from older brother to stand-in dad. But it was the most uncomfortable conversation they'd ever had. Until this one, maybe.

"Come on, Garrett. I'm all grown-up now. We don't need to have any more *talks*."

"Doesn't matter. We're having this one. It's way overdue. And you've been cutting yourself off for way too long."

"And you've been hanging around your boss too much."

"This isn't coming from Jed. This is from me. Your brother. Mark and Tracey's uncle. If you can't listen for your own sake, then do it for theirs."

Maybe they're concerned about your kids, too, Cara had told him in a soft voice.

Garrett resettled his hat. Years ago, that sight would have given Wes a sure sign his older brother was about to lay down the law to him. Too bad. He no longer had to answer to anyone.

"You ought to get out more," Garrett said.

Wes had. The afternoon he had met Cara. Little did he know their meeting would lead to this. "I took Mark for ice cream just the other day."

"Okay, it's a start. But not enough. If you're not interested in seeing that woman—" this time, doubt laced Garrett's tone "—at least get out once in a while. Visit with folks. Go into town for a beer with the boys. Come to a cookout at Jed's. Take Mark to the Bowl-a-Rama. Do anything that will get you away from the ranch for a while. Everybody but you can see you're spending all your time here."

"Then that ought to prove to everybody I'm doing fine."

Fine. Just what he'd told Cara.

He was doing fine. Why didn't folks believe him?

CHAPTER NINE

LIKE A PARCHED HORSE catching sight of a creek, Wes found himself drawn to the room at the end of the hall. What was wrong with him?

To his credit, when he had gotten home a few minutes earlier, he had done better than this. After calling out to Cara to let her know he was there, he had gone to take his shower. Had somehow managed to avoid walking down this hall. Those good intentions hadn't lasted long.

Well, it was only polite to check in on her, wasn't it? And to see if there was anything she needed.

Inside the office, half turned from the doorway, Cara sat cross-legged on the floor. Patty's laptop sat on the dresser. A second computer rested on Cara's lap. The wires of a pair of earbuds disappeared beneath her long hair.

He hovered in the doorway, not wanting to startle her. Not wanting to admit—again—he and Garrett had both been right. She was a good-looking woman. And he shouldn't be standing here looking.

Bad enough he had spent so much time thinking about her the past couple of days. Even this morning, sitting alone in the truck before Garrett arrived, he'd acted like Mark, running through a never-ending list of questions about her.

What had she thought about finding the house empty? Where had she gotten to in her sorting and typing? Had she managed to start on the office closet? He looked across the room. The door was closed tight, which only led to more questions. Why did she seem so reluctant to go near it? And why couldn't his curiosity let that fact alone?

Last time they'd talked, the conversation hadn't ended well. How would she act around him now? Not that he'd lost sleep worrying about it. No matter what Cara thought, he always did his best for the kids.

Computer keys clacked beneath her flying fingers. She hummed a couple of times, then sang a few words under her breath. He recognized the lyrics. She sang off-key, making him want to smile. Instead, straight-faced, he cleared his throat and for good measure rapped a few times on the office door.

She looked up, giving him the smile he wouldn't give her. And it was something to see.

He leaned against the door frame. "Thought you said you'd be leaving early today."

"I planned to, but I want to get as much done as I can."

He nodded as he glanced around the room. "How's it going?"

"Good. I still need to start on a price list, then talk it over with Andi. But I've got everything in the room sorted and entered on the computer."

"Everything in the room," he repeated.

She glanced at the closet. Yeah, that closet… She'd definitely reacted oddly yesterday, nearly jumped backward out of it as if she'd stumbled across a rattler with its tail buzzing in the air.

"I'll get to the closet," she said.

Once again, he shrugged off his curiosity. The boxes and bins and dressers held larger crafts. Maybe she didn't want to have to deal with a load of tiny clothes.

She would probably like another postponement. "There's always tomorrow."

To his surprise, she shook her head, sending her hair rippling against her shoulders. "Not tomorrow. I won't be here. I've got good news.

Andi called a few minutes ago to tell me she's leasing a store."

"Here in town?"

"Yes. She found an available storefront right on Canyon Road, prime real estate, she says."

"Almost the only real estate, when it comes to local businesses."

She laughed. "Andi said that, too. Anyhow, she's insisting we have lunch in town tomorrow to celebrate, then go look over the store after she gets the keys. It's right down the street from the Big Dipper."

"That'll make it handy for anyone who likes ice cream."

"And you know *I* do. I told her that's why she leased a place close by. She wants my help with the layout of the store, so she's going to bribe me with ice cream."

"Will that work?"

"I think you know the answer to that one, too."

He did. He had learned a lot about her in such a short time. She was loyal to her friends. She loved ice cream, especially chocolate. She liked soft rock music and sang off-key. She wasn't comfortable around kids but made an effort with his son. Despite their last conversation, that item alone had him feeling grateful to her.

"But don't worry," she added, her eyes gleaming, "I'm a good negotiator. I told her she'd have to throw in a dessert or two at SugarPie's before I would agree to give her a hand. That sealed the deal. At least for as long as I'm still around." She hesitated, then went on. "Give me a second to power down." She returned her attention to the computer.

He couldn't tear his gaze away from her. He had learned a lot about himself in this short time, too. He liked this woman's gleaming eyes and golden-red hair. Her smile and her sense of humor. Her loyalty to her best friend.

When she closed the laptop, he reached out to help her to her feet and found more to like. Though her hand was small, her grip was strong. Her fingers, slim and warm, fit perfectly in his.

Part of him wanted to keep holding on. The sane part of him made him release her hand the minute she stood upright.

"Thanks." She spent a while putting the computer on the dresser, settling it just so and fiddling with the lid—all unnecessarily, as far as he could see. Finally, she said, "I have to confess."

That explained the delaying tactics. He waited.

"I'd have made even better progress if I hadn't been online most of the afternoon."

"Don't tell me. You're an internet shopper?"

"No."

"A closet gamer?"

"No, not that."

"Addicted to hanging out outline?"

"Not that, either. I'm looking for a job."

"Sounds like you have one—with Andi." He expected her to laugh or at least smile. Wrong again. Her expression suddenly turned solemn.

"No, that's just temporary. I really need to get back home."

Yet another thing he knew about her—where she lived. "What's the attraction in Phoenix?"

Now she grinned. "Oh…the heat, the saguaros, the local petting zoo. Just think of all the animals Mark could find there to inspire his drawings. Where does he get his interest in art, anyhow?"

Nice. With one quick question—and that stunning grin—she had deftly turned the conversation away from a topic she evidently wanted to avoid. Unfortunately, she had also led them to one he didn't want to discuss.

"Most kids like to draw," he said simply.

"And speaking of kids, I've got to head out to get my two."

After collecting her laptop and a purse from the dresser, she left the room with him. "You go into town every day to pick them up? There's no school bus that could bring them home?"

"No. They're young for that, especially Tracey. And Rhea, the babysitter, runs the day care center from her house. No transportation provided. I drop them off in the morning and pick them up again in late afternoon."

"That must interfere with your schedule."

He shrugged. "When it's especially busy, Rhea will take the kids earlier in the morning or keep them later for me. We make it work." He halted at the bottom of the stairs, expecting Cara to leave through the front door.

She gestured to the kitchen. "I left a bag in the refrigerator. Paz sent along a lunch with me today. She doesn't like seeing anyone go hungry."

"Or thirsty. She sent some of her spicy hot chocolate over with Garrett." *Great.* He hadn't planned to mention his brother.

But Cara nodded. "I met him here this morning."

"Yeah. He mentioned stopping by. I told him

you were here sorting through Patty's crafts, and that's it." *And that I've got no interest in you.*

"Well, if you're wondering, I just said I'm staying at the Hitching Post."

"And he didn't get anything else from you? He's good at sweet-talking his way around women."

She laughed. "Not this woman."

A surge of...something...filled his chest. Whatever it was, it was something he shouldn't have let himself feel. Not for *this woman*, whose laptop and job search and hometown with all its attractions proved how much she liked her big-city lifestyle. Good reason for him to keep his distance. Her eagerness to return to that big city told him she would have no interest in small-town life.

He and the kids had been there, done that with Patty. He wasn't going to risk putting them through it again.

CHAPTER TEN

LATE THE NEXT MORNING, Cara and Andi drove to town with Missy in the back seat of Cara's car.

First they intended to drop Missy off at the local day care center. Then, after lunch at SugarPie's, Andi had arranged to pick up keys at the realty office. She was eager to show off the store she had leased. Truthfully, Cara was just as eager to see it. And they were both ready to get started on the cleaning.

"You were lucky to find a location available and so close to home," she told Andi.

"I know I was. But don't worry, boss, I did have a contingency plan in mind."

"I knew you would. And don't call me boss. You're the owner and CEO of this operation."

"Mmm-hmm…" Andi gestured. "Take a right after that blue house on the corner. Well, anyway, if I couldn't find something here, the next step would have been to start looking in Flagman's Folly. Now we don't need to worry about that. Everything just seems to be falling into place, including finding so much inventory at Wes's house. I can't wait to see it all tomorrow."

After breakfast, before heading to the store, she and Andi had settled down in Tina's vacant office behind the registration desk. They had gone over the inventory file Cara had started.

"It's a pretty impressive list," Andi said again now.

"And it's not done yet. I've still got some things to go through. The rest of the packing boxes, for one thing." And the closet, for another. She hadn't mentioned all the baby clothes yet. She didn't want to talk about them or see them or touch them. Handling all those tiny garments would bring back so many memories she couldn't face.

"It's the third house on the right," Andi directed. "We're here," she said to Missy over the back of her seat as Cara parked the car.

While she unbuckled Missy's car seat, Andi continued, "Your suggestions for prices sound perfect, too. Low enough not to scare away customers, but high enough to bring in a little profit all around—for the store and for Wes and the women who bring things in to sell."

"You *hope* the prices are perfect," Cara cautioned, catching her eye in the rearview mirror. "You may have to make adjustments once you see how everything goes."

"Oh, don't worry about that. I'll be consulting with my closest advisor on a regular basis." She closed the car door and settled Missy on her hip. "It won't take me long to drop this little girl off. Just give me a few minutes."

"No rush. I'm sure there won't be a huge crowd lined up at SugarPie's."

Andi laughed. "You might be surprised." She paused. "You know, on second thought, why don't you come up inside with us?"

"Oh, that's okay." She flexed her fingers—visible proof to Andi she wasn't clutching the steering wheel like a lifeline. "I'll wait right here."

Andi pulled her sunglasses down and stared at Cara over them. "Is that really what you want?"

Flexing her fingers again, she looked across the yard to the day care center. A moment passed, then two.

"Wanna go, Mommy," Missy said.

Cara nodded. "I wanna go, too. I'd like to meet the day care owner." After all, she had been curious about Mark's *Miss Rhea*.

Andi smiled.

The small house they approached looked like any family home—a very large family, considering the row of tricycles lined up at one edge of the walkway and the wooden toy box that took up almost one end of the porch.

She imagined Mark happily drawing at a child-sized table. She could see him sitting amid a group of his friends the way he and Tracey sat surrounded by their stuffed animals in the picture on Wes's refrigerator.

"Wes told me he brings his kids here to the babysitter's every day. He makes two trips, actually, to drop them off and pick them up." He had shrugged that off, assuring her he and the sitter worked things out between them. The woman seemed very eager to accommodate him. Nice of her, since it made life easier for Wes and his kids. "The ride's not as long as I'd thought, but a half hour or more back and forth twice a day has to throw off his schedule."

"That's probably true. But he does what he has to."

What he *wants* to.

"You will, too, someday," Andi added softly.

Cara's throat tightened so suddenly, she couldn't risk a reply. Her *someday* had come and gone. Hopefully, not forever. But it was too soon to think about the future.

"I'm happy Rhea had room for Missy today," Andi said.

"Yes." Cara cleared her throat. "It was a good thing she could fit her in. I have a feeling Missy wouldn't have a bit of interest in helping us clean a vacant store."

"But she would love to go where we're going for *l-u-n-c-h*. So whatever you do, don't mention that in front of her."

The petite woman who greeted them at the door had a kind but lined face and salt-and-pepper hair. She also seemed thrilled to see them on her doorstep. "Well, look who has arrived! How is our little Missy?" Rhea took her from her mother's arms.

Once Andi made introductions, Rhea said, "I was so glad when Jed called yesterday to say you wanted to leave Missy here for the day."

Cara frowned. Why would Jed call, instead of Andi? Was he somehow matchmaking again? And how paranoid was that idea? More likely, since he knew everyone in town, he wanted the chance to chat—in other words, gossip.

"Andi," Rhea went on, "the kids haven't seen this little girl *or* you here for a while. Y'all come back with me to say hi."

The small house they entered was deceiving. Rhea led them through the front room and down a long hallway. The hall ended in a huge room overflowing with drawings, toys and child-sized furniture. A wall of windows showed a well-kept fenced-in yard with a swing set and a jungle gym.

No wonder Mark had sounded so enthusiastic about going to Miss Rhea's.

The room was filled with kids and a couple of older teenagers, probably Rhea's assistants. A woman around Cara and Andi's age stood frowning at a wall clock above a dry-erase board.

Cara recognized her immediately as the woman she'd seen outside the Big Dipper, standing close to Wes, clinging to his arm and smiling at him. The *friend of my wife's*, as Wes had called her, had looked pretty friendly with him at the time. Not that it was any concern of hers.

Rhea took Missy over to join a group of toddlers sitting on the floor.

The woman spotted the two of them standing near the doorway and came toward them. "Andi. What are you doing here? I would think you'd have your pick of babysitters out at the ranch."

"Just my luck everyone's busy today." Andi

spoke lightly, but Cara could see she'd made an effort.

Wes hadn't seemed enthusiastic about Marianne, either. No wonder, if she turned on that sarcastic tone around him, too.

"Marianne," Andi added, "this is Cara. She's here on vacation, staying with me at the Hitching Post."

Marianne nodded shortly. She looked at the clock again, then at Rhea, now kneeling to help Missy gather a pile of plastic blocks. "I have to get going."

A few yards past the group of toddlers, Cara saw Mark. Just as she had imagined, he sat at a long table with a group of kids, working on new drawings.

When he spotted her, his eyes opened wide and his jaw dropped, reminding her of the first time she'd gone to see Wes. Mark climbed from the bench seat and ran across the room to throw his arms around her knees in a bear hug. She took a steadying breath.

Marianne's expression almost matched Mark's.

"Hello, Miss Cara!" he cried. "Did you come for milk and cookies?"

"No, not today. We just came for a visit." Too late, she recalled how he'd responded when Wes told him she was only a visitor at their house. As she expected, Mark's face fell. What if he made a scene? How would Miss Marianne react to that? As tempted as she was to find out, she didn't want Wes to hear she had upset his son at day care. Recklessly, she promised, "I'll see you again this afternoon."

"Yay!" Mark gave her knees another squeeze.

She and Andi had to pick up Missy later, didn't they? She ruffled Mark's hair, then froze when she realized she'd seen Wes do the same. "You go work on your coloring. I want to see that picture done when I come back."

"Okay." He grinned and hurried to the table.

Marianne's eyebrows had climbed halfway to her hairline. "I didn't realize you knew Mark." She sounded horrified, as if Cara's association with the little boy might somehow hurt him.

Andi shifted, ready to jump into the conversation—literally. Cara sent her a quick smile indicating she could fight her own battles. Turning to the other woman, she said sweetly, "Since we just met, there's no way you *could* have realized anything about me, is there?"

Marianne blinked, then frowned at the clock. "I'll talk to Rhea later."

Cara and Andi smiled their goodbyes.

After they watched her walk down the long hallway, Andi said in a low voice, "Don't let her get to you. She has an attitude with just about everybody. And to be honest, I almost feel sorry for her now. She was best friends with Patty Daniels. I can't imagine..." Andi shook her head. "Let's not even go there. Anyhow, Marianne seems crankier than usual this morning, probably because she saw the way Mark ran up to you."

Cara shrugged, not caring how Marianne felt about Mark's welcome. More important, would he remember her own promise to him?

Andi sighed. "She's a single mom, and I think she's got ideas about stepping into Patty's space. She gets...territorial when it comes to Wes and the kids."

"Really? Mark didn't even seem to notice her."

Did his daddy?

The thought suddenly made *her* feel cranky. "She was awfully clingy when I saw her with Wes."

"Really? When?"

Wrapped up in her thoughts, she murmured, "Sunday, when I was at the Big D——" She stopped short.

Andi's eyes rounded. "*Sunday?* You saw Wes—and Marianne—before you came to the Hitching Post? And you talk about *other* people being up to things? I won't even go into the fact you went for ice cream without me."

Rhea joined them again. "So, you two are off now for a girls' lunch out?"

"Yes." Andi laughed. "A *long* lunch, where Cara and I will get a chance to talk without interruptions."

Cara laughed, too, trying to ignore the threatening note in Andi's voice. "And don't forget that dessert you promised me."

"Oh, I won't."

"Well, you just take your time and we'll take good care of Missy," Rhea assured them. "I was thinking, Andi. Since Wes's place is right near you, why don't you do your neighbor a favor and take his kids home when you pick up Missy? Save him a trip. I can call him to let him know."

Andi exchanged a smile with Rhea. "That's a great idea."

Why did this suddenly feel like a setup?

Confirming her suspicions, Andi turned to her. "Cara, you wouldn't mind taking the kids home, would you?"

Where was her steering wheel when she

needed it? Yes, she would mind the idea of taking the kids home, helping them into their car seats, carrying on a conversation with Mark. She needed to come up with a way out… "I'm sorry. I'd be happy to help, but we only have one car seat. Missy's."

"No worries," Rhea said brightly. "Parents are always playing musical cars, and sometimes they leave their seats in the wrong vehicle. Or one parent drops the kids off, but the other unexpectedly picks them up. So I make sure to keep a few spare car seats on hand."

"Very convenient," Cara said.

And maybe this entire arrangement today had been *very convenient*, too.

"Yes, isn't it?" Rhea smiled. "You can just leave the seats with Wes when you take Mark and Tracey home, and he can bring them back to me in the morning. Easy as pie."

"Speaking of pie reminds me I'm hungry," Andi said. "Come on, Cara. We have a lot of eating—and talking—to do."

"I'LL BE RIGHT BACK," Andi said. "I just saw a couple of Grandpa's friends come in and want to bring them up to date."

Cara nodded. "Don't rush. I'm not going anywhere without you."

Left alone at their table in SugarPie's, she looked around the room. The country-café decor gave the sandwich shop a homey feel. The line of booths running along one wall and the many round tables with pink-cushioned chairs offered plenty of comfortable seating. And as usual, the food had been fantastic— though neither she nor Andi had found much time to focus on what they had ordered.

Andi had been right when she said the size of the lunchtime crowd would surprise Cara, yet she was wrong about their uninterrupted time to chat. Word of Andi's business venture had reached SugarPie's before they had arrived. Along with their sandwiches and apple pie, they had spent a long time fielding questions from everyone in the place.

Cara didn't doubt Jed Garland had spread the news. The man had ties everywhere. Could he really have played a role in setting her up at the day care center?

A well-dressed older woman entered the shop. She had snow-white hair and the prettiest complexion Cara had ever seen. After waving to Sugar, the owner of SugarPie's bakery and sandwich shop, she approached Cara. "You won't mind making some room for an old lady, will you?" she asked. Her voice held a hint of a brogue.

Cara fought to keep from looking at the now-vacant tables around them. Back home, she would have been wary of welcoming a stranger to sit with her, but this was Cowboy Creek. Besides, after a second glance, the woman seemed familiar. They must have met at Andi and Mitch's wedding.

"Be my guest," Cara said.

"Thank you. My name's Maureen O'Neill, but everyone calls me Grandma Mo or just plain Mo. I hope you'll do the same."

"Nice to meet you, Mo. I'm Cara."

"Yes, I know. You're a pretty little thing. And with that hair—are you of Irish descent, by any chance?"

"No, I'm not."

"Too bad. Well, you can't be blamed for that."

Now Cara couldn't help but laugh. *We are definitely not in Phoenix anymore.*

"Very exciting about Andi's new venture," Mo said. "I hear you've been spending time out at the Daniels ranch."

The change of subject made Cara blink. Thankfully, the buzz of voices all around them guaranteed no one else had heard the woman's astonishing statement. Maybe the noise had also made her miss hearing it clearly.

"Wes Daniels has had a very hard time," the woman went on, proving Cara wrong. "I hope you don't plan to make things any more difficult for him."

Cara struggled to hide her surprise. This conversation had just gotten better. Or worse.

Noticing her reaction, Mo laughed. "You show nice restraint. A good quality not always attributed to young women with red hair. I should know, as I was once both young and red-haired myself." She smiled. "Don't mind my being blunt, love. When you get to be my age, you don't stand on ceremony. And you don't stand for much. In fact, in our small community, we all tend to stick together. And none of us wants to see Wes hurt."

Cara didn't, either. More than likely, when she and Andi went to pick up his kids later this afternoon, just the opposite would happen. She would be the one to suffer. From the moment she heard Rhea's plan to save Wes a trip to town, she had doubted the wisdom of the idea. Doubted her heart could stand that much time alone with his adorable kids.

Mo eyed her as if she could read her thoughts, pushing her into a reply. "Why would you think I'm out to hurt Wes Daniels? I just met him."

"Yes, I know that, too, which is why I've come to chat while Andi's off on her own. To share a bit of Wes's history with you."

Cara hesitated. Part of her wanted to wake up and find this surreal meeting had all been a dream. The other part didn't want to cut the woman off. Not when Mo could help her learn something about Wes.

Except for asking about his wife's accident, she hadn't talked to Andi much about him. She didn't want to give her best friend any ideas— or to give Andi and Jed together any encouragement, if they really did have thoughts about matchmaking. She wasn't interested in Wes… that way. Yet she couldn't hide the truth from herself. Concern for him and his family had filled her thoughts almost from the moment she had met them.

"Shall I begin?" Mo asked.

Giving in, Cara nodded—hopefully not too eagerly.

"Wes is the younger of two boys. He has an older brother."

"I ran into Garrett yesterday."

"He's kissed the Blarney Stone, that one." Mo's smile erased decades from her face. "He has the gift of gab and lightness in his heart. Wes, poor boy, was always exactly the opposite. Broody as a child and quite a handful for his mother. He hadn't started grade school yet when she passed on."

Cara murmured in sympathy. How sad to think of him losing his mother when he was so young, just as Mark and Tracey had.

"They were left, three men on their own— their father, Garrett and Wes. Wes had barely begun high school when their father died. Garrett grew up in a hurry then, stepping in to become a parent to his younger brother. Wes took longer to settle down. He was temperamental as a teen, too. I'm happy to say he's outgrown all that now—thank goodness, for his own children's sake."

Seeing Andi turning back in their direction, Cara spoke quickly, hoping to hurry Mo along to more recent history. "I heard what happened to his wife."

"A very sad thing. Both boys have dealt with a lot of sadness in their lives. Especially Wes. So you can see why we wouldn't want him hurt."

"I wouldn't, either."

Evidently hearing the sincerity in her voice,

Mo brightened. "That's very good to know, because it may be you're just what he needs."

Did *everyone* in this town work for match-maker Jed?

"No, I'm not. Not at all." She added in a rush, "And please don't say anything like that to Andi."

A moment later, Andi took her seat again. "Hi, Mo. Have you heard about my plan?"

"I have. And the ladies of the knitting circle ought to hear about it, too. You'll come to our meeting tomorrow afternoon, won't you?"

"You bet I will. Then you think the store is a good idea?"

"Yes. I think it sounds like very good news for Cowboy Creek." Mo turned, giving Cara a smile. "Just what *everyone* needs."

Andi couldn't have understood the meaning behind Mo's emphasis, but Cara couldn't miss it. As Andi reached for her purse, Cara shook her head slightly, again telling Mo to drop the subject.

What a crazy idea, that she could be what Wes needed. A man whose life revolved around his children, and a woman who couldn't bear to be with kids.

They couldn't have made a worse pair.

CHAPTER ELEVEN

CARA AND ANDI had finally managed to say goodbye to Mo, Sugar and everyone else still enjoying lunch at SugarPie's. They left the sandwich shop and had gone directly to pick up the keys to Andi's new leased property. The store had sat vacant for a while.

"You weren't kidding about needing to do some cleanup," Cara said as Andi unlocked the front door.

Smudges blurred the glass of the door and the storefront windows, as well as several display cases inside the front room. Piles of debris lurked in every corner, and a thick layer of dust coated everything in sight.

"At least we came prepared." Andi set down the vacuum she was carrying. She had borrowed it, along with some cleaning supplies, from the Hitching Post.

"The floor seems okay," Cara said, "but it needs a good scrubbing. And it looks like you're going to have to paint the interior."

"Agreed. I'll talk to Mitch about that. And I'm sure Tina and Jane can convince their husbands to help with a painting party. Then I can pay them all in pizza and soda."

Cara laughed. "Well, at least you're catching on about needing to watch your budget. I'm glad you passed on the presigning service the realty office offered, too, and opted for the reduction in the first month's rent."

Cara looked forward to working here today, to spending extra time with Andi. And if they kept busy enough, she wouldn't have to worry about what would follow—having to take Mark and Tracey home later.

"Anyhow," she continued, "that was a good choice to turn down the cleaning service. It's much smarter for us to do the cleanup ourselves."

Andi grinned. "I hoped you would approve."

Cara not only approved, she admired Andi's enthusiasm and commitment. Even more, she envied Andi's initiative and independence. The need to regain those herself made her twice as eager to return home to find a new job she loved. And not to mention, a new apartment she could afford. Fingers crossed, some of the résumés she had submitted online yesterday would lead to interviews—though that definitely wasn't her focus right now.

"It was nice of the previous tenants to leave the display cases," Cara said. "They're expensive to buy, and they'll come in handy while you're starting out, until you can afford to look into alternatives."

"See? That's why I'm glad you're here. You think of everything."

"Not quite, but thanks. This is a great location, too, right in the middle of the business district." She set their bucket of cleaning supplies on the floor, then wandered over to look through a wide doorway at the rear of the room.

Andi followed her.

"The perfect setup," Cara said. "Lots of space in the front room for inventory and plenty of storage room back here. The kitchen area in the corner doesn't hurt, either, especially if you plan to work odd hours."

"*Long* hours, you mean. I'm planning to keep the store open all day, and in the evenings, too. I'll always need to be ready for the tourists who roll in once the highway exit's finished."

"And before that happens, what are you going to do?"

"Ask my best friend for advice."

They both laughed, but Andi turned serious immediately.

"Honestly, Cara, I'll need all the guidance I can get if I want to help other women here. You know, Mo said this will be good news for Cowboy Creek, and I think she's right—because she's usually never wrong!" She met Cara's gaze. "And speaking of Mo, when I came back to the table, you two looked very intense. What was that all about?"

"Nothing much, just talking." This time, Cara had to force a laugh. "She did tell me it wasn't my fault my family isn't Irish."

"That's Mo for you. You never know what she'll come out with next. Like when she said *Just what* everyone *needs*."

So, Andi had noticed Mo O'Neill's emphasis. Good thing she hadn't heard the rest of their conversation.

...*just what he needs*.

"The funny thing was," Andi continued, "she was talking to me but looked directly at *you* when she said that."

"Coincidence."

"Right. Like running into Wes and the kids at the Big Dipper the day you arrived in town was a coincidence?"

"Of course." Cara had already received a warning from Andi that they would have this discussion. They might not have gotten around to it at SugarPie's, but Andi's crossed arms announced they were having it now.

"So, what happened?"

"Nothing much. I arrived early, and since I didn't know you were all holding dinner for me, I stopped for an ice-cream cone. Wes and Mark were there."

"You said Marianne was, too."

"Outside the store. She went on her way, and Wes brought Mark inside."

"Well, I'm glad to hear he took Mark out for a treat. But, wait… That means you knew Wes before you went to his house."

Cara shook her head. "We never introduced ourselves. We were both surprised when I showed up that night." And both shocked when Mark came in and asked if she was his mommy. "I'm still not convinced matchmaker Jed isn't in the background pulling strings. Why was he the one to call Rhea about today? I'd have thought you—"

A knock rattled against the front door. Lizzie, the teenager Cara had met at the Big Dipper, stood outside the store.

Andi waved—a little too enthusiastically, as

if she'd been relieved to have their conversation interrupted? Or was Cara's paranoia about Andi and Jed really setting in?

"I was hanging out at the Dipper," Lizzie said, "and I saw you go by and come in here. What's going on?" She must have been one of the few people in town who hadn't heard the news.

Andi described her plans, then explained why they were in the store now.

"Can I help?" Lizzie asked.

"How are you at cleaning windows?" Andi asked.

"Great. At home, my mom gets me to help her with everything. But she leaves the windows to me because she says I do a better job than she does."

"Sounds good. If you can give us a couple hours of your time now, I'll match what you're making at the Dipper."

"Awesome. Do you need any regular help?" Lizzie asked hopefully. "My schedule's wide-open on weekdays after school."

"We can discuss that, too, later," Andi promised.

Cara opened her mouth, then snapped it shut. Once she and Andi were alone again, they would need another discussion about that budget.

"Here." Andi tossed the teenager a clean dusting cloth. "I'm going to walk over to the L-G for some extra spray cleaner. Those windows are dirtier than I remembered. Be back in a few minutes."

The L-G was the most-shopped grocery store in town.

Once Andi had gone, Lizzie looked around them. "Wow. Guess she really left us in the dust."

Cara laughed, grateful to have the teenager there. Lizzie's chatter would chase away her worries, from her reluctance to pick up Wes's kids later to her conviction everyone in town was pushing her together with him. Jed might be uncontrollable, and Mo was probably following his directions. But Andi should realize trying to set her up with Wes was a waste of time for everyone.

Hadn't she made it clear she was done with men for the foreseeable future? Maybe she and Andi needed to have that discussion again. Maybe they—

Lizzie waved, catching her attention. "You okay? I thought you'd gone to sleep standing up."

So much for her distraction from worry.

"Sorry. My mind was wandering." Otherwise known as making a list of suspects. "I'm going to start with cleaning off a display case."

"Me, too. My mom says always dust first, then vacuum, because the dust falls on the floor and you have to vacuum it up, anyway."

"That makes sense."

"Doesn't it? My mom and dad don't always make sense about things, but once in a while they hit it right." She waved the cleaning cloth. "I'd better get going so Andi can see what an excellent worker I am. I've been trying to get more hours at the Dipper, but we already have too many kids working there. Do you think she'll really hire me to help in the store?"

"Well, I can't answer for Andi. But she said you two would discuss it. That sounds promising."

"Yeah," Lizzie said wryly. "I hope that's not like one of my parents' definite *maybes*. But you can help. Will you give me a good reference?"

"How can I?" Cara teased. "I haven't seen you work yet."

"Yes, you have. I made an ice-cream cone for you. Twice."

"That's right, you did." Again, Cara thought about that afternoon at the Big Dipper. Her first meeting with Lizzie. Her first sight of Mark. Her first conversation with his daddy...

"I hope Andi does hire me. I could really use the extra money. Christmas is a long way off, but there'll be a party at school, and I'll need a new dress. And then next year's the prom. I have to start saving for all that now."

She hadn't thought the teen was old enough to go to prom. "You're a junior?"

"A senior. So is my boyfriend, Kyle. Don't tell anybody..." She leaned across the display case. "Kyle and I are going to get married right after graduation."

"And...that's a secret?"

"For now, it is. My parents probably won't like the idea."

"Maybe because of your age."

"Exactly." Lizzie shrugged. "We could hold off till after college, but we're going to the same school, so why wait? Besides, Kyle is the one for me. And you know what *the one* means, right? You just know you're a perfect fit. A forever fit. Isn't that how you felt when you met *the one*?"

"I haven't met him yet," Cara admitted.

"Really? That's too bad."

Go easy. "Actually, it isn't. I thought I'd found the right one, but it turns out I was wrong. Very wrong. Luckily, I had enough time to figure that out before…before it was too late. You don't want to make the same mistake."

"I won't. I love Kyle, and he loves me. My parents just don't get it."

"Maybe they do, only they want you to wait until you're sure. You really need to know a lot about a person before you make a lifetime commitment." Cara had come so close to that mistake, too.

"Right! That's exactly what I mean. Kyle and I know everything about each other. We've been friends since kindergarten and started going out in sixth grade." Smiling, Lizzie returned to dusting the display case. "I'm glad I told you. You make sense, like my mom does with the dusting but not about me and Kyle wanting to get married." She looked at Cara again. "You won't tell anyone, will you? Promise."

Maybe she shouldn't have let the girl talk get to this point. But she wouldn't back out on Lizzie now. "I promise."

"Thanks." Lizzie smiled. "You're so easy to talk to."

Cara nearly laughed out loud. *Talk to* was right, since the teenager had carried most of the conversation. Yet it was nice to know Lizzie felt comfortable with her.

And of course she would keep Lizzie's confidences to herself.

She had spoken to Mo in confidence today, too, and only hoped the woman would honor her request not to talk to Andi. Not to repeat what she had said about how good Cara could be for Wes. But Cara suspected chances were slim Mo would keep their conversation private. If nothing else, the chief matchmaker himself would get a detailed report.

"You can't tell *anyone* here *anything* without it getting out," Lizzie added. "But I don't have to worry about telling you, because you're not staying."

Nice. A compliment and a brush-off in one breath.

Of course, Lizzie didn't mean that the way it sounded.

The statement didn't fall far from the truth, though. Eventually, Cara would leave this quiet little town that somehow managed to stir so many memories. She needed to go back to her world, to being the woman she was before she made the mistake of trusting her heart to the wrong man.

CHAPTER TWELVE

"WE'RE HO-OME," MARK sang out as Cara pulled up to the ranch house.

Home. Something she no longer had. As she unbuckled Mark's seat belt, she made a mental note to add apartment hunting online to tomorrow's to-do list.

"Yes, we're home," she confirmed for his benefit, then quickly changed it to "You and Tracey are home."

"And Daddy." He pointed to Wes's pickup truck.

"Yes, and Daddy."

"And Miss Cara."

Before she could explain this wasn't Miss Cara's home, he had taken off at a run toward the house. She shook her head. Such a smart little boy. And he had an answer for everything.

Between watching the road and keeping up with his conversation, she'd had no time to worry about being with Wes's kids. No time even to think about her own baby.

And she still had Tracey to take care of. Unlike her big brother, the little girl slept the entire time. She had rested her head against the side of her infant seat and tucked one hand between the seat and her cheek. The sight of that little hand made Cara envision those small fingers tangling her hair...that tiny fist clamped around her finger... Wes's hand brushing hers as he attempted to help...

She pushed all those memories away.

Trying not to startle the baby, Cara slowly unbuckled the seat belt. At Rhea's, she had managed to put a wide-awake, wriggling little girl into this car seat. She didn't expect to have any trouble taking a still-sleeping one out.

The danger came when she lifted Tracey into her arms. The little girl snuggled closer, nestling her head in the hollow of Cara's throat. Cara froze, holding the small but solid weight securely, feeling the warmth of that weight against her, inhaling the scents of baby shampoo, clean baby clothes and just plain baby.

Of all the things she had dreaded happening in Cowboy Creek, this was the worst of them. And the best.

"Is she sleeping?"

Wes's voice made her jump. Luckily, her instincts also made her tighten her hold on the baby, who squirmed and began to stretch. "She *was* asleep."

"She usually does nod off when she's riding in a vehicle, especially at this time of day. Here, let me have her." He took Tracey from her arms.

Immediately, she felt the loss of the baby's weight and warmth.

"Hey there, sleepyhead. We'll get you upstairs to finish your nap." He looked back at Cara. "Mark brought in his backpack. Did Rhea send Tracey's diaper bag home?"

"Yes. And another handful of Mark's drawings." Cara grabbed them along with the bag. "I'll carry these into the house since you have your hands full. And speaking of full—" she waved the drawings "—I think you may have to buy a second refrigerator."

Wes laughed. A genuine laugh. She nearly lost her grip on the papers. Not that long ago, he'd refused even to smile at her.

"I'll come back to get the car seats. Rhea told me she offered you a couple of loaners. Did either of the kids give you any trouble on the ride?"

"No. Tracey drifted off almost right away.

Mark talked to Missy nonstop from the time we left Rhea's. Once we dropped off Andi and Missy at the Hitching Post, he didn't miss a beat, just kept the conversation going with me."

"That's my boy. You'd think being at the sitter's all day, he'd talk himself out with his friends. But somehow that only revs him up for coming home."

They bypassed the front of the house and went to the kitchen entrance off the back porch. The room was less neat and tidy than the last time she'd seen it, thanks mostly to Mark, who had already covered the table with his supplies.

The countertop near the sink was cluttered with bowls and spoons and a cardboard carton. A large pot and a saucepan sat on the stove.

"Miss Cara come for supper?" Mark asked. "I help clean." He began gathering up his crayons.

"No," she blurted. Wasn't his cute conversation and Tracey's snuggle enough? She couldn't face dinner with them, too. Judging by Wes's blank expression, he disliked the idea as much as she did. "I'm not here for supper," she explained to Mark.

He stared at her, his eyes wide. "But we have bacroni!"

Bacroni? She looked at Wes.

"Baked macaroni. Known by most people as baked ziti. *Bacroni* is Mark's word. And his favorite food."

He didn't sound at all upset. Maybe her own tension had her imagining his. "Sounds great. It's starting to smell great, too, if that's what you have cooking in the oven. But I should get going."

"Daddy makes lots," Mark said.

Wes ruffled his hair. "What my son is diplomatically trying to tell you is, we have bacroni nearly every week. Even then, it doesn't always turn out right. I'm not much of a cook."

"I'm a big fan of simple recipes." It didn't matter what Wes had on the menu. She needed to leave.

As if he'd read her mind, Mark said pleadingly, "Stay for bacroni, Miss Cara? Please?"

Over his head, she exchanged a glance with Wes, who gave her a small shrug. "Once he gets an idea in his head…"

"…he doesn't let go. I remember." Wes had said that the first night she had come here. She didn't want to stay tonight, but how could she say no with Mark's hopeful face turned up to hers. "Well…" She looked at Wes. "I did lose an entire day in town. I could eat and then do some work upstairs." He nodded, and she smiled at Mark. "Thank you. I will stay for supper."

"Yay!" Mark grinned and began shoving his papers into a pile.

"Yay!" Tracey raised both hands high, then patted her daddy's cheeks.

Wes's smile looked strained. She hadn't imagined his tension, after all.

Why hadn't she gone with her instincts and left while she'd had the chance?

As WES CHECKED on the pan of ziti in the oven, Cara asked what she could do to help. He shook his head. "Nothing. You're a guest."

Thanks to him. And maybe he'd made one colossal mistake.

He hadn't wanted her to stay. Hadn't wanted Mark to get comfortable with someone who would soon walk out of his life again.

Yet, something had kept him from giving Cara the out when she'd so obviously asked for it. His son's plea? The indecision he'd seen in her eyes at first? His gut telling him she wouldn't mind staying? All of the above?

Or maybe he'd just felt it only right to repay her favor—a strictly business favor—with a meal.

And maybe he was just making too much of this whole situation. A simple supper in the kitchen couldn't be that big a deal to anyone.

"I don't like standing around doing nothing," she insisted. "So what can I do to help?"

Giving in, he gestured to the cutting board and knife on the counter beside the salad fixings. He thought again of the work she was doing upstairs. "What makes you so willing to give up your free time to help me out, when you could be relaxing at the Hitching Post?"

She hesitated a while, then finally said, "Just being a good neighbor."

They weren't neighbors. She didn't live in Cowboy Creek. She'd thought up that answer just to get by. He could see the tension in her all-too-readable posture as she stood at the sink rinsing the vegetables.

The obvious answer hit him right between the eyes. She had no job, no income. Andi was probably going to pay her for helping with the inventory.

Everyone had their reasons for needing extra cash.

He glanced over at Mark, busy with his coloring, and then at Tracey, now settled in her high chair after refusing to be tucked in for a nap.

Who was he to question Cara's financial situation, especially when he could relate to it? He wouldn't give up the opportunity to live on this ranch—or to raise his kids here—for anything in the world. Still, along with everything else, the past couple of years, before and after Patty died, had taken their toll. He'd skated as near as he'd ever come to not breaking even.

Time to change the subject. He stirred the extra pasta sauce simmering on a back burner. "This is a first, all right—first time I've had help with making supper."

Instantly, Mark said, "I help, Daddy."

Just as quickly, he regretted his mistake. Of course his son, who paid attention to everything, would overhear. "You're always a big help, pardner. I'm getting everything ready for you to set the table."

Cara shot him a look of surprise.

"Don't worry," he said in a lower voice. "He gets napkins, spoons and plastic cups. All non-breakable and without a blade. And considering my son's normal speed is fixed at a run, I set all that out on the table for him to arrange."

She kept her focus on the vegetables, but her lips curved in a smile.

Wes grabbed a few hot pads from the lower cabinet and set them on the counter beside the stove.

"Spoons go on the napkins," Mark announced.

"That's right," Wes confirmed. As he made a mental note to add extra utensils and dishes for Cara, he tried to remember the last time they'd had company over for supper. Before they'd lost Patty, he calculated.

Had it really been that long?

"It sounds like you've trained him well," Cara said. "Or his mother did. But you said you didn't have help—besides Mark, of course. You and your wife didn't get dinner ready together?"

"No. By the time I'd come in at night, she'd have everything waiting to go on the table. Usually, she would head out soon after we ate. She spent a lot of time in town with her friends."

Another mistake he immediately regretted. Why blurt out all these details to Cara? No doubt about it, he would be better once she went on her way. "Anyhow," he finished in a rush, "lack of experience doesn't improve my skills in the kitchen."

"You and Garrett didn't learn from your mom when you were growing up? Oh." She frowned. "Sorry."

"For what?"

"For asking that. I'm guessing you were too young for her to teach you to cook. I...I heard she passed away a long time ago."

She had probably learned that from the town crier, otherwise known as Jed Garland. The thought irritated him, but he couldn't blame her for Jed's habit of running off at the mouth. "Yeah, I was still just a kid."

"That must have been tough for you to handle."

She didn't look his way. Maybe that made it easier for him to answer. "I won't lie. It *was* tough. But it's worse for my kids. They've lost their mother much earlier on than I did."

"As hard as that must be for them, they seem happy and content. Which means you're doing a great job."

"Thanks. I try." He opened the dish cupboard to collect what they would need for supper. Right now, he needed another change of topic. "How about you? Any kids of your own?"

The knife skidded across the cutting board. A piece of cucumber flew off the edge of the counter.

He caught it in midair. "Hey, we don't throw food around in this kitchen."

Her laugh sounded rattled. "Sorry. You have

good reflexes. And I guess I'm not much of a cook, either."

"Somebody else does the cooking in your house, too?"

"No, I live alone. Though lately, I've been staying at a friend's house and eating all my meals out."

"That must get old."

"It does."

She hadn't answered his question about kids, but her response about living alone covered that. "You must appreciate the homemade meals at the Hitching Post."

"Oh, I do. Everyone there appreciates them. Paz is a fantastic cook."

"Yeah, no matter what she makes, starting with burritos and moving on from there."

"I love b'ritos!" Mark shouted.

"B'itos!" echoed Tracey.

"Me, too," she said. "I hear they're on the menu for this week's cookout."

Wes laughed. "No surprise. They're on the menu every week. Paz is famous for hers. It wouldn't be a cookout without them."

Turning back to the cutting board, Cara said quietly, "You could bring the kids over to join us this Saturday."

She must have taken note of his son's excel-

lent hearing. Wes appreciated that she'd lowered her voice. Even better, she'd spoken at
the same time he'd rattled a handful of cutlery,
giving him a reason to pretend he hadn't heard
her. He didn't need any suggestions from out-
siders. He got enough from folks around here.

No matter what Garrett insisted, he didn't
need to go running to the Hitching Post for
any of Jed's charity. He still had to talk to the
man about his interference, though, and about
sending Cara to his doorstep in the first place.

He didn't much like this arrangement he'd
agreed to with her. The sooner she left, the
better. "I was thinking—"

"Great! I know everyone will be glad to see
you all."

"That's not what I meant." Her happy smile
disappeared. "I was thinking about the office.
You're close to finishing in there."

"Right. I should be done in another few days.
Just a reminder, Andi and I will be here tomorrow, in the morning only. In the afternoon,
she's got appointments in town, and we'll be
doing more cleaning at the store. Plus I need
to set up some interviews for when I get back
to Phoenix."

"You excited about that?"

"Very. A new job, a new home, a whole

new life. Anyone would get excited about that, wouldn't they?"

"Yeah." Another good reminder. She planned to move on again. "Sounds like the right idea to line up those interviews. Since you're apartment hunting, you'll need a job to pay the rent."

Her dimples flashed as she laughed. "Having a paycheck would definitely help with that."

He didn't realize he'd kept staring until she set the knife down and turned to him again.

On the back burner, the pot of spaghetti sauce bubbled and spit. He dropped the handful of silverware onto the counter. Half the utensils clattered to the floor. Stepping over them, he grabbed the pot, managing to burn his hand and spill sauce onto the stove.

Good thing he'd already made it clear he couldn't cook.

MARK CHATTERED ALL through dinner. Cara gave thanks for his energy and Tracey's babbling. Without them, the kitchen would have seemed like the staff break room at the department store after a weeklong summer clearance sale. In other words, deadly silent.

Mark chased the last ziti in his bowl. "You like bacroni?" he asked her.

"I love it," she told him truthfully.

She glanced at Wes. Why he'd kept so quiet, she didn't know. That didn't mean she needed to act like a tongue-tied teenager. "My compliments to the cook. You're pretty good around the kitchen, after all."

"Until I burn things all over the stove." He reached for the serving spoon. "Want more?"

"No, thanks. I can't eat another bite."

"What's for dessert?" Mark asked.

"Pudding."

Mark cheered and, naturally, Tracey did the same.

"That's another one of his favorites," Wes told Cara. "And as my mother used to say, nobody says no to pudding." He frowned. "Funny, I hadn't thought about that in a long while."

"Memories *are* funny that way. Sometimes they hit out of nowhere." And all too often, they came when you couldn't handle them.

"About that dessert," he said.

"I guess that's true about not saying no to pudding. After we're done, I'll help with the dishes to work off all these calories."

"Would it do me any good to argue with

you?" Not a hint of a smile now. As if to make up for that, he gestured to the bowl in the center of the table. "The salad was good. Guess that makes you handy around the kitchen, too."

"Not really. Anyone can shred lettuce and cut up a few vegetables."

"Yeah, but not everyone can make a cucumber fly."

"I didn't do it intentionally." If he hadn't asked her about having kids of her own, she probably wouldn't have done it at all. And though she had managed to change the subject without answering, now she suddenly longed to tell him about her baby.

She'd sworn off men—maybe forever, as she'd told Andi. This urge to confide in Wes made no sense at all.

CHAPTER THIRTEEN

AFTER BREAKFAST, AS the Garlands and their guests left the dining room, Cara stayed behind with Andi at the family table. "We should probably get going soon."

Andi nodded. "Just a few more minutes. It's nice to sit in here while it's quiet, and that doesn't happen too often."

The only sounds came from a few clattering dishes as a waitress worked her way around the room, clearing off the smaller tables.

Cara sipped her tea and watched Andi toying with her fork, reminding her of Mark and his *I help, Daddy* at Wes's house last night.

Once they had finished dessert, she hadn't stayed to work, after all. As soon as they'd cleared away the dishes, Wes had taken the kids upstairs for their baths. If being with them all at dinner made her uncomfortable at times, hearing them just down the hall from the office, going through their nightly family ritual, would have been unbearable.

Then there was her unexpected thought of telling Wes about the baby.

"You're not still thinking about leaving, are you?" Andi asked suddenly. "Because if so, Grandpa made me promise to tell you not to worry about your room. He said if you don't believe me, he'll sit you down and tell you himself."

"I'm sure he would."

"Good. Because the room is yours for as long as you want it. And while you're here, I need your help."

Cara attempted a laugh. "What do you call what I'm doing already? At this rate, you'll have to start paying me a salary."

"I wish. I'm going to have enough trouble paying Lizzie at the end of the week. There's zero income until the store opens, which is where you come in. You can take care of all the pricing."

"It's your business. You should set the prices."

"You're the one with the retail marketing background."

"Well, I can't argue with that." Until she'd quit her job to go to Flagstaff, she had worked at the same department store since before high school graduation.

"After you're done with the inventory, I really could use your help setting up the store and talking to some of the crafters in town."

Not a great idea. Not even a halfway good one. Cara didn't need to get involved in a long-term project. "You definitely ought to be the one dealing with the locals. After all, they'll be your main suppliers."

"I know." Andi grinned. "When I talk to them this afternoon I'm referring them to you at the store. The Hitching Post has got another wedding coming up soon, and *that's* my priority. Besides, while you look over the samples, you'll get an idea of pricing. The sooner we have enough inventory, the sooner we can open the store and start seeing sales."

We had better mean *Andi and Lizzie.*

The waitress approached with a carafe. "More hot water, ladies?"

I'm going to be in enough hot water in just a minute. But Cara nodded.

After a quick sip, she reminded Andi, "I have to go home and find a job."

"You can look from here."

"I already am. But I can't go on interviews long-distance."

"Do you have any lined up?"

"Not yet," Cara admitted, fighting a wave of guilt.

Before their late breakfast, she could have made a few phone calls to her former boss and coworkers, could have reached out to other contacts. Yet something had kept her from picking up the phone or even sending out emails. Just as something had kept her from saying a straight no to staying for dinner at Wes's last night.

She'd never been this indecisive about anything, which only proved her need to get her life in order again.

"You'll stay, then?" Andi asked.

Cara hesitated, weighing her options. Keeping her room indefinitely gave her a temporary solution to her housing problem. It would also give her more time to find a job she really wanted. But the most convincing argument outweighed those options combined.

"I don't like leaving before the store's ready to open," she admitted, "especially since you can't focus on it full-time right now."

Andi had plenty of family, but they were all busy with their own jobs. Cara was the only one without other responsibilities…at the moment.

"Okay. I'll stay—at least until I have some

job interviews scheduled. But I can't hang around here forever."

"Why not?" Andi smiled. "I know you've got lots of friends back home, but after all, I'm your best friend, and I'm here. Where would you rather be?"

"You've got a point. But I also have business contacts there. And…" She stared down into her mug, as if the tea held the answers to all her problems. The steaming water blurred her vision. "It's not just finding a job, Andi. I can't let what happened with Brad make me run. With the move to Flagstaff, I lost everything." Blinking away tears, she said firmly, "No. What I lost was my baby."

Andi squeezed her hand gently.

Cara set the mug aside. "I hate admitting this, but it's true. I didn't lose anything with Brad—I gave it up. My job. My apartment. And most important, my independence. I need to get all that back, to get myself back. To trust myself again. That won't happen if I run away."

CARA AND ANDI arrived at Wes's ranch later than her usual time. Just as Wes had done on her first morning here, she led the way directly upstairs.

In Patty's office, Andi looked around them in amazement. "Unbelievable. With all this inventory, the store will get off to a great start." She checked out one storage box after another of the crafts Cara had sorted, counted and repacked. "I don't want to move this load twice if we don't have to. Could you ask Wes if we can leave everything here until we're ready to take it to the store?"

"Sure. Don't forget, he's entitled to a sizable cut from the sales."

Andi laughed. "No worries. I'm not planning to cheat the man."

"I didn't mean that. I was just reminding you not to factor in a hundred-percent profit for the store."

"Point taken, boss." She eyed the boxes again. "I can't believe Patty ever managed to make all this. She never wanted to sit at home."

"So Wes said. He told me she liked to go into town with her friends."

"Into town and out of town. She drove up to Santa Fe all the time and to the flea market in Flagman's Folly on the weekends. Once in a while she went to Vegas with Marianne and their friends. Before Mark, that is."

"Then she just stopped?"

"Only the trips to Vegas. I wasn't living here

then, but I'd see her sometimes when I visited. She loved telling me about all the fun she had. After Mark was born, I'm guessing money got tight, the way it usually does when you suddenly have another mouth to feed. Or more than one. Remember Mo's granddaughter Shay? You met her at the wedding."

Cara nodded. "I also remember you said she and Tyler had triplets not too long ago."

"Right. The babies coming along was a huge surprise to them in more ways than one—and I don't just mean the multiple birth! Mo's a big help, but I still don't know how she and Tyler manage. Anyway, back to Patty. I'm guessing having two kids and needing extra cash is what gave her the idea to sell things online. Now I see why."

Andi wandered toward the closet, then stopped short in the doorway. "Look at this! There's enough in here alone to stock half the store…isn't there? Cara…?" Andi turned to face her. "Are you okay?"

"Yes, just thinking." Remembering. "When I found out I was pregnant, I started buying a few things for the baby."

That massive walk-in closet made her one dresser drawer seem insignificant. But it wasn't. She had chosen every item with love and care, imagining her baby wearing each tiny outfit and playing with every small toy.

"It was too early to start buying anything," Cara said. Was she making excuses for not doing more for the baby she already loved? Her heart said no. "Maybe I should have waited until I was further along. But I couldn't help myself."

"That's no surprise," Andi murmured. "Baby clothes are hard to resist."

"Exactly. And when I first saw those, they all reminded me—"

"I'm sorry, Cara. I should have realized."

"You couldn't have. I've realized something, though. Every single thing I bought for my baby left me with a special memory. That—" She pointed toward the closet. "That's just a collection of adorable clothes. Seeing them the other day upset me, but now I can tell the difference."

Finally being able to talk to Andi about the baby had *made* the difference.

Jed had been right.

A trouble shared is a trouble halved.

THE NEXT AFTERNOON, Cara worked alone in the back room of the store cleaning wall cabinets in the kitchen area. Twice, she interrupted herself to check her watch. Every time she walked over to the small sink, she looked into the display room.

Lizzie should have gotten here by now.

On their way to town yesterday, she and Andi had discussed the store's finances. As Andi later explained to Lizzie, she would pay her to help with the cleanup. Once the store was open, they would talk about additional hours.

Overjoyed to have any extra income, Lizzie had promised to report in directly after school today. Which made her late arrival puzzling.

Again, Cara checked her watch.

On her next glance into the display room, she finally saw the front door opening. But it wasn't Lizzie who entered.

Patty Daniels's friend Marianne stepped inside and scanned the room, bare except for the empty display cases and extra cleaning supplies. When Cara greeted her, Marianne frowned. "I'm looking for Andi."

"She's taking care of some business right now."

"I heard *she* was the one who rented this store."

Rubber fingertips snapped loudly as Cara pulled her work gloves off. "You heard right."

"And you are…?"

"Didn't we cover that yesterday at Rhea's? I'm Andi's friend, Cara."

"That's not what I meant," Marianne snapped almost as loudly as the gloves. "Andi can't be planning to run a store all by herself."

"Oh, she won't be alone."

"Who's helping her? You?"

"No, as Andi said when she introduced me, I'm only here on vacation." Why did Cara suddenly need that reminder herself? "Andi's already hired someone to help her. Were you interested in applying, too?"

"Of course not. I also heard she's going to be selling some of Patty's crafts. I'd like to know how she got her hands on them."

"She didn't, actually. I did. Wes let me have a look at everything, and it was just what Andi wanted."

"I suppose that's how you got to know Mark."

"And Tracey." *And Wes.*

Marianne must've realized the same things she had. Wes Daniels was a good daddy and a good-looking man. But a troubled one. Too bad Patty's friend didn't understand he wasn't ready for a relationship.

Cara slipped one of her gloves on again. "Is

there anything else I can help you with before I get back to work?"

"I'll get in touch with Andi."

"Perfect." As she returned to the back room, she heard the door close.

She thought again of Wes, then pushed his image from her mind.

She hadn't been to the ranch today and didn't plan to go back until Monday. Would Wes take Mark anywhere this weekend? Or would the little boy spend his days drawing at the kitchen table? He would enjoy that, but he could also have fun spending time with a friend.

It didn't seem likely Wes would be stopping by the cookout this weekend. Oh, well, what he did or didn't do in his free time wasn't any of her business…except, wasn't that exactly why Jed and Andi had sent her to him in the first place?

She heard the door open again. Marianne hadn't gotten very far.

But this time, Lizzie entered the store.

"Am I relieved to see you," Cara said, only half teasing. "I started thinking you found another job somewhere else."

Lizzie didn't seem to hear a word.

Her blank stare reminded Cara of her own

numbness the first time she'd seen the closet full of baby clothes. "What's wrong?"

To her shock, Lizzie's eyes welled with tears.

Cara gestured toward the card table and chairs in the kitchen area. "Come back and have a seat for a few minutes."

She would never cross-examine Lizzie but felt sure that wouldn't be necessary in any case. Considering all the talking the teen had done in the past couple of days, when she felt ready, she would mostly likely share whatever had her upset.

As Lizzie took a seat at the table, Cara said, "I'll work in the display room to give you some space." She backed a half step.

"No. Wait." A tear spilled onto Lizzie's cheek. She wiped it away. "I—I don't know what to do. I've been walking around all day wondering if what I think is really true. I mean, I j-just don't know."

That didn't give Cara much of a clue.

Anything that happened in a teen's life could feel like capital-*T* trouble. Cara remembered her own high school years with all the ups and downs in emotions and changes in relationships. Best friends one day became bitter enemies the next, usually returning to normal a week later. Lizzie might have had an argument with a friend or her boyfriend or her mother. Hopefully, her tears came from nothing worse than that.

"Would it help to talk about it?"

"I should get to work."

"Whatever you want." She paused, but Lizzie didn't respond. Right now, staying busy could be the best distraction from whatever had her so upset. "Then I'll get going, too."

Before Cara could take even another half step away, more tears trickled down Lizzie's cheeks. She twined her shaking fingers together, then whispered, "I think I'm pregnant."

Cara's heart thudded. In that one beat, she knew the thoughts that had to be flying through Lizzie's head. She took a seat across from her. "You said you *think*. You don't know for sure?"

"No. But I'm late."

"That sometimes happens. It doesn't have to mean pregnancy. There's a long list of things that can make us late. Stress. Hormones. Some medications. Losing or putting on weight. And more."

"I'm not sick and my weight hasn't changed. And I'm always on time."

"Always?"

"Well, almost. But it's a week now. I...I haven't told Kyle yet."

Pushing memories aside, Cara focused on Lizzie. "How about your parents?"

"I can't. My dad would kick me out."

Cara sincerely hoped that wasn't true, but without knowing Lizzie's situation, of course she couldn't argue. "The best option would be to talk to your mother, but if you don't want to do that—"

"I can't talk to anybody else right now."

At least Lizzie had confided in her. "Have you thought about making an appointment with a doctor? If you're late because of something besides pregnancy, then you'll know."

And if not, Lizzie and her baby would get the care they needed.

"I can't see a doctor. Then everyone else would know, too."

"No, they wouldn't. Doctors and medical staff follow confidentiality laws."

Lizzie shook her head. "In this place, people talk. Or somebody could see me walking in or out of the office."

Cara thought of her own doctor's office, on the higher floor of a multistory building in a sprawling medical complex in the city. But this wasn't Phoenix. When it came down to it,

Lizzie knew more than she might ever know about small-town life.

"I'll wait," Lizzie said. "A few days. Maybe another week."

At the sound of the front door opening, they both jumped.

"Hello?" Andi called.

"In here," Cara called back.

"Cara, don't say anything," Lizzie whispered urgently, wiping her face with her fingertips.

"Of course not." The situation wasn't hers to share. But she might be able to help.

Regardless of her smarts about small-town living, Lizzie was so young, still a teen. A teen afraid to tell her own parents and refusing to talk to anyone but her.

Though their circumstances were different, she'd been in Lizzie's place, too, late and wondering, waiting for a sign. Keeping things to herself. She had never expected that finally being able to talk about her baby would bring her such relief.

When Lizzie wanted to talk, Cara would be here to listen…until she went home again.

CHAPTER FOURTEEN

SATURDAY AFTERNOON, WES turned the truck down the familiar road leading to the Hitching Post. After finishing up the morning chores, he had picked up the kids at Rhea's. At some point once they'd arrived home, he had made the decision to see Jed Garland.

Mark strained against the straps on his car seat as he looked through the window. "Going to see Miss Cara!" It wasn't the first or even tenth time he had mentioned her in the past couple of days.

"Maybe we'll see Miss Cara," Wes cautioned. To tell the truth, he'd thought about her more than once, too.

He hadn't seen her since supper the other night, when she had mentioned bringing Andi with her in the morning. That next afternoon he'd come in from the ranch to find a note on the kitchen table. She and Andi would be busy at the store, and she didn't plan to return to the house until after the weekend.

Once he'd put the kids to bed, he had wandered into the office and seen proof of their visit. At last, Cara had gotten around to working on the closet. The door stood open wide and half the rods and shelves were empty. Below them, a row of packing boxes lined the floor.

"Going to see Robbie and Trey and Missy," Mark recited, counting on his fingers. "And Emilia and Miss Tina and Miss Paz and Grandpa Jed."

"Definitely Grandpa Jed," Wes said under his breath. He had never gotten—no, never *made*—the time to talk to the man. Their conversation was long overdue.

"Miss Paz will give me cookies," Mark said confidently.

"Sure, she will." Whether in or out of her kitchen, Paz never let them get away without urging them to have something to eat or drink.

Wes parked the truck behind the hotel, not far from the corral outside the barn.

"There's Bingo!" Mark cried, spotting the Shetland pony Jed kept for his great-grandkids and the youngest hotel guests.

Inside the corral, Garrett walked Bingo on a short lead. The little girl astride the pony wore an ecstatic grin. Jed stood watching, leaning on the corral fence.

"Go easy," Wes cautioned once he helped Mark out of the truck. Too late. He hadn't lied to Cara about his son's fixed-at-a-run speed.

Garrett waved at Mark. Then he grinned and tipped his hat to Wes, most likely congratulating himself for getting him away from his ranch—not that the big-brother lecture had talked him into anything he hadn't already planned. Wes had wanted to prove to Garrett he was fine, just as he'd told him.

He intended to prove that same thing, along with a few others, to Jed.

Mark gave Jed a hug, then went to the fence rail to watch Bingo.

"G'ampa!" As Wes approached, Tracey reached for her Grandpa Jed just as she had for Cara the other day. At least Jed, with his short white hair, wouldn't have to worry about Tracey's grabby little fingers.

Jed took Tracey into his arms and repaid her for her smacking kiss on his cheek. "Nice to have you stop by, boy. What brings you here?"

"I was in the neighborhood," he said dryly.

"Well, of course you were. Cowboy Creek is just one big neighborhood."

"Also one big hotbed of gossip, thanks to all

the busybodies around here. And I'm looking at the biggest offender right now."

Jed smiled. "You always were straight spoken. I can respect that. To tell you the truth, I'm inclined to take your words as a compliment."

Wes had to laugh. Nothing shook Jed Garland's faith in his own skills.

"You'll stay for the cookout." It wasn't a question. "On the house, of course. I'm sure Paz has an extra burrito with Mark's name on it."

"Yay!" Mark cried. "I love b'ritos! Daddy loves b'ritos, too."

"That settles it, then," Jed said with a smile.

No doubt about it, the man had set him up. Everyone at the Hitching Post knew how his son felt about Paz's burritos.

"Look, Jed, I know you're up to some of your tricks again. I'd appreciate it if you'd quit. I've got kids to raise and a ranch to run, and I'm not at all interested in getting matched up with...anyone."

"What makes you think I'd try that with you?"

Again, Wes couldn't help but laugh. "How about recent events in Cowboy Creek, including more marriages than I can count on one hand and even more kids now living with a pair of parents."

Jed grinned. "Those triplets of Shay and Tyler's sure were a bonus, weren't they?"

"I suppose you could say that. Here's something I want to say. Cara's been coming over to the house—"

"I know. She's helping Andi. And you. That's what friends are for."

"Maybe so, but they're not for wasting your matchmaking talents on when they don't need your services. And I don't. I'm doing fine on my own."

"So Cara said." At his look of surprise, Jed added, "She passed along your message, in a nicer tone than you stated it just now."

Wes scuffed the toe of his boot against the fence post. "It wasn't my intention to come across as rude. I guess you're not the only one around here with a one-track mind."

"Sounds like it. Only this time you're way off track. I'm concerned about Cara, that's all. The girl's got no place to live and no job."

"She told me."

"So if helping Andi—through helping you— takes her mind off her troubles, don't you think it's only natural I'd want that to happen?"

He nodded grudgingly. Somehow, Jed always made his interference sound reasonable. Honorable, even. You had to admire a man who could manage that. To be honest, it went far beyond admiration. Once you got past Jed's tendency to meddle, you couldn't find a better friend.

Tracey squirmed. "Down, G'ampa. Down, down, down!"

"Let me have her, Jed. For once, she didn't fall asleep on the trip home from town this morning, and she's overtired. I think I'll take the kids up to the house."

"Sounds good." The innocence in Jed's bright blue eyes didn't quite match his triumphant smile. Sure enough, he added, "Cara and Andi are busy getting the fixings ready for the cookout. They won't have much time to chat."

Wes forced himself to say casually, "No concern of mine. I'm just planning to stop by the kitchen. Mark wants to say hello to Paz."

That was true, wasn't it? But those blue eyes acknowledged what Wes didn't want to admit, even to himself. The *no concern of mine* part of his response hadn't come anywhere near the truth. He was much more interested in Cara than he ought to be.

"THE NOISE LEVEL in here could break the sound barrier," Cara said with a laugh as she and

Andi loaded the industrial-sized dishwasher in Paz's kitchen.

"This is nothing. Wait till you're around when we're prepping for a wedding reception. Now, *that's* noise. You can't even hear yourself think."

Today came close. The rattle of silverware, clatter of dishes and raised voices in the room almost drowned out Cara's thoughts. Not quite.

As always, she had spent the first few minutes after waking up thinking about the baby. The sad reminders had stopped crashing so heavily on her and were beginning to blend with happier memories—the joy of discovering she was pregnant, the pleasure of shopping for her baby-to-be. She could only hope this meant her pain would soon start to ease.

Then her thoughts had turned to other things. The list of jobs she had agreed to do for Andi. Lizzie and her worries. Her own concern about Wes cutting his kids off from their family and friends.

Maybe she should have planned to drop by to work this weekend. Monday seemed so far away.

Her next glance across the kitchen revealed she wouldn't have to wait till then. There, framed in the doorway, stood a handsome cowboy with a heart-stopping smile, a child at his side and a baby in his arms.

Wes and his kids made the perfect picture. But she wasn't part of it.

Mark ran toward her, his arms already held wide for a hug. "Hello, Miss Cara!" He waved to Andi, then turned back to her.

"Hi, Mark! Did you come for the cookout?"

He nodded energetically. "Yes. And a b'rito. Daddy wants a b'rito, too." Tugging on her hand, he led Cara to the doorway.

"Hi, hi, hi!" Squealing, Tracey waved both hands.

Cara waved back. "Hi," she said, greeting both Tracey and Wes.

"Hey. I stopped by to see Jed, then decided to come say hello to Paz."

Not a bad start to the conversation. The last time she'd seen him, he hadn't talked much. "Well, I'm sorry to say she's too busy to blink right now. You're probably better off waiting till the cookout's underway and she can catch her breath."

A waitress excused herself to pass by them, and Wes backed out of the doorway into the hall.

"It's crazy in here—obviously," Cara said. She knew another place in the hotel that would interest Mark, and she would go there with them to make sure Wes didn't head to the front door. "Let's take a walk to the sitting room."

After a word of caution from his daddy, Mark skipped rather than ran ahead of them down the hall. She and Wes followed more slowly. Suddenly at a loss for words, she focused on playing one-handed pat-a-cake with Tracey and trying not to pat Wes's arm accidentally.

They found the sitting room off the lobby deserted except for two boys; Andi's son, Trey, and Tina's son, Robbie. Both were only a year or two older than Mark. All three boys already knelt in one corner with Robbie's collection of toy horses. When Wes set Tracey on the floor, she immediately toddled toward them.

Wes moved to the fireplace and rested his elbow on the mantel.

"I'm glad you're here," she told him. "Robbie and Trey have been asking about Mark for days. I didn't say anything to them since I didn't know for sure, but I hoped you'd bring the kids for the cookout." Hoped but never dreamed he would actually show up. Maybe her suggestion had made an impact. When he said nothing, she frowned. "You *are* staying, aren't you?"

He didn't respond. He seemed distracted by the chattering group in the corner. Or worse, pretending to listen just to avoid answering her question.

Finally, he shrugged. "Guess we'll hang around. I told Jed we would. Or rather, Mark told him."

She smiled. *Thank goodness for little boys.*

A FEW FEET away from Wes, Cara stood with her crossed arms resting on the back of a tall leather chair. The stance reminded him of her leaning on the upstairs railing at home, her hair tumbling across one shoulder.

"You still plan on coming to the house on Monday?" he asked abruptly.

She nodded. "Yes, but later in the afternoon. Oh, and before I forget, if it's okay with you, Andi would like to leave everything in your office until we're ready for it. We need to paint the store before we start setting up."

"Not a problem. The stuff's not in the way." Why he had wandered into that room the other night, he still didn't know. "I won't have any reason to go near the office again."

The sympathy in her expression instantly made him want to change his mind and tell her not to bother coming back.

Only the thought of his kids kept him quiet. He needed to do better by them, to make some changes, to get rid of painful reminders. If that meant having Cara around the house for another few days, stirring up memories he didn't want to face, he'd deal with it.

"Most of this week I'll be busy at the store all day. And you know," she added in a rush, as if a thought had just occurred to her, "on my way I can pick up Mark and Tracey for you. I'll be in town anyhow, so it only makes sense to save you the trip."

He hesitated, weighing the options. She'd already brought the kids home once without a problem. Fewer trips would cut down his expenses with the truck. And he could always use the extra daylight time on the ranch.

He wondered about her motives. They weren't friends, yet as Jed had said, she was giving him a hand, the way she was helping Andi. Though he'd let her into his home, he'd never expected her to get this involved in his personal business.

As much as he hated to admit it, he owed her his thanks. Her efforts in clearing out his bedroom and Patty's office *were* helping. And she'd pushed him into action he might never have taken on his own.

He nodded agreement before he could talk himself out of it. "That would work for me. I appreciate the offer."

Too late, he thought about the wisdom of having her spend more time with the kids.

CHAPTER FIFTEEN

THIS WASN'T CARA'S first cookout. The Saturday event at the Hitching Post was always fun, and she would enjoy this one even more with Mark and Tracey here.

The women and men tended to break into separate groups at the long wooden picnic tables set out in the backyard. Babies and kids usually stayed with their mothers.

Today, although Mark joined Robbie and Trey at the "women's" side of the yard, Wes had taken Tracey to sit with him.

More than once, Cara caught herself watching them. Wes didn't seem at all self-conscious about being the only man at the table bouncing a baby on his knee. He didn't seem to care that Tracey smeared barbecue sauce all over his sleeve. Now, shouting with laughter, she shoved her corncob into his shirt pocket. He just shook his head, removed the cob and placed it out of reach on his paper plate.

A while later, she saw him set Tracey on a

blanket spread out for the youngest kids, who were being watched over by the women sitting close by.

When he headed toward the line of people at the dessert table, Cara took a deep, steadying breath. *Now or never.* As she joined him, she gestured toward a group of men across the yard. "No horseshoes for you?"

"Nope. Jed's boys kicked me out of the matches a long time ago. They couldn't handle playing against a champion competitor."

"Champion?"

"County, state *and* US."

"Wow. I'm impressed." Surprised, too. From what she had seen of Wes, showing off didn't seem his style.

"Won gold five times in the horseshoe Olympics, too," he added.

That last statement confirmed her growing suspicion even before she heard the man in line behind them snicker. "That's awesome," she gushed, adding sweetly, "and how many medals have you won for telling tall tales?"

The man behind them laughed.

Wes shook his head. "Okay, you got me. I should have realized an intelligent woman like you would catch on soon enough. But you have to admit I had you along for the ride."

"Yes, you did. Briefly."

He laughed.

Wes might have been putting on an act with her—still, she liked this side of him. He seemed to be enjoying himself. If that encouraged him to bring the kids here more often, maybe being around Jed and his family could help them all heal.

They carried their desserts to a vacant picnic table. From there, they could see the younger kids, including Tracey, playing with a handful of toys. The older kids now had paper and pencils and crayons on their table.

"So, what gave me away about the horseshoe stories?"

She smiled. "Your nose twitched every time you added on to your list of accomplishments."

"It did not."

"It sure did. How else do you think I knew you were…stretching the truth, shall we say?"

"I think you're the one telling tall tales now."

She laughed. "So, what gave me away?"

"Nothing at all." He stabbed his fork into the pie. "But it would come in handy if everybody gave off an obvious sign when they were lying."

"Yes, it would. Or when they were making promises they couldn't keep."

"That's the same thing, isn't it?"

"No. At least, I hope it isn't." She twirled her fork a couple of times before setting it down on her plate and pushing her dessert away.

"Lose your appetite?"

She nodded.

"Must be serious, considering you're turning down chocolate cake. What happened? Did somebody make a promise to you and then back out?"

"You could say that." She struggled to smile.

"Sorry to hear it. Sorry it ever happens, and we have to go along for that ride, too. But I guess in life we take the bad with the good. And sometimes it's more of the bad than anything else."

"Sometimes," she agreed. "You're a man of surprising depth, Wes Daniels." And this conversation had become more serious than she liked. "At the same time, you're pretty corny." She plucked a corn kernel from his shirt collar. "Courtesy of Tracey."

"That girl of mine." He shook his head. "Good thing this wasn't a seafood supper or you'd see me crabby, too."

"Been there and done that—the day we met."

He stared at her so intently, she shivered. "Is that so?"

"Yes. That afternoon at the Big Dipper, I could barely get you to speak to me."

"We've come a long way since then, haven't we? I guess you've managed to get me out of my shell."

"Your *crab* shell?"

That day, she hadn't been able to coax even a smile from him. Now he gave her a genuine grin. His eyes twinkled in the sunlight. He seemed not to have a single care in the world.

And all this from her one silly question.

...it may be you're just what he needs.

Wes was right. They *had* come a long way since that afternoon at the Big Dipper.

Could Mo have been right, too?

The thought left Cara stunned.

"You okay?" Wes frowned as if puzzled about her sudden silence.

She looked across the yard, searching for something to say. When she caught sight of Mark at the picnic table, she smiled. "Your son loves his pictures, doesn't he? Did he always like to color?"

"Since he could first hold a crayon. Once in a while, he and Patty would sit at the kitchen table to draw. Well, more scribbling on his part back then."

"It's nice you've helped him keep up the tradition she started. Was she an artist?"

"No. Just liked to draw."

"I don't know much about crafting, but as creative as she seemed to be, I'll bet she used a lot of her own ideas and didn't just follow patterns." Driven by genuine interest and outright curiosity, she added, "You told me she was good at doing things she liked."

"And not so good at follow-through. Yeah, I remember saying that." He shrugged. "The fact is, she never did any crafts when we first got married. She didn't like anything that involved staying on the ranch. Instead, she'd always run somewhere with her friends. Even after we had Mark and then Tracey, she spent a lot of time in town."

He was fighting to keep his tone neutral, avoiding too many details, holding his emotions in check. Anything to keep from letting her know his true thoughts.

Easy enough for her to recognize all those tactics, since lately she'd become an expert at them herself. "When Patty wasn't there for the kids, you were," she said softly. "I'm sure

Mark enjoyed the time with his daddy. And I can see he still does."

"I enjoy it, too. I spend as much time with him and Tracey as I can."

He turned his head to stare across the yard as if he didn't want her to read his expression. Too late. Long before he'd looked away, she noted his grin had disappeared. The sparkle had left his eyes.

Her throat tightened, keeping her from saying a word. But her heart responded with sympathy and understanding and…something else. There were so many more facets of Wes than the *crabby* one he sometimes displayed.

Too bad she wouldn't be around long enough to discover them all.

WHEN SHE'D ARRIVED to pick up the kids at day care, Cara had found a space directly in front of Rhea's house. Must be her lucky day.

She settled Tracey in her car seat.

Mark had already buckled himself into his seat and held his hand upright, waiting for a high five. Cara double-checked everything before nodding and slapping his palm. "Great job!"

"Job!" Tracey repeated, pounding the edge of her seat. "Job, job, job!"

"Don't remind me, Tracey. In case you were wondering, I didn't get any job hunting done yesterday, either." Instead, after Sunday brunch, she'd spent a so-called lazy afternoon with Andi and her family. She had chatted and laughed and pretended she had nothing on her mind, while putting into practice every technique Wes had used with her on Saturday. That left part of her mind free for thoughts of him.

Since the cookout, she had replayed their conversation in her mind several times. She had also repeated Mo O'Neill's words so many times, they'd become a mantra.

When Cara saw Wes again, would she get more glimpses of his lighthearted personality? Would he share other memories about Mark and Tracey? Did he regret talking to her about Patty? Did he feel at all the way—

Oh, no. Not going there.

Today, while Andi stayed behind to focus on the hotel's upcoming wedding, Cara drove into town. On the go ever since, she had talked to some of Andi's potential craft suppliers, seen Lizzie when she came in after school, and had now picked up Mark and Tracey. And as on Sunday, thoughts about Wes ran through Cara's mind all day long.

A car door slammed nearby. She looked up to

find Marianne walking—no, stalking—toward her. Exactly what Cara didn't need right now.

She'd told Andi about Marianne's visit to the store, but Andi had never heard a word from her. Evidently, Marianne hadn't let go of her irritation, because even from this distance, Cara saw the angry gleam in her eyes.

The upcoming conversation probably wouldn't be pretty. She hurried to the front of her car, putting distance between the kids and Marianne, who started speaking even before coming to a stop in front of her.

"Well," she said, looking through the car's windshield, "I see you're picking up Wes's kids again."

"Have picked them up, actually."

"I heard you had a great time at the cookout on Saturday."

This woman must have a network as wide as matchmaker Jed's. Or maybe Lizzie was right, and in this town, no one could keep anything a secret. "I enjoyed myself very much, thank you."

"I meant you had a great time with Wes."

"That's what I meant, too." *Oops.* Not a nice thing to say, especially not after Andi had told her Marianne's hopes for him. But this woman had pushed too many of her buttons—

deliberately. Thanks to Brad, Cara's days of accepting that had ended. "If you've got something to tell me, why don't you just say it?"

"I will. I'm giving you some advice. Don't set your sights on Wes."

"It was only a conversation." The nicest they'd ever had.

"And you shouldn't expect anything more than that. Wes is loyal, and he's loved Patty since we were all kids in school."

A sliver of sympathy for the woman worked its way into her conscience. After all, she had lost her best friend. "That's nice to hear," Cara said quietly. "But Patty's gone."

"I know that." Marianne's eyes glittered again.

"You know, if you have things to say to Wes or Andi or anyone else, you should talk to them directly."

"Because you're leaving?" She couldn't hide her eagerness.

"No. Because I'm helping Andi temporarily and that's all."

"Really?" She shot a look through the windshield again. "How is picking up Wes's kids helping Andi?"

She stalked away before Cara could respond. A good thing, because what would she have said? At this point she couldn't find answers to her own questions.

CARA STARED AT the file on her laptop. The words and figures on the screen barely registered. She had too many thoughts whirling in her brain. And—no surprise—most of them revolved around Wes.

When she'd brought the kids home, her heart had given an extra-hard beat at the sight of him, hinting at something she refused to believe. Something she didn't want to know.

Afraid he would read something in her expression, she had left the kids in the kitchen with him and come straight up here to work. *Right.*

Mark marched into the room, startling her.

"Pretty picture." He pointed to the colorful disks now floating across the front of the laptop.

"Yes, it is." She hadn't noticed the screen saver had turned on.

"Miss Cara stay for supper?" Mark asked.

Her heart thumped in warning. Yet, crazy as it might be, she'd hoped for the invitation. "Let's go talk to your daddy first, and then I'll tell you yes or no." For all she knew, Mark had come up with this idea on his own.

In the kitchen, she noticed Wes had already set a napkin and spoon at "her" place at the table. Realizing he had taken for granted she would stay warmed her from head to toe.

"We're going gourmet tonight," Wes told her. "Fish sticks and French fries with green beans and a salad. As you're planning to work for a while, you might as well join us, if you can handle the menu."

She did need to eat. "I can probably manage," she forced herself to say lightly. "As long as there's no crab at the table."

He sent her a quick, wry smile, proving he'd remembered their silly conversation. Why couldn't they go back to the way things were that day, before she'd come up with so many unanswered questions?

Why had she spent so much time spinning fantasies about him based on nothing more than a provocative suggestion from one of Jed Garland's assistant matchmakers? Cara didn't want to imagine what Wes would think if he ever found out.

She didn't want to stand here watching him work. "I'll take care of the salad," she offered.

"Fixings are in the fridge."

She kept her eyes focused on the cutting

board, hoping he wouldn't see the hot flush spreading across her face.

When she put the salad bowl on the table and settled next to Mark, he said immediately, "Miss Cara, read me a story?"

Her job waited upstairs. But no matter what else was going on, no matter how awkward she suddenly felt around Wes, she had to think of the kids. "Yes, I'll read a story. After we clean up the dishes from dinner."

"And dessert," he corrected. "What's for dessert, Daddy?"

"The ice cream we picked up from the Big Dipper this weekend. That's for after you eat your supper."

Mark immediately reached for a French fry.

"Did you see Lizzie while you were there?" she asked.

"Yeah. Something going on? She wasn't her usual talkative self."

Not today, either. At the store after school, she'd said only that her situation hadn't changed. Despite Cara's gentle encouragement, she still wanted to *wait and see*.

Wes looked at her, expecting a response. Shrugging, she speared a few green beans with her fork. "Teenagers can be temperamental" was all she could think to say. Too late, she recalled Mo telling her the same about him.

He shook his head. "Don't I know it." He turned his attention to his plate.

Evidently eager to get to dessert or a story or both, Mark kept his focus on his food. Tracey played with her green beans.

Cara gave another shrug—a mental one this time—and asked innocently, "You mean you were temperamental, too?"

"That and other descriptions not appropriate for the family supper table."

She didn't know which she liked more, his inclusion of her with his family or his willingness to talk about himself. "Somehow, I don't get that picture of you."

"Talk to my brother. After our dad died, Garrett finished raising me, and I have to confess to giving him a hard time."

"Why?"

He shrugged. "Teenage rebellion, I guess. Not wanting to be ordered around by anyone, especially not a brother only a few years older than me. Maybe not wanting to follow any rules at all."

"Have to follow the rules, Daddy," Mark told him. "Miss Rhea says so."

"And she's right, buddy. I hope you listen to her."

Mark nodded. "Yes."

"That's good."

Wes tilted his head toward his son but made eye contact with Cara. "I just hope what goes around doesn't come around. Even though it might be what I deserve." As if the words made him uncomfortable, he abruptly reached for his plate and Mark's.

While he took care of dishing up dessert, she cleared the rest of the dishes, then carried bowls of ice cream to the table. As soon as she set Mark's bowl in front of him, he grabbed his spoon and dug in.

She smiled. "Mark, did you tell your daddy about your special day on Friday?"

Immediately, he stilled, staring down at his bowl.

"Mark?" Wes prompted. "Miss Cara asked you a question."

"That's for mommies," Mark said. "I don't have a mo-mmy." His voice cracked and his lip trembled and to her dismay he burst into tears.

She turned, ready to wrap him in her arms.

"I got this," Wes snapped. He reached past her to lift Mark from the bench. He settled in his seat again. Perched Mark on his knee. Cleared his throat…twice.

The seconds ticked away. She bit her lip to keep from speaking. Wes's reaction to her instinctive response had unsettled her, but this nonreaction was so much worse. Mark was upset, and his daddy didn't know what to say.

Finally, Wes ruffled his son's hair. "Hey, buddy, no need to worry. The special day at Miss Rhea's is for mommies *and* daddies. Miss Rhea told us that. Remember?"

"And daddies?" Mark's voice shook.

"Yes. And daddies. We talked about this the other day. Daddy told you he's going to be there. Daddy's always going to be here, because that's what daddies do. You remember that now, too?"

Blinking, Mark nodded.

"Everything okay, then?"

He nodded again.

"Good." Wes hugged him.

"I want my ice cream." Just that quickly, Mark's voice had steadied, his problem was solved and he'd returned to putting his priorities in order.

Why couldn't everyone do all that so easily?

Mark returned to being his usual cheerful self.

Tracey, also as usual, babbled away. She hadn't seemed to notice her brother's tears.

Wes stared silently at his son.

And Cara couldn't come up with a thing to say.

While Mark finished his dessert, Wes smiled at him. "Hey, buddy, it will be time for baths and bed soon. If you want Miss Cara to read to you and Tracey, you'd better go pick out a couple of books."

Mark immediately climbed down from his bench.

Cara picked up her dessert bowl.

"About that episode earlier," Wes said.

She set the bowl down and sat back. "Mark was so upset and I just went on autopilot. Sorry for trying to jump in."

"He doesn't usually cry over anything." He made no comment regarding her apology.

"Maybe he's stressing about the recital."

"I doubt that." He spoke calmly, yet the tiny pulse in his jaw hinted at strong emotion. "He's not used to doing things without his mother around. I don't know how much he still remembers about Patty. Maybe he knows he used to have a mommy and now he doesn't. Or he knows there's a hole in his life he didn't have before."

And in yours. "He's got a connection to her through his artwork."

"Yeah, but who can tell what goes through his mind when he does all that coloring. Maybe he doesn't remember Patty at all, but coloring brings back the same happiness he felt when he was with her. If that's the case, those memories are worth all the paper and crayons I can give him."

"I'm sure he misses her, and whatever memories he has are precious. Wes… This isn't the same thing at all, and I'm not pretending it could be. But it might help. The kids might not miss their mother so much if they had more people in their lives. If—"

"If only I'd get out more with them? Right. Jed's always on me about that. So is his family and Sugar and Mo and almost everyone else I can name. And now you." He grabbed Mark's empty bowl and shot to his feet. "I hate to tell you, but taking the kids to a cookout or for ice cream or to the bowling alley isn't going to bring their mother back to them."

"That's not what I said. You're not hearing—"

"I am hearing. Loud and clear. People don't trust I can do what's best for my family."

"I didn't mean that, and I don't think anyone else does, either."

"Mark cried—which is not at all like him—and I choked. It happens. Becoming a parent doesn't mean you have all the answers near at hand, all the time. If you had kids of your own, you'd know that."

Cara swallowed a cry. Wes couldn't have any idea how much his comment hurt.

He would never admit he hurt just as much.

Mark came through the doorway, his arms filled with books.

Grateful to end this conversation, she caught Wes's attention and gestured toward the door.

At the sight of his son with his armload of books, he laughed. Though it sounded strained, she gave him an A for effort. She could barely manage to smile.

CHAPTER SIXTEEN

ON THE COUCH next to Cara, Mark sorted through the pile of books spilled across his lap. "Which story should we read first?" she asked.

She couldn't shake the memory of his tears. She watched him, his dark head bent over the books as he carefully considered each one. He seemed to have gotten over being upset.

What about Wes?

Though she hadn't said what he'd claimed she had about Patty, he was right. Taking Mark and Tracey for treats wouldn't bring their mother back. He was wrong about the rest, about people not trusting him. He couldn't see that when it came to his kids, no one in Cowboy Creek put more pressure on him than he put on himself.

Daddy's always going to be here, because that's what daddies do.

A loving, beautiful promise from a man who

loved and wanted to do all he could for his family.

Andi had been so right when she'd told Cara Wes needed someone to talk to. She was glad he had confided in her about Mark and his drawing but sad to know he had regretted that so soon. She had read the change in his expression as clearly as she had seen the tears in Mark's eyes.

Maybe as they spent more time together, Wes would open up, confiding without later feeling sorry about sharing.

Maybe she would, too.

"Where's Tracey?" Mark asked.

"She's still in the kitchen with your daddy, getting her hands and face washed."

As she spoke, Wes appeared holding his daughter. He leaned over the coffee table and plopped her onto the couch on Cara's other side.

When he took a seat in the chair across from them, her heart skipped a few beats. Considering the way he'd withdrawn after their conversation in the kitchen, she had never expected him to stay.

He grabbed a magazine from the coffee table. "You got this covered?"

I got this. Consoling Mark had been his job.

It looked like reading to the kids tonight was hers. "I'm good."

"I want this, Miss Cara."

When she took the book from Mark, he gave her his sweet smile. Tracey shifted, snuggling against her and resting a hand on her stomach.

Cara's heart filled with happiness as she realized these two precious babies had come to mean so much to her.

"THAT'S ENOUGH READING for tonight," Wes said to Mark. "It's late. Time to get your pajamas ready for your bath."

"Okay, Daddy." Mark slid from the edge of the couch. He headed toward the stairs off the living room, leaving Cara with the books.

As she straightened the pile, she looked at her watch in surprise. She had read to the kids for nearly an hour. Well, to Mark, at least. In the last few minutes, Tracey, her thumb in her mouth, had fallen asleep slumped against Cara's side.

Wes rose from his chair. "I'll carry her upstairs and tuck her in."

"I'll do it. If we move her too much, she might wake up." Carefully, she took the baby into her arms.

Wes led the way upstairs to the kids' room,

which she had often seen on her trips down the hall to the office.

Mark sat in front of a small dresser, playing with a couple of toy cars. Seeing him sitting on the floor reminded her of the day his daddy had landed on his rear while trying to help her with the sticking dresser drawer. The day she had first gotten a genuine laugh from Wes. The memory made her smile.

Besides the small dresser and a twin bed, the room held a crib and a baby's changing table. Cara settled Tracey in the crib.

"Tracey needs jammies, Daddy," Mark said.

"Yeah, I know. I'll take care of her in a minute. I'll be right back. While I'm gone, you pick out a pair of your pajamas."

Mark nodded. "Okay, Daddy."

Cara scanned the border traveling around the walls, a wide strip decorated with horses and wagons and pint-size cowboys. "Guess your daughter's going to grow up to be a cowgirl, like it or not, huh?"

Wes smiled as they moved out into the hallway. "Well, I hope she'll like horses, anyhow. She's got her own room next door, and that's more girly-girl, as Patty used to say."

That explained the door beside the kids' room. Cara had never seen that one open.

"Tracey hasn't slept in there yet," he said. He glanced back into the kids' room. "Before Patty died, the baby was so young we were still keeping her in with us. A while after that, Mark went through a bad time waking up from nightmares. I moved Tracey in here with him, hoping the company would help."

"Did it?"

"It seemed to. From then on, he settled down again. We haven't had any other issues, except for that crying earlier tonight."

Mark waved a pajama top and bottom in either hand. "I picked my jammies, Daddy."

"Okay, pardner, let's get this show on the road. Say good-night to Miss Cara." He turned to her. "You won't mind finding your own way out?"

"Of course not."

Mark flung his arms around her legs in a hug. "Good night, Miss Cara. See you tomorra, right?"

"Good night, Mark. Yes, you'll see me then."

Wes and Mark headed in the direction of the bathroom. She lingered in the doorway of the kids' room.

Tracey still lay sound asleep with her thumb resting against one cheek, as if she was keeping it close by in case she needed it.

Cara took a deep breath, waiting for an if-only to bring her to tears.

Nothing hit her but the reminder that if-onlys came from the past and she needed to think about now. About moving forward. About *tomorra*.

CARA'S WEEK QUICKLY settled into a routine. After breakfast, she drove to town, where she spent her time at the store talking to some of the local women about their crafts, sketching a floor plan and taking measurements for the shelving units and display tables Andi intended to buy.

She made a point of being there when Lizzie arrived after school every afternoon. While she again seemed as chatty and energetic as ever, dark circles had begun pooling beneath her eyes, and she avoided talking about what Cara most wanted to discuss. She hoped Lizzie would come in one day and either confirm she wasn't pregnant, after all, or say she had made an appointment to see a doctor. Meanwhile, all Cara could do was be there for her.

And every afternoon, Cara made the trip to Rhea's to pick up the kids, then spent most of the evening working at Wes's house.

Once in a while, she felt guilty about not

spending more time at the Hitching Post, but Andi assured her everyone there was busy prepping for the hotel's upcoming wedding.

On Thursday, she stopped by SugarPie's for a late lunch. As usual, the owner of the sandwich shop and bakery greeted her warmly. She followed Cara to a table to take her order. "Y'all going to get that store open any time soon?"

"As soon as we can."

"Good. Anything that brings in new customers will be a benefit for everyone in Cowboy Creek."

As Sugar returned to the kitchen, Mo O'Neill arrived and joined Cara at her table. "I hear you're getting interest from the knitting circle members Andi talked to last week."

"Lots of interest. Judging by the women I've spoken to so far, Andi is going to have plenty of stock for the store. I only hope she'll have lots of customers, too."

"That seems promising, considering the talk at the town council meeting. Once construction for the new exit begins, they plan to set up a detour temporarily. Traffic will come right down Canyon Road."

"That *is* good news. I'll tell Andi when I get back to the hotel…later today."

"This evening, once you return after your supper, will be time enough." Mo's eyes positively twinkled.

Cara barely kept from sighing aloud. Obviously, Mo knew about her evenings with Wes and his kids. But unless she had psychic abilities, even she couldn't know whether or not Cara would be staying for dinner tonight.

That was a given, though. After all, she had been invited to dinner, now followed by story time, every night this week. The thought of taking "her" place at Wes's table again sent a few tingles racing along every nerve.

Right now, she had to stop thinking about Wes and deal with this conversation. Hearing Mo comment on the blush now heating her cheeks would be worse than seeing the woman's all-knowing eyes twinkle. Cara needed a diversion, a topic other than where she spent her evenings.

She needed an answer to a question that had troubled her for days. A question she wasn't comfortable asking Wes or even Andi. "Mo," she blurted, "why does Wes's brother work on Jed's ranch instead of with him?"

"Ah. I wondered if you'd considered that. You remember the other day, I mentioned Garrett's lightness of heart?"

Cara nodded.

"He's too much of a free spirit to tie himself to anything—to property or a family or even to a single woman. Not like Wes. Surprisingly, of the two boys, Wes became the one to settle down."

"And the one with all the responsibility for his family's ranch."

"That's very true, and something no one knows much about. How it all came to happen is between them, which might be where it will always stay."

"Everything must have been so much easier for Wes when his wife was alive. Now he's single-handedly taking care of the ranch *and* his kids. He can't manage all that on his own."

Lips pursed, Mo stared thoughtfully across the table at her.

Cara focused on lining up her silverware on her napkin. Even that reminded her of Mark and Tracey and Wes. Her life was slowly becoming intertwined with theirs—not a good thing when she knew she had to leave.

She did plan to go home. When she was done helping Andi… After she found an apartment… Once she had a job lined up…

Cara had enough on her own agenda to worry about. It wasn't up to her to determine what Wes could and couldn't handle. Still, she couldn't keep from worrying about him, too.

No. She had to be honest, at least with herself. She did more than worry about Wes Daniels.

Wes wasn't ready for a relationship. Neither was she.

And yet…was she falling for him anyway?

No, she couldn't be.

How could she even consider the idea, after Brad? Hadn't she learned anything from that disaster?

CHAPTER SEVENTEEN

As usual, when Cara arrived at Wes's house with the kids, he met them at her car. The rush of pleasure that always followed her first sight of him now hit with triple intensity.

As Wes opened the passenger door to get Tracey, Cara leaned into the back seat to help Mark with his seat belt.

"We're almost done with the cleaning at the store," she reported. "Andi's getting a team together for a painting party this weekend."

"With all those grandsons Jed's got married into his family, she'll have plenty of free labor." Wes laughed. "That's probably the reason he went into the matchmaking business to begin with."

She gathered up the diaper bag and some of Mark's papers. Wes came around to her side of the car with the baby. Cara stared up at him. "You don't think he just wanted his granddaughters to be happy?"

"Maybe. But marriage doesn't always guarantee happiness. Free labor's a surer thing."

"That's kind of cynical, isn't it?"

"Sometimes the truth hurts."

And sometimes love hurts. Especially when it was one-sided. She should have learned her lesson the first time around.

Wes had shared some things with her about Patty, but his comments now stirred her curiosity about his relationship with his wife. He was such a good father, she couldn't imagine him not being a good husband. How happy had his marriage been?

She thought again of Mo's idea that she could be what he needed. Yes, Cara now knew she could be exactly that. Unfortunately, her firsthand knowledge of Wes's needs didn't match Mo's ideas, and she would have to be realistic about the difference.

Or make a difference in his life.

He jiggled Tracey and tickled her under her chin.

"You'd better watch that little one," Cara warned, laughing. "Someone was a little cranky on the ride home."

"No nap?"

"Not a wink."

He gave an exaggerated sigh. "Going to be another one of those rough nights."

On their way to the house, she attempted to say casually, "I saw Patty's friend Marianne this afternoon. She's seems very…interested in you and the kids." *Territorial*, Andi had called it. The perfect description.

"Is that so?" He took more time than necessary straightening Tracey's shirt. At the back porch steps, he halted. After noting through the window Mark was coloring at the table inside, Wes said, "I don't want to say this in front of Mark. Ever since Patty died, Marianne's had her wires crossed. I don't know what the woman's thinking."

Evidently, that she could take Patty's place. "It sounds like she wants to stay friends."

"We were never friends to begin with. And considering how she zeroed in on me like a homing pigeon as soon as Patty passed, I'm not sure how good a friend she was to my wife."

"I think Marianne genuinely misses her."

"That may be. It doesn't give us a connection or her a reason to hang around me every time we run across each other at the sitter's or anywhere else. To tell you the truth, I don't like that she sees so much of the kids at Rhea's.

"You saw how ready Mark was to accept

you as his mother. That's all I would need is for him to get the same idea about her."

A vision of Mark asking Marianne *Are you my new mommy?* made Cara's breath catch.

She'd come to care so much about Mark and Tracey. Maybe too much? Did her dismay at seeing that image mean she wanted something more?

"There's not much I can do about the kids being around Marianne," Wes continued. "I wouldn't pull them from their sitter's. Mark and Tracey have known Rhea since they were born. For some reason, though, Mark's never taken to Marianne. And I'm glad for that."

Cara had always known Mark was a smart little boy. "From what I've seen of him at Rhea's, you don't need to worry about him attaching himself to her."

"Good to know. It's not something I can sit Mark down to discuss. As for Marianne homing in on me, I already set her straight. I have no interest in a relationship with her or anyone. My kids are still getting over losing their mother, and I can't risk them getting hurt." He paused with his hand on the doorknob. "It's different having you around the kids. Marianne's not going anywhere. You're here short-term."

He didn't say the words again, but she heard the *Good to know* in his satisfied tone. Would he be that happy to see her leave?

When they entered the kitchen, Wes went to put Tracey into her high chair.

Cara left the drawings and the diaper bag in their assigned spots. "I'm going to work for a while."

"Okay. You know where to find us."

She hurried from the room and up the stairs. The closer she came to the office, the slower her feet moved.

Once she finished her inventory and she and Andi transferred all Patty's crafts to the store, her job here would be done. She planned to continue bringing the kids home to Wes every day but would have no excuse to stay around. Or to *hang* around, like Marianne.

How could she give up the dinners with Wes and his family and miss their evening story time?

How could she make a difference in Wes's life when he didn't care that she planned to go out of it?

AFTER DINNER, MARK carried a pile of books into the living room. "Read these ones tonight."

Cara took her place on the couch. "Okay. What one first?" She knew which book he would hand her. He chose the same one first every night.

Mark settled on one side of her to turn the pages of the storybook. Tracey, more restless than usual, sat back against the couch with her thumb in her mouth.

Cara finished the first book and the second and the third. Once in a while, she exchanged a glance with Wes. Sometimes, when one of the kids laughed or shouted over the story, they shared a smile.

He always sat across from them in the over-stuffed chair with an open magazine resting on his knees. Cara had noticed lately, though, that he didn't very often remember to turn a page.

When she closed the cover on the fourth book, Wes looked across at Mark. "That's enough reading for tonight."

He said that every night, and she loved those words, choosing to believe they implied that after *tonight* there would be a *tomorrow.*

"Time to go get your pajamas ready for your bath," he told Mark. "I'll be upstairs as soon as I walk Miss Cara to the door."

Mark gave her a hug, then ran across the living room to the stairs.

"Let me take her," Wes said when Cara reached to pick up Tracey. "I can tell she's not ready for pajamas yet."

In the kitchen, he set Tracey in her high chair, adding a couple toys to the tray for her to play with. Then, as he also did every night, he left the kitchen door half-open while they went out onto the back porch to say their goodbyes.

It was cooler than usual outside tonight, and Cara shivered.

"You'll be needing to bring a coat with you one of these days," he said.

She wanted to believe *one* would lead to *many*. The thought made her shiver again, this time in pleasure. He reached out as if to wrap his arm around her to warm her, then dropped his hand. She felt his touch all the same.

No, she imagined she did. And she couldn't stand here making up fantasies. Couldn't spend her nights making wishes that would never be granted.

"In case you don't check Mark's backpack tonight," she said, "there's a reminder notice about the recital tomorrow at the day care."

"Yeah." Wes rubbed his forehead as if trying to wipe away a headache.

He worked so hard all day. It wouldn't hurt for her to take more of the load off his shoulders. "Rhea told me the recital isn't really a big deal."

"It's not. The kids all say the alphabet and a nursery rhyme or two, sing a song, then try to stand still for pictures. And that's about it."

Cara smiled. "It sounds very cute, but short and sweet. I'll be in town all day. If you don't want to take time off to make the trip, I'm happy to go in your place and lend the kids some moral support."

"No." The flat reply made her blink. As if he realized how abruptly he'd answered, he went on, "I need to show up. It may not be a big deal overall, but it is to Mark."

"Of course, it is." The recital was set for late morning. "I assume you'll leave the kids at Rhea's and come back to the ranch. I'll pick them up at the end of the day and bring them… here, as usual."

He nodded.

She would bring them *home*. Just what she said and did every day.

And every day, no matter how many warnings she gave herself about wishes and fantasies, this house felt more like *home* to her, too.

As the Garland family and their guests drifted out of the Hitching Post's dining room the next morning, Cara stayed behind with Andi.

Before breakfast, Andi had said she wanted to get organized for this weekend's painting party. She pulled a notepad and pen from her shoulder bag. "I made up a list last night— with a little help from a couple of the husbands around here."

"You don't think we could have figured out on our own what we needed to buy?"

"Of course we could have." Andi laughed. "But part of convincing them we need their help is letting them see how much they're needed. Which reminds me, I need you here, too. I'm beginning to think I won't have a clue what I'll do when you leave."

Cara hoped someday Wes would feel the same. "I see exactly what you're up to," Cara said, forcing a teasing tone. "You're trying to convince me to stay. And why not? I'm your unpaid errand girl." And Wes's unpaid help. "I'll volunteer to pick up the paint supplies on my way to the store today." Andi opened her mouth but Cara held up a hand. "No, don't thank me. We may as well leave everything at the store, anyway. And it only makes sense for me to pick it up, since I'm going into town. Plus, that will save you a trip."

Hadn't she said the same thing to Wes earlier this week, when she had offered to bring his kids home from day care? And look where that had gotten her. To a place she had never thought she would find, a place that made her feel comfortable and happy and needed.

Yes, she was needed…

She wanted to be here for Wes and Mark and Tracey. For Andi and her kids. For Lizzie. For herself. Ever since her arrival in Cowboy Creek, she had reinforced her goal to go home. Now her goal had changed. She wanted to stay.

Cara looked up to find Andi staring at her. "What?"

"My question exactly. *What?* What are you smiling about?"

"Nothing."

Andi shook her head. "That's not going to work. I *know* what's got you so happy. I'm just waiting for you to fess up, as Grandpa says."

Cara wanted to confess, to talk about exactly what had made her smile. But when feelings were this new, this unexpected and unbelievable, how did you share them with anyone else when you still didn't know if you could trust them yourself?

"Cara…"

She couldn't keep from admitting to what she was sure her best friend had already guessed. "It's Wes."

"I knew it," Andi said. "Grandpa was right again. And here you were, mad at us because you thought we were up to something."

"You *were*."

"Yes, we were." Andi laughed. "And aren't you happy about that now!"

"Either way, it doesn't make a difference. Wes told me he's not interested in a relationship with anyone right now."

"And...?"

She sighed. Andi knew her so well. "Okay, I'll admit it. Yes, I'm happy you and Jed got us together. But considering what Wes said, I should have more sense than to act like a teenager with her first crush."

"Or first real love."

"I don't know. As real as it feels, how can I believe in it—after Brad?"

Andi sighed. "I probably should have said this a long time ago, but when it came to him, it always seemed like you were in love with the *idea* of love. You wanted a relationship. A family. You always have. And when you went looking, Brad happened to be there."

"But we went out for months before I started feeling anything like I feel for Wes."

"I fell for Mitch at first sight. Things didn't

work out for us the first time around, but still…
When you know, you know."

And you know what the one *means, right?*
Lizzie had asked. *You just know you're a per-*
fect fit. A forever fit.

Cara could envision a forever with Wes.

Could he ever feel the same about her?

AT THE STORE, Cara had just set her laptop on
the table in the kitchen area when she heard
the front door open. She found Lizzie in the
display room. "Perfect timing. I only got here
a minute ago myself."

"I know," Lizzie said. "I was waiting across
the street."

Waiting? Cara's stomach clenched. Lizzie
didn't elaborate and suddenly wouldn't meet
her eyes, adding to Cara's unease. Knowing
better than to push the issue, Cara dropped her
shoulder bag onto a display case. "I've got to
bring in some boxes from the car."

"I can help."

"Well, thanks. But you're not scheduled to
work today, you know." As she had hoped, that
got a laugh from Lizzie. Not a very natural-
sounding one, but still a laugh.

"Don't worry—I won't send Andi a time card."

Outside, Lizzie looked into the overflowing trunk of Cara's car. "What's all this?"

"Painting supplies. We're going to have a painting party here on Sunday."

"Sounds like fun. I wish I could help, but I'm scheduled to work at the Dipper."

"That's okay." And maybe a good thing, if Lizzie turned out to be pregnant, after all. "I know you'd be here if you could."

Lizzie took two cans of paint from the trunk. Cara grabbed the box with the brushes and other supplies. As they set everything on the floor inside the store, Cara said casually, "You're around early. No school this morning?"

"I'm skipping my prep hour. Cara…" Lizzie paused, then blurted, "I took a test."

For a second, Cara misunderstood. Or gave in to wishful thinking. But one look at Lizzie's anguished expression assured her the teen wasn't talking about a school exam.

"A pregnancy test," Lizzie said. "I went to Flagman's Folly last night and bought it there so I wouldn't see anyone I knew. And I took the test this morning after my dad went to work and my mom went out. And…and…it was positive." Her voice broke. As if her legs couldn't hold her upright, the teen slumped against a display case. "It could be wrong, couldn't it?"

Or it could be right.

Cara had done a home pregnancy test, too, and had been overjoyed to see the positive result. She had hoped for the news. Had been more than ready to become a mom…

That wasn't true for Lizzie. And judging by her wide eyes and the breaths she was gulping, the girl was in shock and fighting tears.

"There's a possibility it could be wrong," Cara said slowly, not sure how much Lizzie could take in all at once. Or if she was up to taking in anything at all right now. "Those home tests have good track records, but even so, they're not a hundred-percent accurate. Some of the same things that make our periods late can cause false positives." Lizzie seemed to hang on her every word. "The next step would be confirming it with a test at the doctor's office. If you don't want to go alone but aren't ready to tell your mother, do you have someone else you can ask?"

"I don't know. I'll think about it." Lizzie didn't sound convinced *or* convincing. She pushed herself away from the display case and stood upright. "I have to get back to school."

"Lizzie—" From the depths of her shoulder bag on top of the case, Cara's cell phone rang. Ignoring it, she said, "I'd be happy to go with you. Or can you ask your boyfriend? Or a close friend?"

"I'll think about it," Lizzie said again. She handed the bag to Cara. "Your phone's ringing. And I have to go to class."

"Lizzie, wait—"

Instead the teen almost ran from the store, leaving the door to swing shut behind her. And the phone continued to ring.

With her gaze on Lizzie rushing across the sidewalk, Cara pulled the phone from her bag. "Hello?"

"Cara? Wes. You sound distracted."

"I'm okay. You sound stressed."

"Yeah, *stress* about covers it. I'm fine, but I've got an emergency here with a mare, and the vet's running late. I'm not going to get into town for the show at Rhea's. And Mark's not going to handle it well when she tells him. She'll have enough stress of her own trying to calm all the kids' nerves." He paused, then added, "You're in town now, right?"

"Yes."

"I don't like to ask, but if you've got a few minutes, could you run by there and help Rhea explain to Mark that I can't make it?"

"Of course. I'll head over now."

"Thanks. I appreciate that."

The sincerity in his voice told her how much he meant it. The thread of tension told her how hard he was taking not being on hand to support his son.

And her suddenly soaring pulse at this admission he needed her confirmed everything she already knew.

Despite all the warning signs, all the questions without answers, all the worry over trusting her own feelings…she had fallen in love with Wes.

CHAPTER EIGHTEEN

CARA CLAMPED HER hands together in front of her but wished she could clamp them over her ears instead. Wes had called it exactly right about how badly Mark would handle the news his daddy wouldn't be attending the recital.

"But *why*?" Mark cried plaintively for the third time.

"Daddy's still at the ranch," Rhea explained again. "He's taking care of one of the horses." She shot a glance at Cara.

With each wail, Mark's voice had risen and he'd swiped away fresh tears. With each wail, Cara's heart twisted a little more. She couldn't do anything about Lizzie's anguish, at least not at the moment, but she was determined to help Mark here and now.

"Daddy can't come," she said. "He's sorry he can't watch the show today."

"Miss Cara will watch?" He tugged on her hand and looked up at her, his eyes brimming again. "Miss Cara will watch, *please*?"

How could she refuse? How could she just walk away from Mark when he was so upset? Of course, she couldn't do that either. She nodded emphatically. "Yes, I'll watch. I wouldn't miss it." And now she had agreed, she could admit to herself how much she wanted to be there.

"You're a lifesaver," Rhea said quietly, adding in a normal tone, "Ignore the chaos. I've learned it's best to let them all work off their nervous energy so they're calmer when the recital begins. We won't be getting underway for a while yet, but other parents will start to arrive soon. So feel free to hang out."

"Thanks. I'll do that."

Rhea had made a slip when she'd said *other parents*. Cara wasn't a parent. Still, she didn't at all mind being included with the rest.

Full of smiles now, Mark led Cara by the hand over to the bench where the children did their coloring and crafts. "Sit."

Obediently, she sat. He slid a piece of paper in front of her and put a box of crayons on the table. As he took a seat beside her, a few of his friends joined them.

They all worked industriously until parents began arriving and most of the children lost interest in their drawings. She noticed the metal folding chairs set up on the opposite side of the room had begun filling fast.

"Mark, I have to hurry and get a good seat so I can see you in the show."

"Okay," he said. "I clean up."

"Thank you."

She hurried across the room to a chair at the end of one of the rows. Before she could sit, someone tapped her on the shoulder. *Wes*. Cara turned, only to find her quick thought and even more quickly pounding pulse had both let her down. It wasn't Wes.

Marianne stood in the aisle. "*You're* here for the recital?"

Cara blinked. Beneath the noise of the audience, teachers and stars of the upcoming show, Marianne's voice had nearly disappeared. But Cara couldn't miss the venom in that first word.

"No, I'm here for the dinner." She smiled. "Of course I'm here for the recital. Wes couldn't make it, and he asked me to stop by." She hadn't lied. But too late, she realized her explanation would probably give Marianne more reason to hiss.

Sure enough, she said, "He *asked*? Or you volunteered?" As she'd done after their last conversation, she stalked off without waiting for an answer.

Cara focused on the other side of the room and watched the miniature version of Wes. Mark carefully tucked the drawings they had done together into one of the colorful plastic bins lining a low shelving unit.

Rhea clapped her hands and called for attention.

Her assistants led the smaller children, including Tracey, over to a curtain blocking off one corner of the room. Mark and the rest of his friends ran to join them. The curtain billowed from the press of little bodies swarming behind it. Excited, high-pitched voices filtered out into the room.

Cara soon learned she had been right, too, about what she had said to Wes. The program was very cute and both short and sweet.

One of Rhea's assistants played a simple tune on the piano as the older children recited their ABCs. Next came a tentative recital of the nursery rhyme "Twinkle, Twinkle, Little Star," followed by an enthusiastic version of "Itsy Bitsy Spider." Some of the more energetic participants occasionally got carried away, especially while showing the rain coming down to wash away their spiders.

All through the program, camera phones clicked from every angle. Cara took pictures of all Mark's and Tracey's shining moments.

After the entertainment portion, each child marched up to Miss Rhea to receive a certificate of participation and to pose for a picture with her.

There had been very few tears and only a handful of shoves as a couple of students tried to claim more than their share of center "stage." And somehow, everyone managed to stand still long enough for a final group shot.

Cara made sure to take pictures of that, too. Wes couldn't be here, but at least he would get to see what he'd had to miss…

Another thought hit her, one that made her catch her breath and clutch her cell phone in both hands. She'd gotten so involved in recording Mark's and Tracey's special moments, she hadn't once thought of her child. In the room filled with kids, she hadn't once missed her baby-to-be.

The feeling of disloyalty she expected to wash over her didn't come. Instead of guilt she felt a tiny but strong certainty she had begun to heal.

Wild clapping brought her attention back to the presenters, who were bowing and accepting their standing ovation. Quickly, Cara stood along with the rest of the audience.

When everyone began moving around the room, she looked through the crowd for Mark, wanting to compliment him on a job well-done. Instead, she spotted Wes standing alone near the doorway at the opposite end of the room.

Pleasure rippled through her with as much force as the rain coming down during "Itsy Bitsy Spider."

Smiling, she dodged chatting parents and children to get to his side. Halfway to him, she caught a good look at him, eyes dark and expression as blank as an unused sheet of Mark's construction paper. As Cara paused, Marianne stepped in front of her, ignoring her to face Wes. Relieved, Cara realized he'd been directing that look at Marianne.

"Oh, Wes, Mark and Tracey were wonderful. Patty would be so proud. I know you are, too." She rested her hand on his arm. "Why don't we take our kids to supper at Sugar's so we can all celebrate together?"

Cara's stomach clenched. Well, she'd wanted Wes to take the kids out, hadn't she? Though not like this. Not with anyone but her.

He'd told her he didn't care about Marianne.

But people didn't always say what they really felt. Hadn't she been proof of that lately?

If Wes didn't want the woman, why couldn't he tear his gaze from her? When he stepped closer, Cara's heart plummeted. She wanted only to slink away, but Wes and Marianne blocked the exit to the hall. The aisles behind her had filled with proud parents and grandparents. She couldn't go forward or back or cause a scene by running out through the emergency door. She turned again, trapped, forced to listen to Wes's response to the invitation.

"Not tonight," he said gruffly. "Not any night. I've run out of polite ways to answer so I'll be blunt. I'm grateful for Patty's sake you two were friends. But you and I were never that and will never be anything else. As plain as I can make it, I'm not interested."

Marianne dropped her hand and brushed past Wes to move into the hall.

As unfeeling and sarcastic as the woman could be, she'd probably needed Wes's blunt response. Still, Cara winced, knowing just how crushing it was to be rejected by someone you cared about. She was relieved she couldn't see Marianne's face.

As it was, she had to meet Wes's lingering scowl. "I... I'm so glad you could make it. Were you here from the beginning of the recital?"

He stared at her, but his expression didn't change. Her pleasure trickled away along with her voice, leaving her sounding as tentative as the children with their twinkling star.

"I didn't expect to see you." His voice sounded uncomfortable and still carried its gruff edge.

"I didn't expect to see you, either. Mark's going to be so happy you were able to get here." She responded lightly, hoping he would feel more at ease again. False hopes, when she knew nothing she could do or say would help. It wasn't Marianne he was angry with now.

"I asked you to come by and help Rhea talk to my son. I didn't ask you to step in for me, the same way I didn't need your assistance when he got upset about the recital." Every word he spoke made him sound more distant, as if he had taken physical steps back from her. "I'll be around town the rest of the day. I'll pick up the kids myself."

This felt like a dismissal—and she refused to let him brush her off that easily. "Okay. We'll talk later, after I'm done at the store."

"Not tonight. The kids will be riled up enough from the show."

Or would he still be too angry to want her around? "Then we'll talk now. What's going on, Wes? It can't just be what happened with Mark. Was it your conversation with Marianne?"

"Nothing's going on."

"It's not nothing." *Everything* between them at that moment was strained and awkward and confusing. And wrong.

Above the noise around them, she heard Mark shriek, "Hi, Daddy!" from across the room.

He came running up to them and threw his arms around Wes's legs. "You came to the show."

Wes smiled down at him. "I did, pardner. You did an excellent job. And it was a great show."

Yes, a great show. Very cute. Short and sweet. And now also bittersweet.

Mark turned to her, his arms held wide, grinning with happiness. She wrapped her arms around him, but even his hug couldn't make her forget the anger in his daddy's eyes.

MUCKING OUT STALLS was probably one of Wes's least-favorite chores around the ranch. As a kid he had learned the job went by faster when he kept his eyes and ears and mind focused on nicer things. Which was probably why, when he heard a car door slam, his thoughts flew to Cara.

Not smart. At all. Because, one, he'd already recognized it wasn't the sound of her car. Two, since their meeting at Rhea's yesterday, he'd been trying to convince himself to stop thinking about her so often. And three...

Well, weren't two examples of his lack of sense enough?

Disgusted with himself, he set the pitchfork against the wall and stomped across the barn. By the time he changed out of his work boots and scrubbed his hands at the sink, his visitor still hadn't come looking for him.

He walked outside into the sun and relative heat of early afternoon. No vehicle in sight, either. Whoever had come to call must have parked in front of the house. He headed that way, still thinking of Cara.

And cursing himself. He shouldn't think of the woman at all, not when she planned to walk out of their lives before too long.

All week, he'd told himself Mark's tendency to cling to her couldn't be a good thing long-term, but for now having her here gave his son extra attention. Being around his kids appeared to do some good for Cara, too. The more she was with them, the happier and more relaxed she seemed.

Excuses. Since he'd met her, he'd made nothing but excuses for his actions. The list went on. Inviting her to supper because she'd offered to help him without asking for anything in return. Hanging around during story time to make sure she could handle the kids.

He'd never admitted the real reasons for what he'd done. He liked being with her.

What was wrong with him?

He'd kept his distance from Marianne so she wouldn't get involved with his kids but hadn't had the sense to do the same with Cara. Now he'd driven her away because he hadn't liked her stepping over the line, especially since he'd made it clear he didn't want her taking his place at the recital.

Yeah, he'd driven her away…and still he missed her.

Even more disgusted with himself, he nearly raced across the yard.

In front of the house, a familiar old but well-tended pickup truck sat on the driveway not far from the front steps. The truck's owner sprawled comfortably on the porch swing.

"Afternoon," Jed Garland said.

"Afternoon," Wes agreed. He went up the steps and leaned back against the railing. "What brings you over my way?"

"I was in the neighborhood."

He laughed at Jed's innocent tone. They both knew the man was quoting Wes's words—or rather, his lie—from the day of the cookout back at him. Two could play that game. "Well, of course you were."

Jed grinned in acknowledgment of the repeated reply. "Nice to see you haven't lost your sense of humor. Also nice to have you and the kids visiting at the ranch again last weekend."

"I was glad we stayed. We had a good time. Great food, nice company."

"I did take note of the company you were keeping."

Yeah, Jed would. "Then you'd have seen me talking to all the locals and even to a few of your guests."

"Mostly to one guest, which is understandable. As you said yourself, Cara's nice company."

Wes hadn't said that exactly, but trust Jed to rewrite events to fit his own ideas. The only surprise was that the man hadn't gotten over here sooner to state his case. Instead of trying to change Jed's mind, an impossibility anyhow, Wes simply said, "If you can wait a few minutes, I'll get cleaned up properly and offer you a cup of coffee."

"Don't stop what you were doing on my account."

No way would he tell Jed about his activities. Not when he'd lined up chores meant to help him avoid his own home. To get distance from memories, old and new.

"It's near quitting time anyhow. I got off to an early start today so I could tackle some extra work around here." Extra work that would keep his mind focused on his job instead of other things. Or other people. "I'm due to pick up the kids from Rhea's soon."

"Yeah, so I heard."

"Good thing I don't try to hide anything from anyone around here. It would be a losing battle."

"Still, you've managed to keep winning for a while now." When Wes said nothing, Jed continued, "You have a bad habit of trying to derail conversations, too. We were talking about Cara."

"*You* were talking about Cara."

The older man smiled. "So I was. And as I was about to say, you couldn't go wrong by getting to know her better. For the kids' sake."

If Jed only knew. Wes had already gone wrong in that regard, letting her get comfortable enough to make decisions that should have been left up to him.

He crossed his arms as if they could form a shield protecting him from Jed's intentions. "I told you already, we're doing fine."

As Jed stared back at him, for once without arguing, Wes couldn't keep from asking himself, were they really doing that great? Until lately, he'd have said yes. He'd have said he could single-handedly raise his kids.

Now he had to factor in recent events, such as Mark's crying spell at the table on Monday. His refusal to eat supper last night. And Tracey's stubbornness this morning when, completely unlike her, she had grabbed Mark's favorite stuffed bear and wouldn't give it back.

Considering their actions forced Wes to think twice. Just how successful had he been in taking care of the kids this past year? And how capable was he at doing alone what he and Patty used to do together?

As if those worries weren't enough, he had a new one to add to his list. Had his kids' recent behavior issues come from Cara's appearance in their lives—and now, her abrupt disappearance?

"Good to hear things are going well," Jed said, jerking him back to their conversation.

Wes nearly laughed at the irony. Nothing like having someone finally believe you just when you start doubting yourself.

"We're all hoping to see you out for the cookout again today," Jed said.

"Yeah, well—" *Not a chance.*

Luckily, he swallowed those last words in time. No sense taking his irritation over his own actions out on Jed. He had known the man his entire life, and as interfering as he could be, Jed always had the best intentions.

Why couldn't he let himself believe the same about Cara?

CHAPTER NINETEEN

WHAT A DIFFERENCE a couple days could make.

While last Sunday Cara had been happy for a lazy day at the Hitching Post, today she was glad to have the painting party to keep her busy. To keep her mind occupied and her thoughts away from Wes. Now, she threw herself into organizing supplies in the store's back room…and still couldn't keep her mind from wandering.

Yesterday she had half hoped Wes would show up at the cookout. When he hadn't, hope gave way to relief. Anyone seeing them together would easily have figured out something was wrong. She couldn't talk about that, not even with Andi. Not yet. Not when her emotions were all tangled up, like a kitten rolling around with a skein of wool.

And wasn't that an appropriate image? If not for Patty Daniels's knitting and sewing and all her other crafts, Cara might never have spent so much time with Wes and fallen for him and his family.

Without Wes at the cookout, she had managed to keep everyone, including Andi, from getting suspicious. But her ability to fake it had worn very thin.

The weekend made her abrupt schedule change less noticeable. What would happen next week, without her invitations to Wes's for dinner? How would she explain all her free time in the evenings? She couldn't claim a need to work at the store every night.

By the time they'd finished Sunday brunch this morning, Cara couldn't leave the Hitching Post fast enough. She had told Andi she needed to stop at the pharmacy before meeting the work crew at the store.

The pharmacy made her think of Lizzie and the pregnancy test. She hadn't seen the teen at all yesterday and probably wouldn't today, either, unless she stopped by the Big Dipper after they finished painting.

Cara heard the door of the store open.

She hurried out from the back room, expecting to see Lizzie standing in the doorway. Instead, she found Wes. He didn't speak, but who needed words when his hands gave him away, revealing his comfort level by his death grip on his hat brim.

She could have used something to hang on to, too. For her, discomfort and longing and love all blended together. Only pride kept her from letting those feelings show. "Hello," she said coolly. "Did you make a wrong turn on your way to somewhere else?"

He'd asked her that the first night she'd shown up on his doorstep.

Wes's contrite expression confirmed he remembered, too. Today he had turned the situation around and shown up on "her" doorstep.

"What can I do for you?" she asked.

"Hear me out," he said simply.

After a moment, she shrugged. "I've got coffee if you're interested. Only instant right now. Or tea."

"Coffee will work."

She led the way into the back room and gestured to the folding table and chairs borrowed from the Hitching Post. At the small sink, she ran water into the kettle.

"All the comforts of home," he said.

"More or less." She didn't want to think of *home*. And she didn't know what his *hear me out* meant. But she wouldn't ask—no matter how strongly her rabid curiosity tried to push away her stubborn pride. "We don't have a refrigerator yet. Would you like powdered creamer? And sugar?"

"Black's fine for me."

As she put coffee crystals into one mug and a tea bag into another, the kettle let out its high-pitched whistle. She carried the brimming mugs to the table and sat across from him. First things first. "How are the kids?" Only two days since she had last seen them, and it felt like forever.

"They're fine."

No surprise there. Everything with this man was always *fine*. Or so he thought. Or…so he pretended, just as she pretended now?

The possibility made her thaw a few degrees. "You wanted me to hear you out about something."

He nudged his coffee mug on the table and nodded. "Yeah. I picked up the kids from Rhea's last night. The day care's quiet on a Saturday, and we got to talking about the show the other day. Rhea told me Mark gave you both a hard time when he heard I couldn't come to it. That he nearly pitched a fit. That he begged you to stay."

She raised her chin. He wouldn't like hearing the truth but she would tell him anyway.

"I wanted to stay. I wanted to be there for him and Tracey."

"Yeah. And if I'd been thinking even halfway straight, I'd have wanted that, too. You've been good with the kids, and they're used to you picking them up at the sitter's. There's no reason you couldn't have hung around to watch a fifteen-minute show. I…" Staring down at the mug, he nudged it again. "I don't usually get to those things at Rhea's. Patty was always the one to go. But I wanted to be there for this one. Mark's acting up lately, not behaving like himself."

Wes sighed. "It didn't sink in for a while, but I started wondering if you'd nailed it and he'd been worried about the show all along." Still not looking at her, he said in a lower voice, "Like the drawing sessions he had with Patty, I don't know what memories he might have about other recitals. It was his first time presenting without her there to watch him."

Cara's throat constricted. She touched his wrist in sympathy, then retreated to clutch her mug in both hands. "I didn't know," she murmured.

"No way you could have known. Anyway, that was on my mind when I arrived, already on edge, sure I had gotten there too late. Then

I saw Mark up in the front of the room…" He paused for a mouthful of coffee. "With all that, I definitely wasn't thinking straight, or maybe at all, when I saw you." Finally, he looked at her. "You didn't do anything wrong. There's no excuse for the way I reacted. And I'm more sorry than I can say."

At those words, she thawed completely. How could she not? She had already seen so much good in Wes. His heartfelt apology added another point in his favor. But what won her over…what she heard beneath his words…what she had seen in him again and again…was his love and concern for his children.

Wasn't that all she had wanted once she found out she was pregnant—a man who would love and take care of his child? And wasn't Wes all she had ever wanted in a partner—a man eager to raise a family?

"Apology accepted," she said softly. "You didn't have to come all the way into town to tell me that." Yet she was thrilled he had made the effort.

"I was heading this way, anyhow. Jed told me you were all going to be working here today. I want to volunteer my services."

"Really?"

"Really. It's the least I can do to repay you for picking up the kids every day."

And...? Pure greed kept her waiting, wanting to hear him say she had helped him, too. That having her around made a difference in his life.

She didn't get her wish.

Silence dragged on between them. Before it could stretch to an embarrassing length, the door in the outer room opened. Lizzie called her name. After sending Wes a quick, strained smile, she set her tea mug aside and went to the display room.

The moment Lizzie saw her, the teen burst into tears.

Please, no.

Cara hurried across the room. *Don't think. Focus. Breathe.* Her heart in her throat, she put one hand on Lizzie's arm and repeated that last calming word aloud. "Breathe... Deep breath... And now one more... Better?"

Lizzie nodded, wiping away her tears with the back of her hand. She gulped, then nearly gasped, "I told Kyle just now. About the baby. And h-he doesn't want to h-hear about it."

"I'm sorr—"

"He always told me he wanted a family."

The blood rushed from Cara's face. She

shoved away painful memories to focus on Lizzie. "This doesn't mean he's changed his mind. The news was a shock to him, the way it was to you. When he has some time—"

"He doesn't want time." Lizzie's voice broke. "He doesn't want the baby."

Cara pushed that memory away, too.

"He says this will mess everything up—the prom, graduation, going away to school."

"None of that will happen for a while. Once Kyle has a chance to get used to the news, you can talk again."

"He doesn't want to talk, either."

"Well, maybe not this minute. But, Lizzie…" Cara waited until the teen met her eyes again. Then she said slowly, "What's most important right now is to think about you and what you're going to do next. Right?"

Lizzie nodded.

"Have you told your parents?"

"Not yet. I will. I wanted to tell Kyle first." She breathed a heavy sigh. "I'd better get back home."

"Do you want to sit here awhile?"

"No. I need to see my mom and dad."

"All right." She had given Lizzie her cell phone number earlier in the week. "If I don't talk to you later today, stop by here after school tomorrow, or call me. Anytime. Either way, I'll be waiting to hear from you."

"You will. Thanks." Lizzie gave her a quick hug and a wave.

As the door swung closed, Cara wrapped her arms around herself, longing for the pressure outside her body to ease the hurt inside yet knowing nothing could ever take all the pain away.

"Are you okay?"

At the sound of Wes's voice, she nearly shrieked. She had forgotten he was in the back room. He stood in the doorway, watching her.

"Yes, I'm okay." She slipped past him and went to the sink. "I never finished my tea, did I? It's probably cold by now. I'll make another one. The answer to any problem is always a nice cup of tea, isn't it? My grandmother used to say that to me all the time when I was a little girl. And she—"

Wes rested his hand on her shoulder. His touch made her jump. The same nerves that triggered her babbling now left her fumbling with the kettle. She grabbed for it, but he was quicker, wrapping his hands around hers. "Steady, girl."

She laughed unevenly. "Sounds like you're trying to calm a horse."

Yet, his tone *was* soothing. And though his hands were rough from hard work, they were comforting. And gentle. And very warm.

Slowly, he released his hold but continued to stand close to her. Did he still expect her to drop the kettle?

Evidently not, because in the next instant he shoved his hands into his back pockets. "Didn't mean to eavesdrop, but this isn't a big room, and there was nowhere else for me to go, other than escaping through the emergency door. Since the noise would probably have given me away, I figured it was better to sit tight so Lizzie couldn't tell I was here. She didn't need to know she had someone else listening in on her conversation, even accidentally."

Now who was babbling? Obviously, the situation had stressed Wes out, too. And he still hadn't backed away from her.

She set the kettle safely on the small counter, then leaned against the sink, facing him. "You heard the whole thing?"

"Most of it. I didn't hang out close to the doorway trying to catch every word. And I didn't see anything, so don't ask me how Lizzie was doing when she left. But after listening to you then and watching you now, something tells me you're not okay."

He touched her wrist gently, as she had touched his.

Wes had saved her from disaster with the kettle, but he couldn't save her. At his show of sympathy, she fell to pieces, her breath catching on a sob.

"Hey, hey," he murmured, taking her into his arms. "It'll be all right."

A tear slipped down her cheek. He brushed it away, his thumb gentle on her damp skin, his fingers curled beneath her chin. His lips touched hers in a kiss she had secretly wished and waited for. A kiss that held promise and offered hope...

A kiss she had never dreamed would end so quickly.

He lowered his arms and stepped back from her. As if they were dancing, she wanted to follow his lead, to move forward, to ask for more. Instead, she forced herself to stay in place. His retreat was the best thing he could have done. Nothing could come of a ten-second show of support, one she should have refused the moment it began.

She brushed away the dampness still cooling her warm cheek. "Sorry."

"I'm the one who should apologize."

"For offering sympathy? You don't need to

say you're sorry for that. And I meant about…"
She pointed to her eyes. "I'm like Mark. I don't
usually cry. But Lizzie's situation touched a
nerve. I…I've always wanted a family and, like
Lizzie, I had a boyfriend who said he wanted
that, too. Only, even though we had talked
about having kids, he changed his mind—after
I had already moved in with him."

After I was already pregnant.

She exhaled a long breath. "I still can't believe I was weak and stupid enough to fall for
his lines."

"That doesn't sound weak or stupid to me."

"No? You don't know the whole story. I'd
already given up my job, my apartment—
everything in my life—for a man who didn't
plan to give up anything."

"Maybe he thought you'd want him to provide a home for you both."

"Which means that should let him off the
hook for needing to compromise on anything
else?"

"I didn't say it was a reasonable thought."

Despite her stress, his reply made her laugh.

"I might have handled that situation as
badly as he did," he said. "In fact, I know I
would have. I've already got proof of that." He

shrugged. "Men—people in general—don't always understand what other people need."

"Brad knew. I wanted us to be equal partners. That's why I said I was so dumb. I should have seen the warning signs."

As if she had thrown a punch at him, Wes stepped back abruptly, hitting the folding table. The table legs screeched against the tile floor. "If missing the signs makes a person dumb, then neither one of us is too bright. Now... Well, forget *now*. Years ago, I didn't understand half of what I should have known about Patty before we got married. Or after."

He shook his head. "That's beside the point, too. What I'm trying to say is, from what I've seen, you're a strong, capable woman. And you'll get your life back on track as soon as you're home again."

Her heart jolted so hard her chest hurt.

Her heart *and* her home were here, with him.

"I've already made progress. And Wes..." She hesitated, then went on, certain she felt ready for the risk she intended to take. "I have you and the kids to thank. I never thought I'd feel this happy again this soon—"

"I'm glad." He returned to his seat as abruptly as he'd spoken. "Then, like I said, you'll be on track once you get back to Phoenix. You'll find an apartment and a job and eventually have the family you want, too."

She couldn't find words, abrupt or otherwise, to respond. What did it matter when he wasn't ready to listen?

Maybe he needed more time. Maybe he was as afraid to open up with her as she had been with him until now.

Or maybe he still grieved so much for Patty that nothing she could say would make a difference.

IN THE BACK ROOM of the store, Cara stared at the bare wall in front of her. Blinking, she struggled to focus. Letting her mind wander wouldn't get her share of the painting done. On the bright side, if Andi would pay her a dollar every time her thoughts went to the men in the display room, she could earn a full-time salary.

Okay, who was she kidding? Only one man out there interested her. The one who had kissed her not ten feet from where she now stood.

Andi gave her shoulder a nudge. "We like to get the paint on the wall *before* it dries on the brush."

Cara laughed. "I was daydreaming, sorry."

"And we don't keep secrets," said Jane, the more outspoken of Andi's two cousins.

"And we can take a good guess at what you're daydreaming about," Tina said.

"She means *who*," Jane clarified, smiling.

Cara looked at Andi, hoping she would run interference, but her best friend only shrugged.

She glanced toward the door to the display room, where deep voices rose in conversation over the blaring radio. No way could anyone out there overhear. Still, Cara lowered her voice. "Andi, when we break for lunch, I'm making sure you get the biggest slice of pizza. You sure have a big enough mouth to handle it."

"Andi didn't tell us anything," Tina said. "If you're talking about Wes, that is."

"Of course, she is," Jane said. "And Tina's right. Andi didn't have to tell us anything. All we had to do was look at *you* looking at *Wes* today and last week at the cookout."

Cara's entire face flamed. "I can't be that obvious."

"Only to the three of us," Tina said soothingly.

Somehow, Cara wasn't convinced.

Jane looked at her watch. "Time to pick up

lunch." She and Tina had volunteered to get the pizza and soda.

Both women went to the sink to wash their hands—the sink she had stood in front of when Wes kissed her.

She needed to stop obsessing over that. Sure, he *had* kissed her, but obviously, it hadn't meant nearly as much to him as it had to her.

As Jane and Tina left to pick up lunch, loud cheering from the front room startled Cara back to the present.

"Guess that means the guys are hungry," Andi said.

"Sounds like it."

"Now we're alone, we can really talk. And if I don't ask, you won't tell. So, what happened between you and Wes before we got here?"

"What makes you think something did?"

"Umm…how about the way you're answering a question with a question? I'll ask again, what's happening?"

"Nothing. And nothing can."

"Cara, you know you can't hide anything from me. And I already know how you feel about Wes. Why would you leave without giving things a chance?"

Because she had to go home. Home where she belonged, which wasn't in Cowboy Creek.

She was almost grateful to Wes for the harsh reminder of the mistake she'd made and her need to stand on her own.

Her thoughts were too complicated to explain. She gave Andi the simplified version. "Because there's no sense in staying around. Right now all Wes can focus on is taking care of his kids, and of course, I respect him for that."

He'd told her plainly how he felt about getting involved with anyone, and like Marianne, she'd refused to listen.

"He's still grieving," Andi said softly.

Yes, she'd thought that, too. Still grieving, and maybe more. She'd once sensed he was fighting guilt—over his kids, Patty, or someone or something else, she couldn't tell. And he certainly wouldn't tell her.

The guilt and grief combined made it harder to go on with life. Cara ought to know. But when Wes did finally move on, that didn't mean he'd move in her direction.

"Things will change eventually," Andi said. "They've already started. Even though I knew you would make a difference with Wes, I didn't realize how quickly it would happen."

The echoes of what she had said to Wes sent a ripple of sadness through her.

"I have to admit," Andi went on, "I was surprised to see him show up today."

"Me, too," Cara confessed.

"It's great news."

"Why?"

"You've gotten him away from the ranch and going out more. And trust me. Grandpa, Garrett, Mitch and the rest of the guys, too, they've all tried lately and gotten nowhere."

"I'm glad he's made progress." Another echo, another ripple of sadness. "But making a difference with Wes won't guarantee anything will happen between us, even when he's ready for a relationship again. If he had any interest, he'd have shown it when he talked about me going home."

She couldn't count their oh-so-sweet kiss—after which he'd backed away quickly enough to give himself whiplash.

You'll get your life back on track as soon as you're home again.

He'd said it as matter-of-factly as if he'd already written her off. Then he'd cut her off when she'd tried to share her feelings.

She would be lost without Wes and Mark and Tracey. The kids might miss her just as much.

Could anything convince Wes he'd miss her, too?

CHAPTER TWENTY

"Pizza!" Jane announced when she and Tina walked back into the store.

Wes looked up from the baseboard he was painting. Both women nearly staggered beneath the weight of cardboard boxes and plastic sacks.

"Let me give you a hand with those cartons," Jane's husband, Pete, offered.

"Fine. But no hands on the food until we get everything on the table."

Pete laughed.

When they all moved toward the back room, Wes followed. Reluctantly.

If he could have, he would have ditched this painting party, picked up the kids early from Rhea's and headed home. But he had already committed to volunteering his help.

Not that he had a problem with the work or the conversation or the pizza brought in hot and fresh for their late lunch. No, what bothered him was the awkwardness earlier this morning, when he had been alone in the store with Cara. He'd given in to the urge to kiss her, which led to him running off at the mouth, letting his nerves make him even more of a fool.

He'd rather look a fool in front of her now than hurt her somewhere down the road. And he would, because he didn't have it in him to give her what he knew she wanted. An invitation to stay.

Luckily, the work party had arrived to keep him from making matters worse.

Andi's husband, Mitch, grabbed one of the pizza boxes. "I'm moving the male half of this party outside."

Pete grabbed another carton, and they all loaded up on pop bottles.

As Wes headed outside with the rest of the men, he fought to keep from looking in Cara's direction. Looking led to thoughts about other things.

Holding her, kissing her, had turned into pleasures he'd immediately regretted. He had since given himself warnings to keep his thoughts away from her, his hands off her and, most of all, his mouth nowhere near hers.

Outside, Mitch said to him, "Let's settle in over there." He gestured toward a low brick wall in a sunny corner.

A native of Cowboy Creek, Mitch was also a former LA cop. Until coming home and settling down to a job as a deputy sheriff, he had tended to be on the quiet side. Not anymore. Given the opportunity, he would talk all day long.

That worked for Wes. Conversation would keep his mind busy with something besides Cara, since he'd already lost the struggle to ignore his first warning.

Mitch set the pizza box between them. "Women," he said, shaking his head, "they're never happy unless they're putting a man to work."

"You didn't seem unhappy about that this morning."

Mitch laughed. "I wasn't. I'm stretching the truth some."

Exactly what Cara had accused him of that day at the cookout. Of course, she'd been right. The memory left him fighting a smile.

"Like half the people I pull over on radar patrol," Mitch went on. "They can't spin tales fast enough, trying to avoid a ticket. You'd be surprised at some of the excuses I hear. And these are from locals, who ought to know I can see right through their stories. The problem is, they don't stop first to think."

"Yeah," Wes agreed. "Running off at the mouth can get you into trouble."

The way he had done with Cara earlier. Nothing to smile about there.

"I'll be glad when that detour sends traffic onto Canyon Road," Mitch continued. "Maybe I'll get some fresh stories from the tourists passing through. Though I hope for Andi's sake they don't just pass through. She's already stressing over how she's going to handle everything. Good thing she's got Cara here to help."

Yeah, but for how long? And why did that matter to him? He was doing just...

He took a gigantic bite of pizza, saving himself from having to respond to Mitch. He was *fine*. He was happy. And so were the kids. That's what mattered. As for Cara...

I never thought I'd feel this happy again this soon.

He sent himself yet another stern warning, one he'd stick to this time.

He'd done everything he could to make Patty happy, and all his efforts hadn't changed a thing. He wasn't trying that again. Better to let Cara go and force himself to forget her.

CARA STOOD BESIDE Wes on the sidewalk in front of the store.

He hadn't once spoken to her or even made

eye contact with her all afternoon. They had both kept so busy, he hadn't had the chance. Or so she wanted to believe.

Now, for the first time since the painting party had begun, the first time since they had shared that kiss, she was alone with him.

"*Brr-r-r!* It's chilly out here." She put her fists into her jacket pockets but couldn't blame her trembling hands on the weather. She hoped her smile didn't look just as unsteady. "It was warm enough inside. I didn't realize the temperature had dropped."

The sun had fallen, too. A streetlamp a few yards behind him left his face shadowed.

They had all stayed late to finish the job. Andi and Mitch were checking doors and windows before they locked up for the night.

Jane and Tina and their husbands had carpooled into town. As they climbed into Pete's truck, he tapped the horn. She and Wes waved them on their way.

"I know Andi's relieved we were able to get the entire store done this weekend." Cara paused, but he said nothing. "We want the paint to dry completely before I start setting up the display room this week." Another pause. More silence. "Thanks again for today. Having the extra help made the work go faster."

He shoved his hands into his back pockets.

She tried for another smile. "I could use some extra help myself right now. It's not easy carrying on a one-sided conversation, especially when the other person is standing right in front of you."

"Sorry. I was thinking about the kids. They were restless yesterday, probably from not sleeping well the night before, after their big day at Rhea's." He studied his watch. "When I dropped them off I didn't know what time I'd pick them up again. She said not to rush, but I didn't expect to be this late." He took a step away. "I should head over there."

And obviously, he felt the need to escape from here.

Or from *her*?

"Sure," she said as brightly as she could. "And I'll get them from Rhea's tomorrow afternoon, as usual."

He opened his mouth, then closed it again.

Her heart sank. Had he changed his mind about her picking up the kids? "I'll be coming by anyhow," she added. "I still need to finish the rest of the inventory for Andi." It wasn't a lie. She and Andi had boxed up most of the clothes from the closet, but they hadn't gotten to it all.

How could she have managed to squeeze that job in? During her last few evenings at Wes's ranch, she had spent her time helping him with dinner, then eating with him and the kids before cuddling on the couch with Mark and Tracey. Why would she pass up the chance to be with them just to work alone upstairs?

To her relief, Wes nodded.

I knew you would make a difference with Wes, Andi had told her.

That's what counted.

Andi and Mitch joined them on the sidewalk.

Andi turned to Wes. "Paz and Grandpa are watching the kids. Since we knew we'd be working late, we're all going over to Sugar-Pie's. You'll come too, won't you?"

"Yeah," Mitch said. "It's been a long time since that pizza for lunch."

"Thanks, but I've got work to do back at the house," Wes said.

"There's always going to be work to do. Ease up, man. Take the night off. Besides, you've got to eat."

"I guess I do. Let me check on my kids."

"Sounds good." Mitch walked off hand in hand with Andi.

As Cara hesitated, Wes pulled his cell phone from his pocket.

"See you over there," she said. *In fact, I'll save you a seat.*

THE PARKING LOT at SugarPie's was as crowded as Cara had ever seen it. She found an open slot halfway down the length of the lot, between two giant pickup trucks. After finally wedging her car between them, she nearly had to slide sideways to get through the driver's door.

By that time, someone across the lot from her had pulled out, leaving a gaping space. "Thanks a lot."

A second later, Wes pulled his truck into the opening and she gave genuine thanks.

The lot was well lit closer to the front of SugarPie's, but here a row of bushes blocked some of the light. Except for a lone bulb over the bakery's side exit, the area this far back was shadowy. Quiet. Almost romantic.

Too bad the cowboy walking toward her didn't have romance with her on his mind.

She glanced at his truck. "You didn't bring the kids?"

"No. I figured since no one else was bringing theirs, I'd leave them at Rhea's. She already fed them supper, and they're in the middle of watching a cartoon video."

"No story time?" The past couple of nights, had Mark and Tracey missed having her read to them from Mark's storybooks?

A car door slammed, startling enough in the quiet to make them both jump. The noise had come from somewhere at the far end of the parking lot.

"No, wait!" a female voice cried. "We need to talk!"

Lizzie.

Wes either recognized her, too, or reacted instinctively to her obvious distress. He strode toward the back of the lot. Cara followed on his heels.

"I'm tired of talking." Another voice rang out, deep and edged with frustration, followed by the sound of a thump.

Past Wes, she could see a tall male she guessed was Kyle standing with his back to them, half blocking their view of Lizzie.

Wes called her name.

The boy spun to face them.

"Take it easy, Kyle. It's me, Wes Daniels."

Kyle squinted against the lights from the street. "Hey, Wes. I couldn't see who you were at first. There's nothing to take easy. We were just talking."

"Is that so?" Wes said, his voice even. "Sounded to me like you were refusing to do just that."

Cara took a step sideways to walk around him.

"You okay, Lizzie?" Wes asked. Cara's eyes stung. She had opened her mouth to ask the same thing. Again, Wes had gotten there first, his concern for Lizzie obvious, from his half step toward her to his question and even to his lowered voice—clearly aimed at keeping this conversation private.

"I'm okay," Lizzie said. "Kyle's telling the truth. We were just talking…well, arguing, and I guess we both got upset."

Wes nodded. "Lizzie, I don't want to add to your upset, but I need to tell you something. This morning, I overheard your conversation with Cara at the store. Didn't mean to, but I was in the back room. Sorry."

She shrugged. "Everybody's going to know sooner or later."

Even in the dim light Cara could see the tears sparkling in Lizzie's eyes. Brushing past Wes, Cara went to put a reassuring arm around her.

He turned to Kyle and rested his hand on the

teen's shoulder as if to calm him. This close, she could now see Kyle looked scared, and he was as wide-eyed as Lizzie.

"Look, Kyle," Wes said, his voice still low and level, "I know this is all a shock and you're going to need time to take it in. The bottom line is, you need to man up."

Man up. Just what Wes would do. Just what the man she had always wanted would do, too.

"That's not saying you have to make decisions tonight," Wes continued. "But Lizzie's not in this all on her own. You follow me?"

When Kyle nodded, Wes took his hand from the teen's shoulder. "Have you talked to your folks?"

"No."

"Me, neither," Lizzie said. "I was going to, but my mom and dad went out. They'll be home soon."

"Good," Wes said. "First, the two of you need to sit down and talk—calmly—about your options. Then get together with your families to talk everything over with them. Because no matter what you decide, you're going to need help from your folks. And from each other, if you're going to be parents. It's not easy raising a child, even when there are two of you. Take it from me, it can be much harder when you're on your own."

Tears stung Cara's eyes again. If she had managed to hold on to any piece of her heart until this point, she now lost it all. Since she'd met him, Wes had insisted to everyone that his life was *fine*. He refused to admit his struggles to anyone. Yet he'd done just that to help Lizzie and Kyle.

Yes, so like the man she wanted. The man she already loved.

As the teens returned to their car, Cara stepped to the edge of the lot. Wes joined her. They waited until Kyle pulled out of the space and drove away.

"You okay?" Wes asked.

For a moment, she couldn't find her voice. "Yes," she said finally. "I just…" She needed to share her whirling thoughts with him. "Seeing Lizzie so upset made me think of things I've been trying to forget. I've been in the same place. Pregnant, I mean."

She didn't expect a response, but he said immediately, "Being upset's understandable. It's not an easy place for anybody to be. And it must have been hard for you, too, only a kid—"

"No, that's just it, I wasn't a teenager. It

didn't happen that long ago, which is why Lizzie's situation hit so close to home."

His eyes widened but this time he didn't respond.

"I told you about Brad," she said in a low voice, rushing to fill the silence. "We weren't officially engaged yet but that was the plan. If it hadn't been, I would have taken precautions to keep from getting pregnant."

Wanting Wes to know what had happened was one thing. Saying it to him was another. She took a steadying breath. "Brad reacted the way Kyle first did. Once he found out I was pregnant, he didn't want to know anything. Only unlike Kyle, he never changed his mind. So I left him. A few weeks later I l-lost the baby."

Wes muttered under his breath, then reached for her. When she stepped closer, he wrapped his arms around her. She rested her cheek against the front of his jacket.

"If I could take away your pain, I would." His voice sounded gravelly. She could almost feel the rumble in his chest. "That's why you wanted to avoid the office closet."

His immediate understanding brought her to tears. He hadn't made it a question, but, unable to trust her voice, she nodded her reply.

The rough wool of his jacket tickled her skin. She lifted her head to see his face.

His eyes shone in the darkness, twin reflections of the lights from the street. He tightened his arms around her just a fraction. Just enough to let her know he was going to kiss her. He lowered his head and touched his forehead to hers.

She held her breath, waiting.

He waited, too, as if letting anticipation build between them. Seconds later he released her and almost stumbled back.

The cool night air rushed at her, chasing away the warmth of his embrace. She wrapped her arms around her middle, hoping to fight her chill. She failed as miserably as when she'd tried using the same position to ease the pain of her loss.

"Sorry." He held both palms out in a hands-off gesture, then shook his head. "Seems like I've done nothing but say that today. To you, to Lizzie, now to you again."

"You said a lot more than that when you talked to Lizzie and Kyle. You helped them both."

"I hope so. But I'm not helping you—" He waved one hand, indicating her crossed arms, the small space between them he had so recently filled, the kiss he had been about to give her. "I swear, that won't happen again."

"Why not? What if we want that—and more—to happen? I do. Because something already happened between us. I've been denying it, making up reasons not to believe it, but the truth is, something wonderful happened this morning when you kissed me. I think you know that, too."

She touched his arm, expecting some of his warmth to return to her, hoping he would move closer again.

Instead, he took another step back, putting him out of her reach. "You're a special woman, Cara, and any man would be lucky to have something wonderful with you. I'll admit you may not be the only one denying things. But neither of us ought to take a risk on the off chance of *something* that turns out to be *not enough*. Right now, tonight, the only truth I know is whatever this might have been, I can't let it happen again."

He glanced toward his truck. "It's getting late. Probably best I get the kids and take them home. I told you they've been acting up, and throwing them off their schedule won't help."

Throwing her off-kilter certainly hadn't

helped her. But that was what he'd done, from the day she'd met him.

"I'll see you tomorrow," she said evenly. "After I pick up the kids."

She'd expected an argument. Instead, he nodded. He strode the short distance to his truck and hauled himself into the driver's seat as if he couldn't get away fast enough.

She watched him leave the parking lot and drive down Canyon Road. Taillights blinked at her as the truck hit the street's tiny dips and valleys.

Or maybe her eyes had blurred from the moisture suddenly filling them. Tears once again. This time, of frustration.

CHAPTER TWENTY-ONE

CARA HAD NEVER been so glad to have a busy schedule as she was on Monday.

At the store, she worked steadily through the morning into early afternoon. The jobs distracted her from worrying about Lizzie and Kyle and the very high chance they were expecting a baby. The work stopped her from wondering what Mark and Tracey were up to at Rhea's. Above all, it kept her from thinking of Wes, at least for a few minutes every hour.

As she was finishing her late lunch—sandwiches courtesy of Paz—she heard the door open. When she looked into the front room, Mo smiled and waved.

"I'm on my way to the community center. I thought I'd come see the results of the painting party."

"Be my guest." Biting her lip to hide a smile, Cara watched the older woman take her sweet time inspecting the display room. She paid just as much attention to the back room, and even peeked into the small bathroom.

"I like the way you have the display cases arranged. And the entire place looks very nice."

"Thanks. I have to say I agree. Andi was lucky to get such hard workers to help out." Including Wes.

For the ninety-seventh time that day, she fought and failed to block images she didn't want to see. Images of Wes rushing away last night, leaving her in the parking lot. Of Wes holding and kissing her in this small room yesterday morning. Even today, eating lunch alone, she couldn't stop seeing him sitting with her at the table.

She needed to do something to drive away all these visions. Having Lizzie around might help with that, depending on how chatty the teen would feel today. Either way, Lizzie didn't get out of school for an hour or so yet. Meanwhile, here was Mo. "Do you have time for a cup of tea?"

"Yes. That would be lovely."

Relieved, Cara took two mugs from the overhead cabinet. She turned on the kettle, then set a cookie tin on the table, close to Mo.

"Paz's baking, I presume?"

Cara nodded. "Still hot from the oven when I

was getting ready to leave the hotel this morning. She insisted I take some—along with the lunch she packs for me every day *after* cooking my breakfast. She takes very good care of me."

"That's Paz. She takes care of everyone at the Hitching Post."

"Yes." Still, guilt at the reminder of both Paz's and Jed's generosity to her made her cringe. Free room and board was one reason she needed to get back to her long-abandoned job search.

Her frustrating conversation with Wes was another.

Mo smiled over her tea mug. "I noticed you didn't mention supper."

She wasn't falling for *that* opening again. The woman probably knew down to the minute how much time she spent at Wes's house. "Oh, Paz handles my dinner, too, when I'm around. But last night after we were done painting, we all went to SugarPie's." Or to be exact, all but one.

"Yes, I know. I was just there for lunch today." Laughing, Mo reached for a cookie. "So, obviously I don't need any sweets. I met with a few of the girls from the knitting club. They said they had stopped in earlier."

"They've been coming in all day. Last week,

too. They've all brought samples—of beautiful work—but as I'm telling everyone, I can't make any promises. The decisions are up to Andi."

"Of course."

Andi would like what she had seen, too, and the store would have a surplus of stock. But she wouldn't tell Mo that, either, without discussing the details with Andi first. "I just hope enough customers come in so she can get this business off the ground."

"I'm sure they will," Mo said confidently. "Once she's set up, we'll all get the word out to everyone in the county, if not the state. They'll come by the carload. You'll see."

Mo was wrong. Cara wouldn't see. By the time Andi was ready to open the doors to all those customers, she would be gone.

You'll get your life back on track as soon as you're home again.

Wes had been wrong, too. Her life might never get back on track.

FROM AS FAR AWAY as the kitchen, Wes had somehow gotten tuned in to Cara's car door closing when she arrived. Today, he had dreaded hearing the sound, yet he forced himself to head outside. Why had he ever started this ritual in the first place?

Skipping the reason he refused to admit, he went straight to the easy one. His son thrived on routine.

Even this morning, when he delivered the kids to Rhea, Mark had asked for the third time, *See Miss Cara after school?* Wes had assured him Miss Cara would come to pick up both him and Tracey.

Now she'd brought them home and he had to face her again.

At the car, she leaned down looking into the back seat. The open door blocked his full view of her, but he couldn't miss the hair flowing across her shoulders, the golden red muted from the late-day shadows filling the yard. That long, soft hair had spilled across his hands when he'd held her.

He pushed away the memory, which wasn't his to enjoy.

He never should have touched her.

"Don't forget your backpack," Cara said to Mark.

She spotted Wes approaching. Standing upright, she brushed her hair behind her. Out of the way of temptation?

"Hi." Her cool smile almost made her a stranger.

"Hi, Daddy!" Mark's energetic hug sent the backpack crashing against Wes's legs. The boy took off at a trot toward the back of the house.

Wes turned to Cara. "Hey. How…" *was your day?* Another routine he shouldn't have started. "…were the kids on the ride?"

"The same as always. Tracey slept. Mark talked, though not as much as usual."

"Yeah. He was quiet off and on this morning, too." Except for asking about his Miss Cara. "Did you hear anything from Lizzie?"

She nodded. "A phone call after school let out. She was on her way to meet her mom. They were heading for a doctor's appointment."

"That's good."

"Very good. And last night, she and Kyle talked to her mom and dad. If the test results confirm she's pregnant, they'll all sit down with his parents." This time her smile looked more like the Cara Wes knew. "All your suggestions were very good. Lizzie and Kyle were so understandably upset, they needed help figuring out what to do."

She had done as much and more, wrapping herself up in concern for a couple of kids she barely knew. Who had helped her when she needed it?

"I should have an update by tomorrow." She glanced into the car. "Tracey's still asleep. Give me a minute."

As she turned away, Wes touched her arm. When her gaze shot to his, he immediately dropped his hand. "How about giving me a minute first."

She nodded, waiting. Her blue eyes appeared darker in the shadows, too, but just as beautiful. He wished—

Self-preservation instantly made his mind go blank. When he could finally think again, he blurted the first thing that came to him. "Yesterday."

"What about yesterday?"

"I shouldn't have held you. Or kissed you. Or made you think there was a chance of anything between us. I think it's best we keep away from situations where what happened yesterday could happen again."

"You're saying we shouldn't get close? Like we are right now?"

He took a quick step back. Obviously, she didn't intend to help him here. Didn't she realize this conversation was tough enough?

"Yes, I'm saying we shouldn't get close.

The kids won't understand and they're already confused with you here." Not just his kids. But he'd worry about his own problems later. "Mark's clinging to you because he's missing his mother. I'm sure of it. And both kids are getting too used to having you around.

"This is on me, not you. I should have seen it coming sooner. Or maybe it's a case of that denial we talked about last night." Or his inability to ask her to stay away. "You're going home eventually. When doesn't matter. The point is, the more attached the kids are to you, the worse it's going to be when they lose you."

Like they lost their mother.

Cara's suddenly glistening eyes said either she understood and cared that much about his kids or he'd stupidly but unintentionally reminded her of her own loss. Either way, he had never wanted to take her into his arms more than he did right now. And now was the one time he most needed to stay away.

"You're right," she said finally. "We can't let things go on like they have."

"It would be better if you don't just walk out on the kids."

She gasped. "I would never do that."

"I know you wouldn't. That came out wrong. These aren't situations I deal with every day."

He exhaled heavily, wishing they could end the conversation now. Not an option. And he'd started them down this road. "What I meant was, it would be better, especially for Mark, if we could ease into the idea you're leaving."

"You mean… How, exactly?"

She was determined to make him lay everything out. And why not, when none of this was her fault? "You could pick them up and stay for supper a few more nights. Finish out the week. Over the next few days, we'll talk to Mark to get him used to the idea you won't be around here much longer."

"If you think that's the best way to handle it."

She sounded as enthusiastic as he suddenly felt about the plan. Which meant not at all.

"A-A-AND…YOU LIKE BACRONI?" Mark asked.

Cara smiled and pointed to the plate in front of her. "I do." She had barely touched her baked ziti. No one seemed to notice.

To keep everything "normal" for the kids, she and Wes agreed she should eat dinner with them, as usual. Tonight was more uncomfortable than the night they talked to the kids but not each other.

Wes barely spoke at all. As if he'd flipped

a switch, he'd again become the quiet, withdrawn man she had met on her first day in
town.

"A-a-and…you like tomatoes?" Mark asked.

"I do."

They had played this game almost since they
had sat down at the table, with Mark more than
likely running through a list of every food he
could ever remember eating. At least he was
smiling again.

By the time she arrived home…*here*…with
the kids, Wes had everything prepared and
ready. The table had been completely set. After
he learned there was nothing left for him to do,
Mark cried in disappointment.

"A-a-and…you like spaghetti sauce?" Mark
asked.

"I do." If this game kept him happy, she
would gladly stay and play it with him all
night long.

Wes hadn't needed her help with anything,
either. Considering their conversation outside,
she wasn't surprised. The fully set table could
have passed for a visual version of the speech
he'd made.

When he laid out his plans, he'd left nothing
for her to do either except spend a few more

nights here working upstairs and then go on her way.

"A-a-and…you like milk?" Mark asked.

"I do."

Wes still focused silently on his dinner.

No matter what he wanted, right now, she just couldn't force herself to talk to Mark about the fact she would be leaving. And why should she without Wes's support?

Instantly, her face burned. She stared down at her plate. She should never have asked that question, even in her own mind. This situation was as hard for Wes to deal with as it was for her. And hadn't she created most of it herself? Hadn't she been the one to volunteer—and keep volunteering—to pick up the kids?

"A-a-and…you like ice cream?" Mark asked.

"I *love* ice cream." Deliberately, she broke the pattern with her enthusiastic response. When Mark laughed, she took a deep breath. Now or never. "Mark, do you remember when I met you at the Big Dipper?"

Wes froze with his fork halfway to his mouth.

Mark nodded. "I spilled your ice cream on the floor. Daddy bought more."

"That's right. And do you remember when

I told you about my home? I said I lived in Arizona."

He nodded again.

"Well… I have to go home."

"When?"

Still not a word from Wes. "Soon."

"Okay. Time for dessert yet?"

She almost laughed. So much for worrying about upsetting Mark.

Her glance at Wes showed he'd zeroed in on his ziti. Tracey frowned as she pushed green beans around the edge of her tray. Cara would get no help from either of them. "Your sister looks like she's not hungry tonight. She may not want dessert."

"*I* want dessert!"

"Mark," Wes said quietly.

She hesitated, but he didn't seem ready to answer Mark's question about when they would have their dessert. Sure, over this small unimportant matter, Wes would let her have a say. Her stomach clenching, she turned to Mark. "Yes, I know you want dessert. And it will be time to have it when we're all done with dinner."

Now, as much as she liked Mark's game, it was also time for her and Wes to make adult conversation. Spearing a piece of her almost forgotten ziti, she said casually, "I'll work up-stairs after dinner. That will put me one night closer to finishing."

"No!" Mark said. "I want books."

Of course, she had meant after story time. Before she could explain, Wes spoke up.

"Hush." He frowned. "You're not behaving well tonight. And Miss Cara was talking to Daddy."

"I want story time!"

"Mark." This time, Wes's voice held a warning tone.

"I don't want dessert. I want *books*." Mark pushed his bowl, which knocked over his half-full plastic cup.

Milk splashed everywhere, including onto her plate. Grabbing her napkin, Cara tried to catch a quickly moving stream before it could run off the edge of the table.

Wes set his fork on his plate. "Mark," he said mildly, "you just ruined Miss Cara's supper. What do you think you ought to do about that?"

"Go read books."

Wes sighed. "Okay, my boy, that's it. Somebody's ready for an early bath and bedtime. Two somebodies." He undid the buckles on Tracey's high chair. "Let's go. Say good-night."

"No."

"Mark." Now Wes's tone said this wasn't open for argument.

Mark must have caught this warning. "G'night, Miss Cara."

His mumbled words and the way he avoided her eyes clearly announced she had lost the chance to get a hug from him tonight.

He stomped toward the door. Halfway across the room he turned and ran back. He threw his arms around her, squeezing harder than he ever had before, until she could barely catch her breath.

CHAPTER TWENTY-TWO

AFTER WES LEFT the kitchen with Mark and Tracey, Cara wiped up the spilled milk. She cleared and washed the table, rinsed the dishes and loaded the dishwasher, all to leave the room looking as neat and tidy as Wes had it when she'd arrived.

Finished straightening up to her satisfaction, Cara wandered around the room. How many more times would she see this kitchen with its picture-covered refrigerator, piles of art supplies and baby toys all seen from "her" place at the table? If Wes had his way, not nearly enough times to satisfy her.

Well, she had news for him. She had given in earlier but wouldn't walk away that easily now. Yes, she had agreed to his plan for the kids' sake. They came first, no doubt about it. She and Wes had thought of the kids. Now they needed to think of themselves.

Wes's footsteps sounded in the hallway.

Why couldn't he trust her enough to let

himself get close to her? No sense asking that question, since he wouldn't answer.

When he entered the kitchen, she said, "Everything go okay with bath time?"

"Yeah. After, Tracey nodded off before I finished getting her clean pajamas on."

"And Mark?"

"He's sound asleep already, too."

"I feel terrible about what happened at dinner." *Feel terrible* didn't come close to describing the guilt that had flooded through her as quickly as Mark's milk spilled across the table. "I didn't plan to go upstairs to work until after I read to the kids. But Mark couldn't know that. No wonder he got upset."

"Not your fault. He should've known better than to misbehave that way."

"Wes," she said softly, "he's only three going on forty."

"Yeah, I suppose." He answered grudgingly, but one corner of his mouth twitched as if he fought to hold back his half smile.

"Well, I guess I'll get to work upstairs."

"Sounds good. I'll be down here if you need anything."

I need you.

She couldn't say that right now, either, with

their earlier conversation still hanging over their heads.

How could two people desperately have the same goal but disagree completely about the way to reach it? How could Wes ask her to help ease the break between her and his kids, while her heart told her she could be the best thing for them all?

She'd made one mistake with Brad, but Wes wasn't another. She refused to stop believing he would change his mind, give her a chance, give *them* a chance. Sooner or later, he would be able to listen to his heart again, too. When that happened, she wanted him to turn to her.

WAS THE WOMAN never coming back down again?

Standing at the bottom of the stairs, Wes noted the occasional faint sound of her footsteps moving back and forth in the office.

Since her first night here, she had walked into almost every room in the house one step at a time. And once she left he'd have to deal with all those memories.

At least she was still here tonight. After their talk earlier and then the scene with Mark, it wouldn't have surprised him to find she had slipped out the front door while he was with Mark and Tracey.

The empty couch made him miss the kids. Putting them to bed early tonight left the evening extra long. Or maybe it only seemed that way to him.

Still, enough was enough.

He found Cara sitting on the floor with her laptop. "Still working?"

She nodded. "I wanted to get…well, as much done tonight as I could."

"Even after cleaning up the kitchen. Which you didn't have to do."

"I don't mind. I wanted to help. But you know, now you've mentioned it, you didn't leave anything for me to do before dinner. And…"

"And, what?"

She hesitated, her brow wrinkled in concern. "And you didn't let Mark do his usual job, either. That's partly the reason he had that meltdown, I think. Helping you gives him a chance to feel, well…helpful. And maybe important. When he didn't get that, he was disappointed."

"Is that how you felt, too?"

She shook her head. Light from the overhead fixture bounced off her hair, turning it a crackling red, threatening to burn him if he touched it. Struggling to heed the warning, he curled his fingers against his palms.

When he didn't respond, she gave a shaky laugh as if the delay unsettled her. Or as if she'd read his thoughts. "Okay, yes, I did feel disappointed when you didn't need me to help with dinner. But not anymore. Because when we talked outside, you kept saying we shouldn't get close to each other. But we already were, and now here we are again. Because you kept insisting nothing else would happen between us. And now, call me crazy but all that emphasis gives me hope."

He sighed. "Cara—"

From across the hall, Mark screeched in terror.

Her eyes widened. Before Wes could say a word, she hurried toward the doorway.

He followed. "He's having a nightmare. Yelling in his sleep, the way he did a while back."

After his mother had gone away.

When they reached the kids' room, Cara stepped aside, giving Wes space to pass by.

Mark sat straight up in bed staring into space, his covers thrown off, his breath coming in gasps.

Wes took a seat beside him and wrapped one

arm around his shoulders. "Hey, buddy, Daddy's here. You were dreaming. Everything's okay."

His eyes wide now, too, Mark held out his hands. But not to Wes. "Miss Cara," he sobbed. "I want Miss Cara."

CARA'S ARMS WENT NUMB from holding and rocking Mark. He didn't talk, just gripped her wrist in both hands.

Startled by her brother's shrieks, Tracey had stirred but drifted off again almost immediately.

Wes leaned against the door frame, watching over them, his expression blank.

Mark's grip on Cara's wrist relaxed. He had finally fallen asleep again. She eased him onto the bed and tucked him in, helping with the bedtime ritual just as she'd imagined.

But not like this.

Wes backed silently from the room.

When she went down the hall to the office again, he followed her into the room. She looked around. "I've got a few more things—"

"It's late. Don't worry about the rest tonight."

He kept his voice down, probably to avoid waking the kids. But she couldn't miss his expression, the same blank look that had closed him off to her ever since Mark had called for her instead of his daddy, had reached for her instead of him.

That look had struck right to her heart. She couldn't let him think his own son put her above him or that she was trying to take his wife's place with his kids. She couldn't let his family stand in for the baby she'd lost.

No. She would never have to worry about that again, not because Wes refused to get close to her but because she'd let herself fall in love with him. She didn't need a replacement family. She needed the one she had found right here.

At the moment, she needed a way to erase that blank look from Wes's face. "I'm sorry for whatever I've done to confuse Mark and Tracey. Hurting any of you is the last thing I wanted to do."

"That's not your fault. I knew all along this wasn't a good idea, but I...I just didn't want to admit it. And I was dead wrong about the kids getting used to the idea of not seeing you. Dragging it out isn't going to help at all. They need a clean break."

"No!"

His eyes looked as unseeing as Mark's had after his nightmare.

Why couldn't this *all* be a bad dream?

"What I mean is," she said, "I don't think that's the answer. Having me just go out of their lives wouldn't be good for them, either. That's how Patty left them. I don't want to leave them—or you."

"No worries. We're fine, just as I've been telling you and everyone else all along."

Did he deliberately misunderstand? Or… "Maybe I'm not doing such a good job of explaining. I've known you and the kids for such a short time, but to me it feels like…forever. And I don't want to leave. Not tomorrow, not at the end of the week, not ever. I don't want to leave because I love Mark and Tracey. You must have figured that out already."

"Wouldn't be much of a daddy if I said my kids weren't lovable."

"No, you wouldn't." She took a deep, shaky breath. "But it's more than that. Yes, I love them both. And I love you."

"Don't."

"Too late."

His eyes gleamed but his expression stayed the same. "Then I'm sorry for anything I did to confuse you."

"But—"

"Cara, I'm not the man for you. A long time

ago, I might have been, and to tell you the truth I'd like to go back then to give you what you want. To be the man you want me to be. But that time's past. My life has changed." He looked at her with the same steady blank stare. "I'm doing what I have to do."

He believed in his plan and wouldn't change his mind. And hadn't she known he had already shut her out?

She nodded stiffly. "I still need to come back to work on the inventory, but I'll make sure it's when the kids are at day care. I'll come early tomorrow morning to talk to Mark. To tell him why I won't be picking him and Tracey up at Rhea's again."

"I can tell—"

"No. Like it or not, we're in this together. You had to explain to Mark that I wasn't his new mother. That I was only here for a visit. It's up to me to tell him the visit's over. I love Mark and Tracey, Wes. It's the least you can let me do before I go."

He didn't reply, just gave her a silent nod of agreement and turned away.

SHE REACHED THE Hitching Post at nearly midnight. The welcoming light over the front door greeted her.

Inside, the desk lamp cast a glow over the lobby, as it did every night. Not so usual, a couple of the sitting room lamps still burned, and someone in the room called Cara's name.

Andi had curled up on one of the couches near the fireplace, a book in her hands and an afghan tossed over her legs. "It's about time you got home." She laughed. "Can't you just hear me saying that to one of my kids someday?"

"Yes. And probably sooner than you expect."

"I know. They'll grow up so fast."

Mark and Tracey would, too. Cara would miss hugging them over lost baby teeth and skinned knees, watching them in their recitals at Rhea's, celebrating their graduations from day care and kindergarten, and more.

Pushing the images aside, she said, "What are you doing out here so late?"

Andi held up her book. "Reading. And waiting for you." She put the book on the couch beside her and sat up. "I couldn't wait till the morning to tell you the big news."

Good, because Cara's own news could wait forever.

She sank onto the chair across from the couch. "What's up?"

"Well...we haven't even stocked our shelves

yet, but the store is expanding! Remember your suggestion about adding southwestern-themed gifts?" When she nodded, Andi went on, "There's a place I shop at every time I go up to Santa Fe. It's that kitchen and novelty store I told you about."

"I remember that, too. Don't you buy a lot there for the hotel?"

"We do. I didn't say anything to you because I didn't know if my plan would work out. But I talked to the owner last week and again today about carrying some of the handcrafted local pottery they sell. And he agreed to a deal! Isn't that fantastic?"

"It's great." Especially if the customers arrived by the carload, as Mo anticipated. But as far as Cara knew, Andi hadn't been out of town. "You settled this with a handshake?"

"A phone call, actually." When Cara's jaw dropped, Andi shook her head. "Don't worry—I haven't signed anything yet. Grandpa has a lawyer friend who will be looking over the contract. But there's more. Everyone I've talked to in town is excited about the store. It's going to do well, I just know it." She leaned forward, her eyes shining. "And I want you to come in as my business partner."

"I can't."

"Why not? You're between jobs and you don't have a lease. And you're not in a relationship… yet. It's the perfect time to make the move."

"I can't do that."

"Look, I know you'll be taking a risk. The store may get off to a slow start and money will be tight until we're established. But once we have everything up and running, I'm sure it's going to be a big success."

"I still can't do it, Andi."

"All right, then I'm going to play the emotion card. The kids and I miss you and want you with us."

"You know I miss you all, too." Just as she would now miss Wes and Mark and Tracey. "But I can't stay here."

"What happened? Something with Wes?"

"Nothing with Wes. That's the problem." Cara wrapped her arms around her waist. "I… I told him how I felt, and he told me straight out he's not the man for me."

A long time ago, I might have been…

"Oh, no."

"Oh, yes." Cara's laugh sounded strangled. "And you and I both know it's probably a nice way of saying *I'm* not the one for *him*."

"Well, you still have us." Andi's attempt at lightness failed, too. Her eyes were as tear filled as Cara's own. "I do mean that, you know," she added softly. "We're here. Please stay with us."

"It's better if I don't." His claim that she would leave again would come true sooner than Wes thought. "I was going home eventually. This just gave me the push. And if I don't leave, Wes might stop coming here with the kids, when he's finally starting to reach out again."

"He can learn to deal with that."

"But can I? If I stay, how will I feel about seeing them? In this small town, it's a given our paths will cross."

"I can't argue with you there."

And Cara couldn't argue with Wes.

I'm not the man for you.

She could prove to him he was exactly the man for her. That wouldn't matter if he could never bring himself to believe it.

She had cut her ties with Brad. She would have to walk away from Wes and his family, too. But how could she leave when they meant everything to her?

CHAPTER TWENTY-THREE

As MUCH AS she longed to see Mark and Tracey again, Cara found her footsteps slowing the closer she came to Wes's back porch. She faced a first and a last experience this morning—her first time at Wes's house while he was getting the kids ready to go to the sitter's and her last time to be here with them all.

Wes opened the door. "Good morning."

After her long night, there was nothing good about this morning. One glance at him said he'd missed out on sleep, too. Lines bracketed his eyes and pale shadows smudged the skin beneath them. She had no delusions about him tossing and turning over her.

"How's Mark?" she asked quickly. "Did he have any more nightmares?"

"No. He seems okay." He closed the door behind her, then went over to the sink.

"Good morning, Miss Cara!" To her relief, Mark looked bright-eyed and happy and seemed to have forgotten all about last night.

He gave her a huge smile and came toward her, his arms spread wide.

"Good morning, Mark." She knelt to hug him, resting her cheek against his hair, hiding her face for a moment while she blinked away a rush of tears.

"You will drive to Miss Rhea's today?" he asked.

She shook her head. "No. I just stopped by to do some work."

He climbed onto his bench again. The remains of milk in the bowl in front of him showed he'd already eaten breakfast. A plastic cup gave off the tangy scent of orange juice. Tracey had her own bowl on the high-chair tray and dipped her fingers into the dry cereal. Her diaper bag and Mark's backpack sat on the edge of the counter near the door, ready to go.

Cara stopped to play pat-a-cake with Tracey before taking "her" chair.

As Wes now stood at the counter with his back to the room, she knew not to expect any help from him. Swallowing a sigh, she turned to Mark. "I can't come to pick up you and Tracey from Miss Rhea's today."

"Why?"

"Well… I have to go back to Arizona."

"Oh. Next door."

"That's right. Next door. That's where I live. And I have to go home."

"That's good."

Not the answer she had expected…or wanted. "Why is that good?"

"You can come back tomorra."

"When I go to the Hitching Post, I can come back tomorrow. But Arizona is too far away."

"No, it's not. Grandpa Jed lives next door. Grandpa Jed's not far away."

Using that logic, he made perfect sense.

"It's more than that, Mark," Wes said. "You know when we drive to Miss Rhea's, the sun's coming up, and when we drive home, the sun's going down?"

Mark nodded.

"Well, all that time in between, all day when you're at Miss Rhea's, that's how long it will take Miss Cara to drive home."

"All day?" His eyes opened wide. "That's far away!"

Too far away.

Mark noisily drained his cup and set it back on the table. "All done, Daddy."

"Good. Time to brush your teeth."

"Okay." He scooted off the edge of the bench.

She watched him run from the room. After

a long moment of silence except for the rattle of Tracey's dry cereal, Cara carried his empty bowl and mug to the counter.

"I'd have taken care of those," Wes said.

"In other words, *I don't need your help.*"

"I didn't say that."

"You didn't have to," she said sadly. "I'm getting the feeling we've started the day off from where we left things last night, and my apology for confusing the kids wasn't enough for you. Or maybe my confession about how I feel was too much."

"The apology was accepted and over with, and I told you, you weren't the only one at fault."

No mention of what else she had just said.

Last night's brief acceptance didn't seem enough for *her.* Nothing given so grudgingly would satisfy her. And if he thought running it by her again now would send her on her way more quickly, he thought wrong.

Last night, she had given in, believing it was the best choice. The only choice.

On the ride here this morning, she thought about Andi, working hard for her dreams and to help the women of Cowboy Creek. About Lizzie, waiting for confirmation of her pregnancy and prepared to make huge changes in her life to give her baby a family. They were both going after what they wanted. How could Cara do anything less?

"You're right," she said flatly, raising her chin to look him in the eye. "I never meant to confuse Mark or Tracey. But you're just as much to blame for doing the same thing—to the kids *and* to me. Deny it all you want, Wes, but you feel something for me. Mark's a smart little boy. He picks up on your feelings, too, just the way he noticed your—*our*—tension at the table last night."

"No tension on my part. I just didn't have anything to say."

Her laugh cracked in the middle. "Oh, no. I've fallen for bad lines before, but you're not catching me with that one."

"It's not a line. Or at least wasn't intended that way. Even if I were looking for someone— and I'm not—I've got my kids and my ranch here. You've got your job search and your apartment hunt and your life somewhere else. That ought to prove to you we're not a good match. That we don't have much of anything in common."

"You're right. Not much in common. Except for liking cookouts and burritos and bacroni. Ice cream and corny jokes and tall tales. Fun dinners around the kitchen table and quiet nights in the living room with the kids."

"Those kids are my priority. Right now, they're all I can think about."

He shifted as if planning to move away. She rested her hand on his arm. The warmth of him against her palm gave her a jolt, reminding her of him holding her. Kissing her. He refused to admit it, but those actions showed he did feel something for her, something much more than the same sympathy and compassion she felt for him.

"Do me the favor of hearing *me* out this time." She dropped her hand and stared up at him. "You know what happened to me with… with everything. What you don't know is why I came to Cowboy Creek. Of course, I wanted to visit Andi and her family. But that's not the only reason."

She paused, gathering strength. His face wore last night's blank expression, but at least he wasn't backing away. Yet.

"When I first got here, there wasn't much of anything left in my life. There still isn't, if you consider I haven't found that job and apartment. Worse, after losing the baby, there wasn't much of *me* left."

This time, he reached out to her, a quick

brush of his fingertip to wipe away the tear from her cheek.

"Now I've learned the joy and happiness of loving my baby will always stay with me, because my baby will always be part of me. That's given me the courage to move on, to think about the future. And to tell you how I feel." She took a deep breath. "I needed to heal my heart, not lose it. Since meeting you and the kids, I've done both. I didn't come looking for a family to love, but that's exactly what I've found."

She blinked away another tear. "I've been where you are, Wes, falling apart after a tragedy that changes everything. You helped me deal with my loss. I wish I could be here to help you work through yours. For your sake and, I'll admit, mine. But mostly for Mark and Tracey."

His eyes hadn't left hers. She only hoped her words were registering.

"There's something else. When I lost my baby, I struggled with more than grief. There was so much guilt that came along with it. Guilt from getting pregnant with a man who wasn't who I thought he was. From believing I'd done something to bring on the miscarriage. From thinking I wasn't capable of carrying a baby at all. I recognized those feelings in me and finally let go of them."

What she said next would make him want to run. "I know you're dealing with some guilt, too. I don't understand exactly where your feelings come from, but I know you need to find a way to resolve whatever is weighing you down."

"You can't know that."

"Oh, yes, I can. Because I see them in your face and hear them in your voice." She tried to smile. "It's thanks to you I've finally figured all this out. I hope you can at least try to let what I'm saying help you."

Realizing Mark could come back into the room at any minute pushed her to share everything she needed to tell him. "I love you, Wes. And you care about me, too. Maybe it's not love now. Maybe it can't ever be. I don't know. But if there's one thing I can tell for sure, it's how much you love Mark and Tracey. You said they're your priority, and of course they should be. If you didn't feel that way I wouldn't love you as much as I do." She took another deep breath, then blurted, "Just promise me one thing."

"What?"

"I'm leaving because you asked me to, for

their sake. But that's just a small part of the solution. You're the much bigger part. The most important part. You need to do something for their sake, too. Please promise me you won't go backward. Back to being a hermit isolating yourself and the kids. It's not fair to you, and it's not fair to Mark and Tracey."

"I wouldn't do that."

"You already have," she said softly. "At dinner last night, you barely spoke at all. It wasn't because you had nothing to say. You just retreated into your shell."

Your crab shell. Once, they had both laughed at that silly joke. Now she would give anything to have one of those—to have *something*—to make her smile.

As if in answer to her silent plea, Mark ran into the kitchen, showing off his just-brushed teeth in a gleaming grin.

LATE THAT AFTERNOON, seeing Lizzie and Kyle arrive at the store holding hands finally gave Cara another reason to smile. Their linked fingers had to prove they'd found a way to work things out.

If she could only say the same about herself and Wes…

"Wow!" Lizzie eyed the stacked storage containers and piles of plastic bags lining the walls in the display room. "What're all these?"

"Inventory for the store." Once Wes left to take the kids to Rhea's, Cara had spent a long, active and busy day. "These are the clothes and crafts I told you about, from Wes Daniels's house."

"There's so much!"

"Tell me about it. It took me most of the day to load up the car and drive back and forth to bring it all into town in batches."

"But your car's so small. Why didn't you ask Wes to help?"

"Yeah," Kyle agreed, "he probably could have filled up the back of his pickup a few times and saved you a lot of trips."

"He wasn't around," Cara said truthfully.

Each time she returned to the house for another load, she made sure to check that his truck wasn't in the driveway. She made up her mind not to go downstairs or even to call out to him if he stopped by while she was there. But all her care and planning had been for nothing since he hadn't come home...hadn't come back to the house at all.

He'd either found a reason to stay in town or gone directly to work somewhere on the ranch.

Obviously, he wanted to stay away from her as much as she wanted to avoid seeing him.

Then all day, why had she ridden a roller coaster from relief to irritation to sadness to regret?

"Is Andi going to want me to start working soon?" Lizzie asked. "To help get all this set up?"

"I think so. But you'll have to check in with her."

"Yeah, I know. The budget."

Kyle gestured over his shoulder. "I'm gonna run to the L-G for a soda. Anybody want anything?"

"Not me, thanks," Cara said.

Lizzie looked at her. "Do you have time for a cup of tea?"

She smiled. "I thought you'd never ask."

"Then I'll stay here."

When Kyle left, the two of them moved into the back room. Cara filled the kettle to heat water.

As Lizzie took a seat, she laughed. "Talking about budgets must've reminded Kyle he should have his soda while he can. We're both giving them up. Once we get our next paychecks, we need to start saving."

That could mean for anything from a baby to prom night.

"Saving's a good habit." One Cara had to get back to as soon as she found a job. Which now, unfortunately, might happen much sooner than she expected. "Nickels and dimes and pennies add up."

"Yeah, they do, and that's why I hope Andi will give me lots of hours. I'm going to need them." Lizzie crossed her arms on the tabletop and leaned forward. "My new test came back positive, too, Cara. Kyle and I are really having a baby! We talked to my parents and his parents together, and everybody's okay with it. No, everybody's good with it."

Lizzie's face glowed with her own happiness and excitement. She had gone back to her usual chatty self, speaking even more quickly than usual, barely pausing for breath. "When the baby comes, we're going to live with my parents for a while, and both moms said they'll babysit when Kyle and I start college next fall. And we're going to get married. Soon. We don't know when yet, because we just started talking about all this last night!" Lizzie laughed again. "You'll be here for the wedding, right?"

"How can I answer that when I don't know the date?" Cara teased. Then she smiled. "You know I'll want to be here for it."

She set Paz's cookie tin on the table and went to the counter to pour water for their tea.

"Mmm. Are these from the Hitching Post?" Lizzie asked. When Cara nodded, she said, "I'll just take two. The doctor said I can have sweets if I don't overdo it. But I'm not just giving up soda. I'm going to stop eating fried chicken and a bunch of other things. And take these *huge* vitamins. There are so many rules you have to follow when you're having a baby. Wait till you get pregnant, Cara. You'll see. But first you can learn all about it from me. I'll let you in on *everything*."

"Thanks." She turned back, hoping her smile looked natural. "I'm sure I'll need all that info, too. Someday…"

Everything was working out for Lizzie and Kyle and their new life, and Cara couldn't be happier for them both.

Or more dismayed by the comparison to her own situation.

The first day she had come to this store, Lizzie—teenage, talkative, excitable Lizzie—had shared words of wisdom with her about finding *the one*. Cara *had* found the man she loved, right here in Cowboy Creek.

And he had made it all too clear she had no future with him.

CHAPTER TWENTY-FOUR

"LOOKS LIKE I'M the last to pick up my kids tonight," Wes said to Rhea when she came up to him at the day care holding Tracey.

He needed to get back on track. All this week, he'd left the house later than he had before. Before Cara. In such a brief space of time, he'd gotten used to working longer hours since he could rely on her to bring the kids home. A luxury he didn't have anymore.

Pushing away memories of their last two conversations, he made a joke of his late arrival. Not as corny as the ones Cara said they both liked, but still... "You know how wild Canyon Road gets at rush hour on Friday night."

Rhea laughed. "That might actually happen once they open the highway exit. Can you imagine Cowboy Creek in gridlock?"

"No. And let's hope it doesn't come to that. We're not the big city here." If they were, maybe Cara wouldn't be going home to Phoenix.

Not that he'd given her a reason to stay.

By the time he had returned home on Tuesday, she had left the house. To be honest, he'd stayed away after bringing the kids here to Rhea's. He'd gone back to the ranch but nowhere near the house until late afternoon. Considering everything Cara had said to him and knowing everything he couldn't say to her, what point would there have been in talking again?

But of course she would be back.

She'd need to come by to pick up all the bins and bags of crafts she'd organized in the office. Maybe he ought to contact her and volunteer to drop them off on one of his trips to town to pick up the kids. Not that he wanted to see her. But no sense having her come to the house, running the risk of Mark and Tracey thinking she'd returned for good, then getting upset when she left again.

No sense running the risk she might bring up all those thoughts and feelings of her he could do nothing about.

Across the room, Mark knelt beside the kids' table stuffing papers into his backpack.

Rhea handed Tracey over to Wes. He tickled his baby under her chin. She squirmed, turning her face away, then slumped against his shoulder. Frowning, he looked down at the top of her head.

"Actually," Rhea said, "I'm glad you're here later tonight. With everyone else gone, we can chat for a minute. If you have time, that is."

"No problem." But a request from the sitter for a chat normally meant just that. A problem. "Is it Tracey or Mark?"

"Both," she said promptly. "Tracey's been cranky all this week, not sitting still long enough to eat much of anything, and restless during nap time. Well, she's never been a good midday sleeper, you know that. She likes her late afternoons."

"Yeah. In a moving vehicle or at the supper table." Yet night after night, his little girl had managed to stay awake almost until the end of story time.

"But the rest of it's not like her." Rhea shook her head. "And then Mark. He's not mixing much with the other kids, not interested in his drawing and just dragging himself around all day. Is he getting enough rest at home?"

"As far as I know. He's not waking up during the night for water or bathroom trips." Or nightmares, fortunately. "And whenever I check on the kids, he's sound asleep. Too sound asleep," Wes admitted. "Some mornings, I've had trouble getting him moving."

Rhea sighed. "You know, Tracey was so young when you lost Patty, we didn't see much change in her personality. But Mark's acting like he did around the time his mother passed away."

Because now his Miss Cara had gone away?

As if she'd read his mind, Rhea said, "I noticed Cara's stopped coming for the kids at the end of the day."

"That was just a temporary arrangement. She won't be picking them up anymore."

"What a shame. She's a nice, friendly girl, and pretty, too. I'll bet both the kids got attached to her."

Yeah. The kids and their daddy.

And you care about me, too. Maybe it's not love now...

It was love on Cara's part, or so she said. But she'd also said she'd broken up with her boyfriend not long ago. How could she even know yet how she really felt?

"Sometimes children don't react well to change," Rhea went on. "I'm sure that's what's got them both out of sorts this week."

"Probably," Wes agreed. What else could he say?

To tell the truth, he'd had his own issues lately, feeling crankier than his son had been when he'd acted out at the supper table earlier in the week. Naturally, Wes managed to keep himself from having a full-out tantrum. But it worried him to hear how listless both kids had been.

Mark crossed the room toward them.

"Hey, buddy." Wes smiled. "Ready to go home?"

Mark shrugged. "Okay."

Once they said their goodbyes and went outside to the truck, Mark looked up at him. "Do we have to go home, Daddy?"

He frowned. "Well, sure we do. We need to get supper going. And you need to help me set the table, right?"

"Right," Mark agreed, though he didn't sound at all interested.

Wes swallowed a sigh. He didn't much like the idea of going home to an empty house, either.

As Cara came down the stairs to the first floor, she saw Jed near the registration desk in the otherwise deserted lobby. He held his Stetson in one hand and jiggled a key ring in the other. He smiled when he saw her, almost as though he'd been waiting for her to arrive.

"Are you going or coming?" she asked.

"Going."

So was she, just a couple of days from now, though she doubted Jed was on his way to Phoenix.

"I'm having supper at Sugar's with Sugar and Mo before we head over to the town council meeting. I've got time for a chat before I go. The porch swing ought to be empty at this hour. How about it?"

"Sure. I'm ahead of schedule for dinner."

Outside, she took a seat beside Jed on the swing. She had joined Andi here the first night she'd come back from Wes's house.

Frowning, Cara mentally pushed the reminder away. She'd last seen Wes just a few days ago and hadn't been able to get him out of her mind. Was his name forever going to pop into her head as part of almost every thought?

"You've been less of a stranger around here lately. Andi tells me you're getting all those crafts from Wes's in order."

And was Wes going to be the topic of her every conversation?

"The inventory's done. I'm at the pricing stage now."

"Sounds like it won't be long before Andi will be able to open up the store. You know she's got her heart set on you working it with her."

"I know."

"But she tells me you're determined to go home again. She'll miss having you here. We all will. I suspect you realize that, as well."

"I do. I'll miss you all, too. It's been a... It's been great to see everyone. And, Jed, I really do appreciate the room and the meals."

He waved one hand as if swatting her words away. "You're always welcome. You have a funny way of repaying your debts, though."

Her jaw dropped. "Repaying? But Andi said—"

"I don't mean the room or the meals. I'm talking about you and Wes. Between the pair of you, you're ruining my reputation."

Her laugh sounded more like a sob. "I'm not sure what to say."

"Yeah, plenty of folks around here get struck that way."

Including Wes—the day Mark had been so upset about the recital and his daddy hadn't known how to handle the situation.

"Fortunately," Jed continued, "talking's never been a problem for me. Getting people to listen can present a challenge at times, though. Some folks would rather run for the hills than take advice."

"I know what you mean." *Or who you mean.* Wes, when she'd tried to talk to him about his feelings. Or was Jed thinking about anyone foolish enough not to take him up on his matchmaking services?

"Then there are the folks who would rather run than face up to a problem."

He meant Wes again.

He couldn't be referring to her. Yes, she had run from Phoenix to Cowboy Creek. Now she was going in the opposite direction. *Going.* Not running. Resolving a problem, not avoiding one.

Getting her life back on track.

As Wes had said.

ALMOST DONE CLEARING the dishes, Wes looked over his shoulder at Mark, alone at the table.

Thanks to his delayed arrival at the day care and his conversation with Rhea, Wes had gotten supper ready later than usual. Halfway through, Tracey had nearly fallen asleep over her tray, and he'd taken her upstairs to tuck her into her crib.

Over the past few nights, with Cara gone and only him and the kids at the table again, their meals had gotten lonelier. He made sure they hadn't gotten quieter. Or at least, he tried. Most of the time Mark barely spoke, just poked at his plate with his fork as if he'd never seen food, while Tracey babbled to herself and mashed vegetables with her hands instead of chewing them.

How could Wes blame the kids, when even he had to force himself to eat?

He heard footsteps on the porch, followed by a knock on the back door. A male, he judged by the heavy tread, trying to push away his foolish rush of disappointment. Still, grateful for the distraction of an unknown caller, he went to the door.

"Howdy," Jed Garland said.

"Grandpa Jed!" Mark yelled. He slid from the bench and ran to hug the older man.

Wes smiled broadly at Jed. This week, he'd have shaken the hand of his worst enemy— if he'd had one—if that person could get this much enthusiasm out of his son.

Mark leaned over to look past Jed. "Where's

Miss Cara? Did you bring Miss Cara with you?"

Great. Wes clamped his hand on the doorknob. Here, he'd thought the older man would add a diversion for the kids...and for himself.

Jed removed his Stetson and shook his head. "Nope, Miss Cara's at the Hitching Post. I'm here all on my lonesome tonight."

Wincing at the man's choice of words, Wes headed toward the counter. Halfway across the room, he nearly stumbled as Jed's first words finally registered. Of course he knew Cara hadn't left town. She wouldn't abandon her job for Andi. But had Mark picked up on the fact she hadn't gone home to Arizona yet?

"All right if I come in and sit for a while?" Jed asked.

"Sure!" Mark said.

Wes opened the cupboard. "You'll have coffee?"

"And dessert," Mark added as he led Jed to the table.

Jed patted his belly. "I'll skip the dessert, thanks. Had a slice of Sugar's pecan pie earlier. But I'll take you up on that cup of coffee."

"Sounds good." Wes filled their mugs, then brought them to the table.

"Can we have chocolate ice cream, Daddy?"

"Of course." Mark hadn't asked for that flavor since Cara had left. Maybe he just wanted a taste of it again. Or maybe he had learned to associate both chocolate ice cream and his Grandpa Jed with Cara.

"You're running around late tonight," Wes said as he dished up Mark's dessert.

"I am. I went into town for the council meeting and thought I'd stop by here on the way home. Though I shouldn't stay long. I've got good news for Andi and Cara. Very good news. Work's going to start on the exit in the next few weeks. That means traffic will be diverted down Canyon Road sooner than we expected."

"Mitch told me the other day about the new detour. Andi will be even more eager now to get that store all ready for her customers." Then Cara would be done helping out her best friend, and there would be nothing keeping her in town. No surprise. He'd known from day one she was only visiting, hadn't he?

As if Jed had read his mind, he said, "We're having an extra-special cookout tomorrow before Cara heads home."

She was going already? Would he even see her again before she left?

He wouldn't ask. If he showed Jed any interest in her at all, the man would be reserving the Hitching Post's banquet room for their wedding.

"Why don't you drop in?" Jed asked.

"B'ritos?" Mark asked, his spoon clattering into his empty bowl.

"Plenty of 'em," Jed confirmed. "And a lot more."

"Don't count on us," Wes said flatly.

Mark must not have heard the response, as he grinned and pushed his bowl away. "Daddy, can I draw upstairs?"

"Sure, as long as you don't wake up Tracey." After Rhea's report on Mark's lack of interest in his artwork, this came as a welcome burst of enthusiasm. Or it did, until the next "maybe" hit him. Maybe Mark's sudden excitement again tied in to Cara, this time to his belief he would see her again tomorrow. "The lamp's on upstairs. Grandpa Jed and I will be down here if you need anything."

You need to do something for their sake, too.

Why couldn't he keep the memories of those conversations with her, long over and done with, out of his head?

Once Mark left, Wes looked at Jed and almost choked on his mouthful of hot coffee. The older man had crossed his arms and set his face in the sternest frown Wes had ever seen on him. "What's the matter?"

"Wish I knew," Jed said. "All week long, whenever Cara's not at the store she's moping around the Hitching Post. And nobody's seen hide nor hair of you anywhere. You know, it wasn't that long ago you were telling me to mind my own business. Well, when it comes to my friends, their happiness *is* my business. And you're not happy." He sighed. "I know what it's like to lose a wife. Not a day goes by that I don't think about my Mary. Son, nobody's expecting you or the kids to forget their mama. But you've got to go on with your life."

Please promise me you won't go backward.

Cara meant well. So did Jed. Wes had acknowledged that to himself before. But their ideas of getting on with his life didn't match his. "I am going on. At my own speed and in my own way."

"A lonely way, seems to me." Jed eyed him thoughtfully. "Have you asked her to stay?"

"There's no point. Even if I had a reason to ask her, I wouldn't. We're not a match, Jed."

"You're a stubborn one, aren't you?"

"Stubbornness has nothing to do with it. I'm doing what's right for my kids. So is Cara."

I'm leaving because you asked me to, for their sake.

But that's just a small part of the solution.

SOON AFTER HE had laid out the truth to Jed, the older man went home.

Wes could still see him sitting at the table, shaking his head sadly.

Much as he'd have liked to cheer Jed up, Wes couldn't change reality, could he? He and Cara were completely wrong for each other, and matchmaker Jed would have to live with the single failure on his record.

So would Wes.

Trying to ease the tension tightening every muscle, he stomped up the stairs. He walked more quietly only as he got closer to the kids' room.

Tracey lay curled up in the same spot he'd left her earlier, with her thumb now in its nighttime position, resting on her cheek, ready to be popped into her mouth as needed.

Mark lay on his belly on the floor with a piece of construction paper in front of him and crayons in a heap beside him.

"Time to clean up your mess," Wes said.

"Not a mess. A picture. Almost done." When Wes took a step forward, Mark slapped his hands down on the paper. "No peeking. I have to finish, Daddy."

"All right. I'll give you another couple of minutes."

Wes left the room and looked down the length of the hallway. Jed had never said exactly when Cara was leaving. Maybe he should have asked, after all. Maybe he ought to follow through on his idea to call her about all those boxes and bins she'd piled up in the office.

As if a strong magnet drew him there, he paced to the end of the hall and opened the office door. He flipped the wall switch, then blinked, half from the sudden bright glare and half in surprise.

The desk and dressers Patty used for storage were still there, but the crafts Cara had organized and inventoried were gone.

She had taken time away from the store to finish her work here while Mark and Tracey weren't around. Not because he'd asked her to do that but for the sake of his kids.

He shoved his hands into his back pockets and shook his head. Everything she did showed she cared, yet after saying she didn't want to leave, she was going anyway. And she should. She might also say she'd be happy in Cowboy Creek, but what were the chances that happiness would last? He couldn't risk finding out she'd rather be anywhere but here.

"Pssst."

At the sound of his son's hiss, Wes turned. Mark stood in the hallway, holding the construction paper clasped against his chest.

Wes smiled. Looked like his pardner was back. "You made a surprise for Daddy?"

"No." Mark flipped the paper over to show off his crayoned artwork. "For Miss Cara."

His stomach knotting, Wes forced a smile as he inspected the picture in the light streaming through the office doorway.

In front of a squat, boxy house stood a row of stick figures. A man wearing a cowboy hat and boots. A little boy, the man's pint-size twin. A baby gripping what looked like a giant green bean in one fist. And a woman with a generous smile and long red hair.

Mark frowned. "You like my picture, Daddy?"

"Yes." The word came out in a croak. He cleared his throat. "Yes, I like it. It's very nice."

"I have to give it to Miss Cara."

"We'll need to see about that. Miss Cara's… going to be back in Arizona."

"Okay. We can go tomorra."

"No, not tomorrow, son. And for now, we want your picture to stay nice and clean right?"

Mark nodded.

"Good. First, put the drawing on your dresser. Then grab your pajamas."

"Okay, Daddy." He went down the hall.

Wes turned and walked to the center of the office. Every last box, bin and plastic bag from the room and the closet had disappeared. Cara had cleared everything out, most likely when he'd left her here on Tuesday and then refused to come near the place.

Jed hadn't missed the mark about his stubbornness. That stubborn streak had saved him before. And now. He dug in his heels over issues only when he knew he was right, and he'd definitely called it right about keeping his distance from Cara.

Why did that certainty have to come at such a high price?

CHAPTER TWENTY-FIVE

CARA AND ANDI carried the last of the casserole dishes from the Hitching Post's kitchen out into the backyard.

"So, what did you decide?" Andi asked. "Are you packing up tonight so you'll be ready to go in the morning?"

Cara nodded. "I want to get an early start." Just as Wes had explained to Mark about their trips to Rhea's, she'd be leaving when the sun was coming up.

"We're going to be busy once you get back." Andi smiled. "I'm very glad you made up your mind to become my partner."

"I am, too." Cara set her foil-covered dishes onto one of the picnic tables reserved for food.

She looked from one table to another. The dessert table where Wes had told her the tall tale about his horseshoe championships. The men's table where Tracey had stuffed a corncob into his pocket. The table-for-two they had shared where she had wondered if Mo had been right about her being good for Wes.

When Wes was ready, she would be here to find out.

She looked over at yet another table. "It's getting crowded already. We'd better go sit."

"No worries. Tina and Jane are saving seats for us."

"Good. Paz really went all out today. What's the occasion?"

"Grandpa's expecting some of our favorite guests, and I think he and Paz might feel the need to make an impression." Andi inspected the table in front of them. "Looks like everything's out and we're done for now. Let's go grab those seats."

Cara turned to follow her. Instantly, she noted three things. First, Mark running toward her waving a sheet of construction paper, his latest creation, no doubt. Second, Tracey on the blanket reserved for the babies, happily playing pat-a-cake with Andi's daughter, Missy. And third…

The third person she longed to see was nowhere to be found.

"Miss Cara!" Mark shouted. His enthusiastic hug nearly knocked her off her feet. "Look what I brought you!" He held the construction paper face out against his chest.

With her first glance, her eyes watered so quickly she barely had time to take in the drawing before everything blurred. "Oh, Mark, that's so nice." *Nice? Try perfect.*

"Beautiful," Andi agreed. "And, Cara, that looks just like you. Is it, Mark?"

"Yes!" He handed the paper to Cara. One arm wrapped around her legs for another hug, he stared down at his work of art.

She ruffled his hair. A few extra blinks finally helped clear her vision. His drawing hadn't changed. It showed a row of four stick figures lined up in front of a small square house.

Wes and his kids *did* make the perfect picture. And now, she was part of it.

At least, on Mark's drawing.

"Is this for me?" she asked.

He nodded. "You can have it in Arizona."

"Oh…thank you very much."

Over his head, Andi's gaze met hers.

A moment later, Cara saw the third person she so wanted to see.

Wes seemed deep in conversation with Jed near the back steps of the hotel, but as if he felt her gaze on him, he looked up and met her eyes.

"Mark," Andi said, "let's go put Miss Cara's picture in a safe place for her."

"Okay." He took the drawing and followed Andi.

Cara waited as Wes crossed the space between them.

The last time she had seen him felt like a lifetime ago, yet in reality only a few days had gone by. She was shocked by how much he had changed. His face had thinned. Worry lines crossed his forehead. The dark shadows beneath his eyes belonged on a man wearing a football jersey and helmet.

"Are you okay?" she asked in concern. "Sorry, but you look…ragged."

"Good description. That's about how I feel, like a worn-out rag. Losing sleep is not the best way to gain energy."

"Is Mark still keeping you up with his bad dreams?"

"No. Nothing after the one he had the other night."

"I'm glad for that." Then why the lost sleep? Had she been wrong when she'd seen him Tuesday morning? Since then, had he actually tossed and turned at night, thinking about her…the way she'd thought about him? "So, what made you come to the cookout today?"

"I told you I didn't plan to go back to being a hermit." After a hesitation, he added, "And Jed told me you were leaving. I thought this might be the last chance I'd get to see you."

She knew better than to let this admission excite her. "You wanted to say goodbye?"

"That and a few other things."

"Oh." She glanced at all the hotel guests milling around them. "Maybe we should go for a walk."

"That might be best," he agreed.

When she looked across the yard at her picnic table, she found Andi and Tina and Jane looking back at her. And when she gestured toward the kids' blanket and the younger kids' table, the women all nodded in understanding.

"Guess we won't need to worry about the kids for a bit," Wes said dryly.

"Guess not."

Andi flashed her a quick familiar grin, confirming Cara's suspicion that Wes and his family were Jed and Paz's favored guests.

They wandered away from the crowd, ironically in the direction of the group of small honeymoon cabins behind the hotel. At least there they would have seats, privacy and quiet.

Too much quiet. An occasional shout or laugh from someone at the cookout made its way across the space. Otherwise, nothing but silence and the scent of pine surrounded them.

At the first of the cabins, she settled on the top step.

Wes stayed at the foot of the steps, resting his elbow on the end of the railing.

"You said Jed told you I was leaving." Which had given him the reason to come to the cookout today. "If you're here so I can see the kids, I appreciate that more than I can say. But Jed may not have told you everything. I have to be honest. I'll only be gone a few days."

"You'll...*what*?"

She nodded. "I'm coming back next week. Andi and I agreed to go into a partnership with the store. I'm going home to get more of my clothes and personal stuff from storage."

"And Jed knows this?"

"Of course."

Wes laughed shortly. "Wait till I get my hands on that matchmaking, interfering busybody. I just got done talking to him, and he didn't say a word about it. He had me thinking I might never see you again."

Her heart tripped a beat. Maybe he had come today to tell her just what she longed to hear. But as this conversation proved, people didn't always mean what you imagined they did. "Jed does have a way with words, doesn't he? When he first mentioned you to me, he gave the impression you were at least double your age."

"You're kidding. Why?"

"I'm not sure. Maybe he was afraid I'd refuse to go near you if I thought he was being a matchmaking, interfering busybody."

He laughed sheepishly. "I guess I deserve that one."

"And maybe he deserves more credit than we're giving him."

"Yeah. Let me just get this clear. You're staying in Cowboy Creek?"

"Yes. I'm staying because I need a job and because I want to help Andi and because I genuinely believe the store will make a difference to so many people here." She took a deep, shaky breath. "And mostly, I'm staying because of you and the kids. I told you, Wes, I know caring about me doesn't guarantee you'll ever love me. But you can at least give me a chance. Give *us* a chance. I'm not going anywhere. No matter how much time you need to think it over or to feel ready, I'll be waiting for you."

"Cara…" He spread his hands in front of him as if groping for answers out of his reach.

She wrapped her arms around her knees and hung on tight. Would that keep her from falling apart if he refused to give her any hope? "Now you know I'm staying, do we still need to talk about those *few other things*?"

"Now more than ever. There's been a need almost from the first time I met you. But I was too stubborn to admit it. When I get done talking, I'll be the one waiting for an answer, and you might have changed your mind about giving me a chance."

"I doubt that."

"We'll see."

WES TOOK A LONG, deep breath to ease the band tightening his chest. It didn't help. That tightness didn't come from tension but from the weight of guilt and the confessions and apologies he needed to make.

Above Cara's eyes, clear and blue and trusting, her raised eyebrows showed a let's-get-to-it impatience. He didn't blame her. "You've waited long enough for some explanations. And you deserve 'em. I just hope I can deliver without also making a complete jackass of myself. Again."

She must have remembered the day he'd landed on his butt in the office, sending balls of yarn bouncing all around them, because she laughed softly. "Hang on to the railing, cowboy, and you should stay on your feet."

"I will if you promise to hang on to your hat. This will be a rough ride and it's about to last a while."

"I'm not going anywhere," she said again.

Why couldn't he have listened the first time she'd told him she didn't want to leave?

"I meant it when I said my priority has and always will be my kids. It's been a hard year for us, and as I told you, all that concerned me was keeping them safe. You never know what can happen from one minute to the next. We found that out with Patty."

Now Cara's eyes suddenly sparkled with tears, making his hand itch to reach out to her. Instead he gripped the railing. He'd barely started talking. If he stopped now, he might never finish what he needed to tell her.

"That's when I lost interest in going anywhere or being around anyone but Mark and Tracey. Not Garrett or Jed and his clan or any of my friends.

"Jed's right," he blurted, "about thinking I need to get out more. So are you and Garrett.

Heck, everybody in Cowboy Creek most likely has the right idea. Not for me, but for my kids."

"You brought Mark and Tracey to the cookout today. And a couple weeks ago."

"And it had been a while," he confessed. "Except for a couple of trips here to the Hitching Post and a few stops for ice cream, they haven't been anywhere much besides their sitter's."

"That's understandable. You're busy."

"I could have made the time. Should have made the time. Instead, I've kept them home, cut off from family and any friends except those at Rhea's. I didn't understand that until that Saturday here at Jed's when I saw Mark excited at being around his favorite pony again. And then Mark and Tracey playing with Robbie and Trey."

And in the Hitching Post's kitchen when he'd felt the kick in his chest as his son hugged Cara.

"I guess I thought keeping my kids near home would help me protect them."

"That's understandable, too," she said softly. "It's like what you said that afternoon. Sometimes life throws more bad than good at us. You've had a lot of bad happen, and it takes time to get past it. Now you realize that, it means you're on your way to seeing the good."

"Does it?"

"Definitely," she said. "You'll find out soon enough. I have the advantage since I fell in love with you first."

"Don't be too sure about that." He smiled. "I started to see some good, too, the day you came ringing my doorbell. I didn't recognize it as my good fortune at first. Having your help with clearing out all Patty's things, then coming to the house to work on the crafts, brought up a lot of memories about Patty I didn't want to think about."

He took another deep breath. That band around his chest held tight. "You were right about guilt I didn't want to face, and it all involved Patty. Growing up, she was never happy at home with her folks, then she carried those same feelings over to me. I knew that but never realized how deep the unhappiness went. Since she's been gone, I've spent a lot of time second-guessing myself for not understanding her needs.

"She was a town girl, and I lived out on the ranch, taking the school bus back and forth. In high school, I fixed up an old car and we started dating, but as I once told you, I didn't know her well."

She nodded. "I remember."

"Not long after graduation, we got married, and while I worked the ranch, she spent most of her time with her friends. Even then I didn't know much *about* her, but once she got pregnant with Mark, I started to learn a lot *from* her. Having the baby seemed to stir up a lot of feelings for her, none of them good, and she wanted to make sure I knew every last one."

"She...she didn't want the baby?"

"No, it wasn't that she didn't want Mark, she just didn't want anything interfering with what she liked to do. She hated being tied down, hated living on the ranch, resented me for not having enough money for us to go out and have fun.

"If I had realized earlier, I would have tried to do something to change things, to make them better. Make her happier. But the truth is, I didn't have any idea how she felt. And things got worse after Mark came along. She stayed home more but started buying all those clothes and craft supplies. We weren't in bad financial trouble, but we were always riding on the edge. Once we had Tracey, I tried to talk to Patty about the money situation. She lost it, ranting about me having her on a financial leash so I could keep her tied to the ranch."

One more admission and he could be done with the past once and for all.

"A few days before that trip to Santa Fe, she sucker punched me with another piece of news. She'd never loved me and only married me for an easy escape from her problems at home."

Cara raised her fingertips to her mouth as if she could block the cry of dismay he'd already heard. "You must have felt so betrayed."

"That's a word for it. And I should have known you'd understand. Because you felt the same when your man wouldn't compromise. And when he changed his mind about wanting kids."

Her eyes teared again. "Yes."

They reached out to each other at the same time. Again her small strong hand fit perfectly in his. "Cara, I'd never want to be that guy, the one who can't compromise and meet you halfway."

She squeezed his fingers. "There's a huge difference between you and Brad. You'll never be like him. Not when you love your family so much."

"There's a big difference between you and Patty, too. She didn't make communication easy, like you tried to do with Brad. And with me. Patty didn't talk to me upfront about how she felt and what she needed. All I heard were the complaints about what she didn't like."

He rubbed the back of her hand with his thumb. "You're not like that. You're a beautiful woman, inside and out. And though I could see that plainly, the minute I heard you were a city girl heading back home as soon as you could, all I could do was compare you to Patty. To make assumptions about you from the minute you walked into my living room, to figure you'd be like her—angry to be stuck on the ranch, unhappy with me, indifferent to the kids.

"I was wrong to do that. Even my three-going-on-forty-year-old son seems to have more sense than I do."

"He's a smart little boy. Adorable, too."

"Takes after his daddy in that respect."

She laughed.

"You were right about something else," he admitted. "After I accused you of confusing the kids, you hit the mark by turning it around on me, calling me just as guilty of doing the same to them and to you. This isn't a defense, at least not a good one, but my only excuse is I've been confused myself for a long time.

Too confused to think straight about much of anything."

He shook his head, recalling the belief he'd held about Cara early on. "Talk about confusion. I didn't want anyone in my life. But once you got wrapped up in Andi's project, I got the idea you needed the income, and I didn't have the heart to change my mind about you working on the crafts. Even then, I knew you would turn my life upside down if I let you.

"Not that I allowed myself to think about you that way. I tried not to think about you at all. I didn't want you around the house but at the same time it felt comfortable having you there. And I didn't want to get to know you, but, before too long, I'd done much more than that. And I fought every feeling for you as hard as I could.

"Mark and Tracey need a new mother, and I know nobody could fill that role for them better than you. But I'd told myself I'd do anything for the kids—except let myself get involved with another woman. I'd done so much wrong when it came to Patty, I didn't think I deserved a wife."

"Oh, Wes, that's not true. I felt the same way when things didn't work out with Brad. Does that mean I deserved to lose my baby?"

The break in her voice and the pain in her eyes sent him to the top step beside her. He slipped his arm around her shoulders. "It doesn't mean that at all."

"Then it's not true for you, either."

He took a deep, satisfying, unrestricted breath, yet he had to stop and swallow hard before he could continue. "What's true for me is this—I walked into the office last night and saw the room and the closet both empty, and it made me realize how empty our lives would be without you. Then my son showed me his family picture, and I knew our family wouldn't be complete until you took your place in it."

With his free hand, Wes ran his thumb down her soft cheek. "Cara, I hope you can forgive me for all I said about you confusing the kids. You didn't do anything wrong by trying to be there for Mark and Tracey. You were just being you—kind, loving and concerned. You'll make a great mother for any child, and a wonderful wife for any man who can win your heart."

"Like you have."

"Like I have. Just as you've won mine. And in this long-winded, roundabout way, I'm saying I love you and I hope you'll marry all three of us."

She rested her head against his shoulder. "I thought you'd never ask."

"But what's your answer?"

She pulled back to stare at him. "My answer is yes, of course!"

EPILOGUE

Two weeks later

CARA LOOKED AROUND the Hitching Post's banquet hall, a room transformed by thousands of white lights into the perfect setting for a fairytale wedding reception.

"Andi and Tina and Jane really made this one special," Cara said to Jed. "It's just what Lizzie wanted. She hasn't stopped smiling since she and Kyle made their entrance."

"I second that," Wes said.

The newlyweds had originally planned a small party at the community center. Thanks to Andi, Cara knew Jed had offered Lizzie and Kyle the banquet hall without charge, then surprised them by giving them the reception as a wedding gift.

Andi had sworn her to secrecy about Jed's arrangements, which turned out to be unnecessary since the bride had charmingly and publicly thanked Jed the minute the reception began.

Every time Cara thought of his generosity, her eyes misted with tears.

Every time she thought of his matchmaking skills, she gave thanks.

She smiled at Jed. "You've made Lizzie's day complete."

"Glad to hear it. But that girl needs to learn when to keep things private," he pretended to grumble.

"In *this* town?" she asked in mock surprise.

They all laughed.

With a smile of farewell, Jed wandered away.

The deejay had started a slow song, and in Kyle's arms, Lizzie nearly floated around the dance floor in her simple but elegant white gown.

Cara sighed happily. "She looks like a princess, doesn't she?"

"Yeah." One arm around her waist, Wes kissed her temple and gave her that half smile she loved. "The maid of honor's not too bad, either."

"Well, thank you for the compliment, cowboy."

"You're not sorry we're waiting?"

She shook her head. "Not a bit."

Wanting all the attention to go to Lizzie's special day, she and Wes had decided to hold off on their own wedding. In the meantime, Cara worked at the store during the day, then spent every evening at the ranch with Wes and Mark and Tracey before returning to the Hitching Post for the night.

Jed now sat at a table with Paz, Mo and Sugar.

"I'll bet they're up to some matchmaking business again." Wes leaned closer and murmured, "Don't ever tell anyone I said this, but I don't know what I'd have done without that man's interference."

Cara smiled. "Same here."

After all, thanks to Jed, she had the family she'd always wanted.

* * * * *

Get 4 FREE REWARDS!

We'll send you 2 FREE Books plus 2 FREE Mystery Gifts.

Love Inspired® books feature contemporary inspirational romances with Christian characters facing the challenges of life and love.

FREE Value Over **$20**

YES! Please send me 2 FREE Love Inspired® Romance novels and my 2 FREE mystery gifts (gifts are worth about $10 retail). After receiving them, if I don't wish to receive any more books, I can return the shipping statement marked "cancel." If I don't cancel, I will receive 6 brand-new novels every month and be billed just $5.24 for the regular-print edition or $5.99 each for the larger-print edition in the U.S., or $5.74 each for the regular-print edition or $6.24 for the larger-print edition in Canada. That's a savings of at least 13% off the cover price. It's quite a bargain! Shipping and handling is just 50¢ per book in the U.S. and $1.25 per book in Canada.* I understand that accepting the 2 free books and gifts places me under no obligation to buy anything. I can always return a shipment and cancel at any time. The free books and gifts are mine to keep no matter what I decide.

Choose one: ☐ **Love Inspired® Romance**
Regular-Print
(105/305 IDN GNWC)

☐ **Love Inspired® Romance**
Larger-Print
(122/322 IDN GNWC)

Name (please print)

Address   Apt. #

City   State/Province   Zip/Postal Code

Mail to the Reader Service:
IN U.S.A.: P.O. Box 1341, Buffalo, NY 14240-8531
IN CANADA: P.O. Box 603, Fort Erie, Ontario L2A 5X3

Want to try 2 free books from another series? Call 1-800-873-8635 or visit www.ReaderService.com.

---

*Terms and prices subject to change without notice. Prices do not include sales taxes, which will be charged (if applicable) based on your state or country of residence. Canadian residents will be charged applicable taxes. Offer not valid in Quebec. This offer is limited to one order per household. Books received may not be as shown. Not valid for current subscribers to Love Inspired Romance books. All orders subject to approval. Credit or debit balances in a customer's account(s) may be offset by any other outstanding balance owed by or to the customer. Please allow 4 to 6 weeks for delivery. Offer available while quantities last.

Your Privacy—The Reader Service is committed to protecting your privacy. Our Privacy Policy is available online at www.ReaderService.com or upon request from the Reader Service. We make a portion of our mailing list available to reputable third parties that offer products we believe may interest you. If you prefer that we not exchange your name with third parties, or if you wish to clarify or modify your communication preferences, please visit us at www.ReaderService.com/consumerschoice or write to us at Reader Service Preference Service, P.O. Box 9062, Buffalo, NY 14240-9062. Include your complete name and address.

LI19R3

THE FORTUNES OF TEXAS COLLECTION!

18 FREE BOOKS in all!

Treat yourself to the rich legacy of the Fortune and Mendoza clans in this remarkable 50-book collection. This collection is packed with cowboys, tycoons and Texas-sized romances!

Get 4 FREE REWARDS!

We'll send you 2 FREE Books plus 2 FREE Mystery Gifts.

FREE
Value Over
$20

Both the **Romance** and **Suspense** collections feature compelling novels written by many of today's best-selling authors.